ADRIANA PRIDEMORE

# THIS JOB *Sucks!*

For Frank, Leah, and Mom.

Thank you for putting up with my insanity and sticking with me.

I could never have made it this far without you.

# CONTENTS

# WORST DAY EVER

Whitney Martindale's lip quivered as she knocked on the door of Mrs. Myers' office at the Orchard Employment temp agency.

"Yes?" Her boss looked up as Whitney stepped inside.

Whitney parked her suitcases next to the door and plopped down like an unloved puppy in the chair facing Mrs. Myers.

The older lady studied her for a moment, then asked quietly, "Are you okay?"

That was all it took, the dam broke. Whitney's worst day ever spilled out in a river of tears.

"The recording studio fired me. Justin didn't pay my car payments like he said he would, and they towed my car. In front of everyone! It's been repossessed! Then I get home, and my suitcases are in the hallway with a break-up note from Justin! A note!" She held up the note, then read it, "See ya, found a better offer." With a feral sob, she ripped the paper into tiny pieces. "I'm homeless, jobless, and... and... carless!"

She let her head drop into her hands.

Mrs. Myers came around the desk and sat beside her, handing her a box of tissues. "I can't say that I'm sorry about Justin. I never thought he was good for you. As to the studio, I am sorry. I thought it was going to be a more permanent opportunity than just a few weeks. I had no idea they were planning to close."

Whitney viciously pulled a tissue out and blew her nose.

"Well." Mrs. Myers shuffled her paperwork as if she were dusting her hands. "There is always the possibility of another opportunity. That is what I always say."

"And is there another opportunity?" Whitney dabbed at her mascara.

Mrs. Myers smiled at her favorite employee. "Actually, there is. I just got a call; there is an opening at InfiniCorp."

"What's InfiniCorp?"

"InfiniCorp is an investment firm with a few subsidiary companies tied into it. Mr. Ravilla is the CEO. He is in need of a receptionist. He does most of the work himself, and the rest is through telecommuting."

"Doesn't sound too bad," Whitney shrugged. "I can start in the morning. Maybe I can stay with Lisa."

"Oh, that won't be necessary, dear. This job comes with an apartment."

"Why would a receptionist job come with a place to stay?"

"Mr. Ravilla is," Mrs. Myers gave a little shrug, "a bit eccentric. He doesn't keep normal business hours. Most of his staff have apartments there."

"Sounds kinda ominous," Whitney said. "What else do I need to know besides the fact that he's nuts and can't use a clock like a normal person?"

"Whitney!" Mrs. Myers scowled at her.

"Sorry, I'm just out of sorts. Suddenly being homeless and unwanted will do that."

"You are not unwanted, my dear." Mrs. Myers leaned over and patted Whitney's knee, then glanced at her watch. "We could head over there now if you like."

"Why not? It's not like I've got anywhere else to go."

Whitney swiped at her smudged mascara with one finger. *Nothing like a red nose and puffy eyes to make a great first impression.* Whitney looked down at herself. She suddenly felt really self-conscious. She glanced at Mrs. Myers, who looked every inch a lady in her matching blue suit and pearls.

"Uh, Mrs. M? I'm not exactly dressed for a job interview."

"Oh." Mrs. Myers suddenly seemed to notice what she was wearing: high tops with mismatched shoelaces, striped socks, purple leggings with a denim mini-skirt and jacket, and a long, belted, purple shirt with skulls on it. "Did you wear that to work today?"

"Yes," Whitney blurted. "It's a recording studio, everyone dressed like this."

"I see," she said in her 'I don't approve but I understand times change' voice. "Do you have anything suitable to change into?"

"I don't know. I haven't had a chance to check through my suitcases. I don't know if he gave me all my clothes," she gave a little chuckle, "or even if I have a hairbrush."

"Oh dear." Mrs. Myers frowned and led Whitney out of the office. "We will make the best of it. As you say, we will spin it."

Whitney grabbed her suitcases and followed her to the parking garage.

"Are you sure?" Whitney knew what a stickler for proper dress Mrs. Myers was.

"Well, in my past dealings with Mr. Ravilla, his interview methods have nothing to do with outward appearances," Myers explained as they got into the car.

"Is he one of those inner beauty fanatics?"

Mrs. Myers gave Whitney a stern frown as they slid out into traffic. "There is nothing wrong with inner beauty, Miss Martindale."

"Sorry, Mrs. Myers." As they traveled toward downtown Denver, Whitney wondered how that frown made her feel so guilty, but it did, every time.

"Ah, here we are," Mrs. Myers said as the car rolled to a stop.

Whitney stared up at the skyscraper as she got out. "I thought these were all office buildings. I didn't know you could live in one of them."

"You'd be surprised what's in some of these buildings."

"I already am," she mumbled as they entered the lobby and crossed the marble floor.

"Now, Whitney, he may seem a bit forward, so please don't take offense."

"Forward, huh? He isn't some kind of weirdo, is he?" Whitney squinted sideways at the older lady.

"No, dear," Mrs. Myers gave her an indulgent smile, "not in the way you are thinking."

"What's that supposed to mean? He's not going to jump on me and drain my blood in the middle of the night, is he? Or sacrifice me to a chicken or some other horrible thing?"

"Come along, dear."

"That wasn't an answer," Whitney said as she looked around.

A few people were milling around, mostly leaving for the day. Despite the impressive gray stone and metal lobby, Whitney was not impressed with the elevator ride. It went way too fast, and it was dead silent; the combination gave her an instant headache and a queasy stomach.

They stepped out into a small lobby with a red carpet so thick it seemed to suck up every sound in the room. Deep leather armchairs and a few potted ferns occupied two of the corners. In the center of each wall stood dark wood doors.

"Door number one, door number two, or door number three?" Whitney smirked.

A small sign that said InfiniCorp was next to the only open one. She followed Mrs. Myers into it and almost laughed when she saw the décor. It looked like an office from an old black-and-white detective film.

The blinds on the windows were closed, giving the room a gray, hazy glow. A couple of wooden chairs sat along the wall with a rack of magazines between them. An old wooden desk stood in the center of the room; behind it stood four large wooden filing cabinets. There was even a slowly turning ceiling fan. Except for the computer on the desk, the room probably hadn't changed in fifty years. She rather liked it.

Mrs. Myers' heels clicked on the hardwood floor as she crossed to a door behind the desk. She knocked lightly and then returned to Whitney's side.

One of the biggest men that Whitney had ever seen stepped through the door. His skin was dark but not quite black, and tattoos covered his cheekbones. She couldn't tell if his head had been shaved or if he was naturally bald, but somehow it made him look even more intimidating. The unimpressed sneer that he directed at the two women sent a chill down Whitney's spine. She hoped desperately that this was not the man she had to impress.

"Hello, Rami." Mrs. Myers smiled up at the giant. There seemed to be genuine affection in her tone.

"Mrs. Myers?" his deep voice rumbled. Whitney saw a sudden smile, and a twinkle filled the man's eyes.

"I have brought a new candidate for your receptionist position," she said, gesturing toward Whitney. As he ran his eyes up and down her in a once-over perusal, the twinkle increased.

"This way," he rumbled again and led them out the side door into a luxurious hallway that matched the lobby in style. Wood paneling ran halfway up the wall, then changed to a creamy, patterned wallpaper. Rami seemed to fill the hall as they followed him, making it impossible to see around him. A short distance down the hall, he turned into a room.

Mrs. Myers and Whitney followed him into an absolutely beautiful, dimly lit study. The dark wood paneling was in here too, but the top section of the wall was deep cobalt blue. Floor-to-ceiling bookcases lined one wall, filled with what looked like ancient books. A Persian rug covered the floor. There were matching overstuffed leather armchairs flanking an ornate chess set on an elegantly carved table. On the opposite side of the room was a carved wood desk. Everything in the room seemed to be from another era, one that believed in beauty before function.

Whitney had been so busy gawking at the furnishings that she hadn't noticed that everyone was silent. The lack of noise finally permeated her brain, and she turned to find Mrs. Myers and Rami watching her. Whitney just rolled her eyes and turned to find there was someone else in the room. He was sitting behind the desk. She was a little disconcerted that she hadn't noticed him before.

He was nearly as impressive as his study. He sat with his fingers steepled, staring at her. He had a lean face and a sharp nose and chin.

His hair was dark and closely cropped. He remained perfectly still, watching her with intensely dark eyes.

# LOST AND FOUND



"If you are through ogling my study, you may sit." The words seemed to roll out of him like silk.

He had a smooth, deep voice with the hint of some sort of accent, but she couldn't tell where it was from. His tone, however, grated on her nerves, and she couldn't stop her tongue.

"Well, if you are going to have a study this gorgeous, then you should expect people to gawk and give them time to appreciate it," she snapped and plopped down on the chair in front of his desk, glaring at him.

For a moment, the man just stared at her. Mrs. Myers sighed behind her, and she realized that was probably not the best thing to say if she wanted this man to give her a job. Her gaze faltered. She sat up a little straighter.

"Mr. Ravilla, this is Whitney Martindale," Mrs. Myers offered from behind her as she passed Whitney's resume to him.

She knew she had to look up now. Mrs. Myers always said to look the prospective employer in the eye when giving your resume.

Whitney raised her eyes, and thankfully, he wasn't still looking at her. He was, however, frowning at her resume. Seemingly satisfied by his unhappy perusal, he tossed the resume on his desk.

It shone like a beacon of failure against all the darkness of the desk. Whitney stared at it. Suddenly, it seemed like her whole life was that piece of paper. Outside of what was written there, she was nothing. She had done nothing, been nowhere, and didn't even have a boyfriend now. She sighed and tore her gaze away from the paper and found him watching her.

"Do you always dress like this for an interview?" His condescending look following her own self-condemning thoughts was just too much for her tongue.

"Oh yeah, I always try to look like an incompetent idiot for a first impression."

His frown deepened. It was obvious that he was not accustomed to being spoken to like that. Inwardly, she cringed. Her grandmother always said that she should learn to think before speaking.

"Well, I wasn't going to use those exact words…"

Before she could respond, he spoke again.

"Why did you leave your last job?"

"It left me," Whitney snorted.

"I would imagine that was an act of desperate self-preservation," he said, glaring at her.

"Oh really?" Whitney leaned forward. She wasn't going to just sit here and be insulted, not after the day she had had.

"Ray? May I speak with you?" Mrs. Myers asked quietly. He shoved his chair back from his desk and followed Mrs. Myers to the far corner.

Whitney frowned and crossed her arms, feeling petulant. She didn't need any help getting a job from a jerk. She had done it plenty of times, just look at her resume. At least half of her bosses had been obnoxious.

This guy was no different. Normally, it wouldn't be a big deal, but today she just wasn't in the mood to deal with self-important ass-holes.

She didn't need this job that badly. Just because she had nowhere to stay didn't mean that this was the only job for her. She could take any job and just stay with friends. That's what she would do. *Screw this Ravilla guy and his attitude.*

Whitney started to stand up when she caught Rami staring at her again. This time, there was sympathy in his stare instead of amusement.

"Whitney?" Mrs. Myers said quietly from right beside her chair, making her jump.

"Yes?" Whitney glanced over to see Ravilla standing behind Mrs. Myers with his arms crossed, glaring at her again.

"Mr. Ravilla has decided to give you a trial period."

"Really." Whitney's tone was more sarcastic than surprised.

Mrs. Myers nodded. "Yes, dear. So, I will leave you to it. Do try to get along." She started to leave but turned back and laid her hand on Whitney's arm. "Call me if you need anything." The way she said it made Whitney want to leave with her.

"I'll have your bags sent up," she called as she left. When the door closed behind her, it sounded so final. Whitney turned to find herself alone with Rami and Ravilla. A wave of unease washed over her.

For a moment, they watched each other: gaging, judging. Then he moved around the desk and sat down, motioning her to take her seat. Slowly, she obeyed.

"Miss Martindale. Your duties will be to answer the phone, file, make appointments, and sometimes run errands. For the most part, you will be working days. We don't open until ten, so you will have most of the morning to yourself. There is an apartment on the other side of the hall. It will be yours until you leave us. No live-in boyfriends or visiting overnight friends. I keep varying hours and may have need of you at any time, including in the middle of the night. You will be expected to come immediately if you are called," he said, pulling a cell phone out of the drawer and sliding it to her.

Reluctantly, she picked it up.

"You will direct anyone who comes to the office to wait, and then notify Rami or myself via the intercom. Under no circumstances will anyone pass your desk and enter the hall unless I say so. Rami or someone else will be on hand to back you up if necessary. Some of my clients are... insistent, you will be more so. Do you understand?"

He paused for her confirmation but instead heard her mumble, "Woof. Woof. Grr."

"Pardon me?"

"Fetch, carry, guard. Gotcha." She almost wanted to salute. Ravilla's gaze narrowed, and he flicked a glance at Rami, who was standing behind Whitney's chair. Ravilla frowned and then continued.

"You are not to pass beyond this study without escort. My living quarters are beyond that door, and I don't allow visitors."

At that point, he gave her such a pointed stare that she felt like he was already accusing her of poking around.

"Now about your wardrobe—"

"I have better clothes!" Whitney cut him off. She had had about enough of his insinuations. "They are just..."

He held up his hand. "Yes, I know about your circumstances."

She wasn't sure, but she thought that she heard some sympathy in his tone.

"Rami will go with you and retrieve the rest of your belongings."

Whitney's mouth dropped open. She had not expected sympathy or help from this arrogant man.

"Ah," she said, "thanks."

Ravilla waved her thanks away absently. "I was going to have you start tomorrow, but there is a dinner meeting that I must attend tonight, and I need a plus one. Get your things and then be back here dressed for a semi-formal dinner at eight." He paused and looked at her appraisingly. "You think you can handle that?"

Rather than roll her eyes, Whitney only frowned back at him. He took it for a yes.

With that, she was suddenly dismissed. His attention was on a file that had appeared on his desk at some point, although she couldn't remember when. Rami stepped forward and motioned her to follow him out.

Whitney followed Rami back down the hall, through the reception office, and back to the lobby outside the elevator. Everything was so quiet. Rami led her to the door on the left and motioned her inside. She stepped into the darkened room, once again questioning her own intelligence for blindly trusting these people.

Rami switched on the light, and Whitney blinked at the sudden brightness. When her eyes adjusted, she had to smile. The room was gorgeous. A cozy little living room with a big, soft couch faced the TV. Tiffany lamps stood on the end tables. A Chinese screen separated the living room from a small office, complete with a computer.

"There is a kitchen through there," Rami's deep voice rumbled from behind her, "and a bedroom and bathroom are over there."

She followed where he pointed, finding a beautiful marble-finished bathroom with a tub and separate walk-in glass shower in the corner. She giggled in girlish delight. Then she came back out and stepped into the kitchen area. It was very modern with stainless steel appliances, all done in black, white, and silver.

"I've never lived anywhere this nice in my life!"

"We take care of our own," Rami said from the kitchen door.

Braving the giant, she asked, "So what happened to the last receptionist?"

"She stopped coming to work."

"What," Whitney glanced at him, "like Ravilla scared her off? Or did the workload kill her?"

Rami studied the carpet at his feet.

She moved into the bedroom.

It was just as beautiful as the rest of the apartment. There was a huge four-poster bed with lots of pillows and two long windows on each side with heavy curtains. A cozy armchair that matched the salmon-colored comforter on the bed sat in the corner next to a huge ornate dresser with a carved mirror. More Tiffany lamps sat on the dresser and nightstand.

She returned to the living room to find a man standing in the door with her suitcases. His black leather jacket and sunglasses made him look like a hoodlum.

"Whitney Martindale, meet Philtzer," Rami rumbled.

"Hi," he said. "You the new receptionist?"

Whitney nodded, eying him skeptically.

"Good, I'm not cut out for desk work. Well, good luck. I imagine we'll be seeing each other a lot."

"Yeah? Why?"

"Philtzer works for Mr. Ravilla," Rami supplied. "He has been filling in as our receptionist."

Philtzer popped his sunglasses up onto the top of his head. His eyes were a very pale blue and contrasted strongly with his extremely black hair. The combination reminded Whitney of a Husky dog. He was good-looking enough to be a model, except he was too short. He smiled at her.

"Shall we take you to retrieve your belongings?"

"I guess," Whitney shrugged, "although I am not that optimistic about coming back with anything."

They closed up the apartment and walked to the elevator in silence. As they were riding down, Rami finally spoke.

"Why do you think we will not be able to collect your things?"

"Well, for starters, I don't even have a key."

"Is your name on the lease?"

"No," she frowned. "Technically, I have no right to have the manager let me in."

"Not a problem," Rami exchanged a mischievous grin with Philtzer.

"Wait!" Whitney exclaimed as she caught his meaning. "We can't just break in!"

"Why not?"

"Duh! It's illegal!"

"He'll never even know we were there," Philtzer reassured her.

# CHIVALRY IS UNDEAD

MADRAEUS KNOCKED ON WHITNEY'S door again. She hadn't answered the first time, but now he was hearing movement from the other side of the door.

"Coming, coming, coming!" He heard her call.

The door jerked open. She was still in the process of sticking a last pin into her hair. Then she turned to grab her purse and hit the lights.

"Sorry, I was trying to get ready as fast as I could. We only got back a few minutes ago," she puffed as she shrugged on her black velvet jacket.

Madraeus ran appreciative eyes over her. Mentally, he took back what he had said about no sense of style. Her young punk look from earlier was gone. She was now dressed in a classy black and green dress with her hair swept up into a French curl. She looked every inch a lady.

His eyes strayed to her neck, where she wore a string of green and black jeweled beads. She had a beautifully slender neck. He could see her pulse fluttering just under the skin, tempting him.

"Shall we go?" Whitney waited for him to move.

Madraeus shook himself, realizing that he had been staring at her neck for too long. He grunted and motioned her toward the elevator.

The meeting was in the conference room of a nearby hotel, so they walked. It had stopped raining, but puddles still lined the curbs. They walked in silence until they neared the hotel.

"This is an investor's meet and greet, so you won't really have to do anything. Just be polite and vague. Don't give any details about me or my company." Madraeus slid a glance at her.

"Well, that should be easy. I don't know anything about you or your company."

"You'll be fine; just mingle a little," he said, holding the door for her.

Madraeus handed his invitation to the door attendant and ushered Whitney into the conference room. The roar of wheeling and dealing surrounded them. People in suits were everywhere, laughing and talking.

Madraeus offered her his arm and started snaking his way through the room. Periodically, he would stop and speak with someone, and then they would move on. She watched Mr. Ravilla as he spoke. Everyone seemed to defer to him. He was wearing a suit just like everyone else, but he was more elegant and less Wall Street banker. He looked slightly out of place despite being completely at ease. Whitney got the sudden impression that he was humoring them all. He wasn't loud and boisterous like everyone else, and he wasn't drinking as much either. In fact, Whitney was sure that he hadn't even taken a sip of the drink that some guy had placed in his hand earlier.

The noise level increased. Most of the conversations were just innuendos and bad jokes that seemed to get worse as the alcohol consumption increased.

By the end of the night, Whitney was beginning to feel uneasy. She was grateful to Mr. Ravilla for keeping her with him, unlike some of the men who shooed away their escorts only to pursue others, like they were just some decoration or entertainment. Whitney had several lewd offers as they moved through the crowd, but her employer just kept walking as if he hadn't heard.

Suddenly, he turned to her and scanned her face intently. "I've had enough of this, shall we go?"

"Yes, please!"

Madraeus led her through the crowd. As they neared the door, one of the more drunk businessmen grabbed Whitney's rear end. She jumped to the side, stumbling into her employer.

"What's the matter?" he hissed as he tried to keep her upright.

"He grabbed me," Whitney whispered back, her face flushing red.

Madraeus frowned and Whitney thought that he was upset with her, but he moved around her toward the man who had grabbed her. Madraeus leaned in close and started to speak to him. Several people had noticed the commotion, and a small group of spectators was starting to gather.

Whitney glanced around as the crowd got bigger and wished that they could just leave. She turned her attention back to her boss. She couldn't hear what he said, but the other man suddenly turned pale and backed up, staring at Madraeus. Then he looked at Whitney, gave her a quick nod and muttered an apology, then turned and practically ran for the door.

The crowd started to murmur as Madraeus turned back toward Whitney. As he turned, she thought his eyes looked black for a moment, but when he looked at her, they were merely brown again.

"Come on," he growled, slipping a hand behind her and guiding her toward the door.

Whitney could feel the anger radiating out from him as they left the hotel. She was almost scared to talk to him. A chilly wind hit her as they rounded the corner. Crossing her arms to ward off the cold, she hurried to keep up with him as he strode toward home.

"What did you say to him?" she asked as she caught up with him.

"Who?" He sounded as if he could kill something.

"Who? That guy," she said as she hopped over a puddle.

"Nothing," he growled, trying to discourage her questions.

She trotted beside him for a moment in silence.

"Thank you."

"For what?" he growled again.

"For..." she didn't know exactly how to put it, "you know... back there."

"It doesn't matter." He waved her thanks away.

"It does to me."

He stopped suddenly in the middle of the sidewalk and looked at her. He studied her face.

"Look, that guy was an ass. I'm sorry that we had to go to that meeting, but it's over now, and we can forget it. I found out what I needed." He turned and started walking again.

"And what was that?" she asked, hurrying to catch him. She couldn't believe how fast he walked. She was starting to have trouble keeping pace.

"Information."

"Duh! What kind of information?"

"Why do you need to know?" he snapped.

"Because good receptionists hear lots of stuff and I wanted to know what to keep my ears open for," she explained as they reached the doors of his building. Once they were in the elevator, he turned to her and frowned.

"Good receptionists know when to keep their noses out of things." Before Whitney could reply, the elevator doors opened, and he stalked out, throwing a 'Goodnight' over his shoulder. He disappeared through the office door, leaving her standing alone in the lobby.

"Goodnight," she mumbled in disgust as she entered her apartment, feeling a great satisfaction in slamming the door behind her.

# YOU BUG ME

Whitney awoke puffy-eyed and groggy. She felt awful after staying up half the night and then crying herself to sleep. At first, she couldn't sleep because she had been angry with Ravilla, but then she started to think about going to sleep in that big bed alone. She hadn't slept alone in a year. She had always been with Justin. So, she had wandered around the house, stalling, but eventually crawled into those empty covers. Now she was paying for it.

After a nice hot shower and a comforting chocolate donut, she called her grandmother.

"Hi, Grammy," she said with faked enthusiasm.

"Whit? How are you?" Her grandmother's soft voice almost made her start to cry.

"OK, I just wanted to let you know that I'm not living with Justin anymore." She tried to say it matter-of-factly so that her grandmother wouldn't worry, but she should have known better.

"What! Tell me what happened. Did he hurt you?" Her grandmother sounded like she was ready to come through the phone.

"No! No, he just broke up with me." She couldn't bring herself to tell her that he had done it by leaving her suitcases in the hall with a note on top.

"Well, you need to just come on home then. I knew that he was no good for you."

Whitney rolled her eyes. "I'm not coming home, Grammy, I got a new place."

"That was fast."

"It is actually part of a new job."

"I thought you liked it at the recording studio."

"I did, but they got bought out and then closed down, so now I have a new job as a receptionist at an investment firm," she said, picking at a spot on the counter.

"What kind of receptionist job comes with an apartment? Whitney, are you sure that this is a legitimate company? You know, there are a lot of weirdos out there."

"I know, but this is legit. Mrs. Myers found it for me."

"Hmm, sounds a bit shady to me."

"Well, it seems to be a good job." Whitney glanced at the clock, "Speaking of which, I gotta go, Grammy, so I'm not late. Love you."

"Whitney, you be careful. I'll come see you soon and check out this job for myself."

"OK, talk to you later. Bye!"

She groaned. The last thing she needed was for Grammy to come and get into the middle of her new job, but she also knew that there was no stopping that woman.

She picked her outfit with vengeance in mind. Ravilla hadn't said anything bad about her dress last night, although he hadn't said anything good either. Armored in business attire, she headed over to the office. It took all of a minute.

"I'm certainly not going to lose weight walking to work," she chuckled.

Rami was waiting for her. He took in her crisp blue suit and smiled approvingly. They spent the next hour going over logins and passwords, procedures, and general duties. Then he disappeared through the door behind the desk, which she now knew led to his office.

She sat down and arranged the desk to her liking and then sat back to wait for the first client. However, as the hours crept by, no one came through the door, and no one called. She began to get bored.

Whitney explored the desk drawers. She poked into every nook and cranny. All she found was a lot of dust, a fashion magazine from two years ago, and a jumbled mess in the filing cabinet. Eventually, she was going to have to sort that out. Whitney decided that this was the most boring job she had ever had.

*Maybe that's what happened to the last receptionist*, she thought, *she died of boredom.*

It was nearing six p.m., and she was entangled in a gripping game of solitaire on the computer when a smooth voice made her jump.

"I see that daylight has improved your wardrobe."

As if sneaking up on her wasn't bad enough, he had to start out being rude.

"It apparently hasn't made you any nicer though," Whitney frowned at him.

"Do you speak to all your employers that way?"

"No, only the ones that have no manners," she said sweetly, turning back to her game.

"I have manners." He glared at her. At her lack of response, Madraeus frowned. He walked past her into Rami's office. He shut the door with a satisfying thump, imagining her head in it.

"What was that for?" Rami asked without glancing up from his paperwork.

"That girl is intolerable!" Madraeus snapped.

"What girl?"

He had known Rami for over 700 years, and he had seen his deliberately obtuse act before.

"What girl? What girl? That bloody Whitney Martindale!" He stamped back and forth.

Rami finally looked up. "I like her."

"What?" Madraeus stopped. "How could you like her? She is obnoxious!"

"She is actually quite nice and very intelligent."

"She is a harpy."

"And you are acting like a child. You have not even gotten to know her." Rami went back to his paperwork.

Madraeus threw himself into the chair and scowled. "I'm not acting like a child."

Rami merely sent him a speaking look and resumed his work. Madraeus waited for Rami to add another defense of the harpy, but when he remained silent, he gave up. It was obvious that Rami was not going to be baited. He leaned forward and fiddled with the glass paperweight that sat in the middle of Rami's desk.

"Is there something you wanted, or are you just here to annoy me?"

"Last night went pretty well," he said after a minute.

"Really? You and Whitney had a good time?" Rami asked.

"I wasn't talking about her. I meant the meeting." Madraeus watched Rami grin knowingly but ignored him. "They are going ahead with the deal. I think we should be able to get back about ten times our original investment."

"Good." Rami had never become as good as Madraeus at the investment game. With Madraeus in charge of their finances, they had increased their wealth exponentially in the past 200 years.

"So, you and Whitney had a good time then?" Rami grinned at him: the grin he used when he was going to let you find out for yourself what he already knew.

Madraeus growled and looked away. He wasn't about to tell Rami about the events of last night. He wasn't sure he even wanted to think about them. She had been the perfect escort. Her manners were impeccable, and she was very pleasant to look at. He still didn't know why he had jumped to her defense against that drunken buffoon.

A crash and a yelp from the outer office cut into the silence. Both men were instantly on their feet. They rushed into Whitney's office. She was backed into the corner, staring at the ceiling.

"What's wrong?" Madraeus demanded, searching for the cause of the crash.

"Wasp!" Whitney squeaked, pointing toward the light.

He turned to look where she was pointing. At that moment, the wasp dipped down toward Whitney, making her shriek and launch herself behind Madraeus. She huddled behind him, holding handfuls of his suit, steering him to stay between her and the wasp.

Madraeus was at a complete loss.

He was a 1,766-year-old vampire responsible for the safety of the entire population of immortals, and he was being used as a human shield against a bug. Madraeus looked toward Rami for guidance, but Rami was too busy controlling his laughter.

"Whitney, it's a wasp."

"I know! Kill it!" She pushed him forward, realized she wouldn't have her shield, and pulled him back with a squeak. "No! Stay here!"

"But it's just a wasp!"

"I know!"

Madraeus sighed, picked up the fashion magazine off the desk, and smashed the wasp in mid-flight, ricocheting it off the filing cabinet beside Rami.

"There! No more wasp!" He tossed the magazine back onto the desk.

"Are you sure it's dead?" she asked, peaking around his shoulder.

Rami reached out a toe and squished it.

"Yes."

Madraeus felt Whitney relax her hold. She leaned her head into his back.

"Thank you," she murmured.

Madraeus froze. He had not played the role of the rescuer in so many years. Now twice in twenty-four hours, he had. He felt uncomfortable with the idea of being anyone's knight in shining armor. His armor had been tarnished black decades ago. Now, of all people, Whitney was making him feel almost...

*No. I'm no one's hero. I'm a monster.* Madraeus shook her off and stalked out of the room.

"What did I say?" Whitney looked to Rami.

"It is alright. He is just..." Rami shrugged as if that explained everything. "It is very quiet. You can go home."

"Am I in trouble?"

"No, you are not in trouble." Rami smiled.

# FUZZY BUNNIES

"Is there something I can help you find?" she asked Madraeus.

"Where the Hell did you learn to file?"

Papers were sticking up in all directions, and nothing seemed to be labeled or organized. He slammed the filing drawer shut as he turned.

"Excuse me?" Whitney crossed her arms.

"It is part of your job to file things, is it not?"

"That filing cabinet was like that when I got here, so don't blame it on me." She held up her hands.

"I need the receipts from Gloria's shop," he snarled as he leaned an elbow on top of the cabinet. "I don't suppose you know where they are?" He made a grand invitational gesture with his hand.

She shoved her chair back, frowning at him the whole time. She stalked over to the filing cabinet and opened the drawer as if demonstrating how it was supposed to be done.

The clean scent of her perfume engulfed him. It was like being hauled in with a net. He swayed toward her.

After a moment of digging, she pulled out the file he wanted.

"Anything else?" She handed it to him with a sweet yet determinedly vacant expression.

"Find some time to fix the rest of it." He scowled to cover his momentary attraction to her. Then he turned and stalked into Rami's office.

"Bite me." He heard her mumble as he left.

"Don't tempt me," he muttered.

A couple hours later, Madraeus came out of his study and stood in the hall. His sensitive vampire's sense of smell had caught the whiff of something as he had been working. He wrinkled his nose. It smelled like it had been sweet and spicy at one time, but now it just smelled burnt. The whole hall was filling with the awful stench.

"Whitney," he growled and stalked down the hall to the door at the end. It led to her kitchen. He knocked, but there was no answer.

He could definitely smell smoke now. "She's going to burn the whole place down and never even notice."

Madraeus strode back to the study and dug through his desk drawer until he found the spare key. He marched back to her door, intent on draining every drop of blood from her body, no matter what Rami said.

He unlocked the door, threw it open, and stopped dead.

Smoke curled out of the open oven, escaping out the door above his head. In the midst of it all stood Whitney. She was holding the charred remains of her dinner, waving the smoke out of her eyes. She blinked in surprise at his sudden entrance. Her wet, uncombed hair was dripping a little puddle around her bare feet. She had obviously dressed in a hurry because only a couple of her buttons were fastened on her fuzzy pink pajamas. She set the smoking lump on the counter and closed the oven door.

"Sorry about the smoke," she coughed, waving some of the fumes away. "I guess I took too long in the shower."

He couldn't tear his eyes off the little white bunnies spaced out all over that pink flannel.

Whitney cleared her throat nervously as he continued to stare. She followed his gaze, glancing down to her nearly open front. With a gasp, she hurriedly finished buttoning her pajama top.

She shoved the wet hair back from her face and looked up at him.

"You have pink bunny pajamas."

"Yes?" Whitney looked down at her favorite pajamas.

He took the opportunity to flee.

Madraeus paced his study like a caged lion. He didn't know what to think. He hadn't thought about women in decades. The sight of Whitney dripping wet and wrapped in pink flannel stirred up forgotten feelings and almost had him marching back down the hall.

*No.* He couldn't afford to get involved with a mortal. *Not again, not like last time when Cecelia had...*

"No, never again." He knew it was too dangerous.

"I don't even like her. She's a harpy." With a frustrated snort, Madraeus plopped down at his desk. He tried to work on some investment files and the report from the council, but everything seemed to have a pink-flannel tinge.

"I'm just hungry," he muttered to justify his lack of concentration.

Madraeus walked out of his study into his apartment. He grabbed a bottle from the refrigerator on his way through the kitchen.

He stalked into his bedroom. It was blue like his study. It always reminded him of a midnight sky lit by moonlight. He had never taken to the whole Gothic theme that some vampires favored. He'd had enough damp and cold in the Dark Ages.

He opened the bottle and poured some of the dark red liquid into a glass, then flicked on his gas fireplace. He slid into the overstuffed armchair and stared at the fire.

Madraeus swirled the blood around the glass in disgust. He remembered a time when drinking blood from a glass had been an entertaining party trick.

"So much for progress."

Times had changed. It was evolution.

Madraeus glared at the liquid in the glass. He was a predator; he wanted to hunt. It was moments like this that made Madraeus question whether or not Cecelia was right. Maybe they should just take over the mortal world. Madraeus could easily imagine the chaos that would ensue if the council let the vampires and werewolves loose. It would be a carnival of blood.

He sighed.

Where would that leave the Pixies or the Witches? The Weavers would never forgive him. There were only seven of them left anyway. No, the council must maintain control.

It had been a long 220 years since Madraeus had been chosen to lead the council, especially when vampires like Cecelia pushed for less restriction. He sighed again. It seemed like a lot more effort to stop Cecelia's little schemes than it used to. It used to be a challenge, now he just felt tired.

Maybe he just needed a break, not that he was likely to get one. No one had the ability to handle Cecelia better than him. Long ago, when she had been new to this dark world, Madraeus had tried to guide her, but she wouldn't listen, and she wouldn't be tamed.

Madraeus slid further down into his favorite chair and sighed. He wasn't just stuck with a lunatic as a nemesis; he had one as a receptionist too. The thought of Whitney brought images of pink flannel back to his mind.

"Why did she have to be wearing pink pajamas?"

It had been over a hundred years since he had seen a woman's nightclothes.

He looked toward the wall on the far side of the room. She was on the other side of that wall, all snuggled up in her fuzzy bunny flannel, curled up under that fluffy comforter. Her dark brown hair splayed across one of those soft pillows.

He found himself in front of the wall. He laid his hand against it and closed his eyes. With his vampire senses, he could hear her heart beating steadily as she slept. He could feel the rise and fall of her breathing. Madraeus stood still, simply listening. There was such a pureness to her life as it pulsed through her. Longing filled him that had nothing to do with blood. He missed home and family.

He jerked back from the wall. Sick that she could bring up all that pain he had buried a thousand years ago.

*Damn her!*

Madraeus turned and stalked out toward the elevator. He needed to get out. He needed the night.

# WEIRD DAY AT THE OFFICE

WHITNEY SAT AT HER desk, drumming her fingers and glancing at the clock. Time crept by as she waited for the inevitable embarrassing confrontation with her boss. They didn't have the most cordial working relationship to start with, and now it was going to be really awkward too.

It wasn't every day that your employer sees you in your pajamas, *and* only half-buttoned, *and* dripping wet. She had lain awake most of the night, wondering what to say to Mr. Ravilla when she saw him again.

She was also a little concerned that he had a key and obviously felt no qualms about using it. Maybe she could put a chain on the inside of the kitchen door. It might keep him out, but it would probably piss him off. He might even get mad enough that he would fire her.

Whitney heard the elevator and panicked, wondering if that was him. She glanced at the clock again; it was almost six.

Luckily, it was only a deliveryman pushing a dolly with three large coolers on it. He carefully navigated her office door and then set them down next to the door leading to the hallway. He came over to her desk and handed her a clipboard, pointing to a line with his pen.

"Sign," he said in a bored voice. She did, and then he went to open the hallway door.

"Excuse me." Whitney jumped up. "What are you doing?"

"I'm going to put these away."

"I'm sorry, I can't let you go back there without Mr. Ravilla's consent, and he's not here."

He turned and looked her up and down. "You're new, huh?"

"Yeah, so?"

"Look, honey, I've been delivering here once a week for several years. I bring the coolers and I put them in the fridge in back. Now you're telling me I can't?"

"I'm sorry, but those were my instructions."

He looked around the room and then blew out a sigh. "Fine. I don't have time to argue. You put 'em away and I'll see you next week."

With that, he took his dolly and strode out the door. Whitney watched him go, wondering if she had just made a mistake. She walked over and looked at the coolers.

A large sticker on top said 'Refrigerate Immediately.' Now she really felt bad. She had no idea where this fridge was that he had mentioned, and there was no one to ask.

Whitney wondered what was in them. Technically, it was none of her business what Ravilla had delivered, but on the other hand, it might make a difference how long they could stay out of the fridge.

"Crap." Whitney glanced at the door again, and feeling a little mischievous, she cracked the lid and peered inside.

"Hey, sugar-pop, whatcha doin'?" a playful voice asked. Whitney jumped backward, and the lid slammed down.

"Philtzer! Damn it! You scared the hell out of me!" Whitney glared at him over the top of the cooler. "Where did you come from? I didn't hear the elevator."

"Undoubtedly, you were distracted." He gave her a toothy knowing grin.

"Don't look at me like that." She quickly poured out her story about the deliveryman and her worry about messing things up.

Philtzer listened to all of her ranting, patiently smiling and nodding sympathetically. He leaned his elbows on the cooler and rested his chin in his hands.

"How was I supposed to know what to do?" Whitney threw her hands in the air.

Philtzer smiled at her again.

"Do you know how cute you are when you're flustered?" He wiggled his eyebrows at her.

"It's not funny," she protested, smiling in spite of her worry.

"No, it's not," he said almost seriously, and came around behind her. He took her shoulders and guided her to her desk chair.

"Hmm, you smell really good," he purred as he prodded her to sit down. He leaned on the arms of her chair and stared into her eyes.

She stared back with one eyebrow up and her nose wrinkled.

"What's that look for?" He cocked his head to one side like a puppy.

"I'm not sure if I should say thank you or slap you."

He grinned wolfishly. "Let's decide that later."

"Ahem." The sound of an angry throat being cleared made Philtzer shoot upright and Whitney jump.

Madraeus stood on the other side of the desk with his arms crossed and his gaze sliding from Whitney to Philtzer to the stack of coolers. The look on his face made Whitney feel like she just got caught making out on her grandmother's couch.

"Care to explain?" he growled. Whitney and Philtzer both started talking at once. Madraeus held up his hand. Philtzer stopped, but Whitney kept going.

"—showed up and scared the crap out of me. Then—"

"Who scared you?" Madraeus demanded.

"Well... he did," she pointed at Philtzer, "then you did."

Madraeus slid his gaze to Philtzer, who immediately backed up with his hands up, deliberately not meeting Madraeus' eyes.

"Not intentionally, she just didn't hear me."

"Hmm," he growled and then asked, "And the coolers?"

"Well, the delivery guy said he was going to put them away, but you said no one goes past me without your permission, and you never gave permission, so what was I supposed to do? And where have you been anyway? The whole afternoon and not a peep, what kind of a way is that to run a business?" She ended her defensive ranting with her hands on her hips, glaring at Ravilla.

Madraeus watched her for a moment. Slowly, her bravado started to slip, and her hands slid to her sides.

"You will have a list of authorized deliveries and those with permission tomorrow." Madraeus turned to Philtzer. "Get those put away."

Philtzer nodded quickly and grabbed a cooler, disappearing down the hall. Whitney watched them, sure that she had missed something. Then Ravilla simply turned and walked away without another word. Whitney slowly sank back into her chair. She wasn't sure what had just happened. She couldn't believe she had let her mouth get away from her again.

She kept one eye on the hall door just waiting for him to come back and yell at her, but when nothing further happened, she started to relax.

Whitney forced her attention back to The Dreaded Filing Project, as she now called it. She had hoped that maybe it would suddenly get easier, but it seemed to get more confusing. There were references to so many different countries, and names, and companies that she was beginning to think that every person on the planet was going to have a separate file. Eventually, she figured out a system and started making piles. She would have to sort them by region, then by business, and then re-label everything. Everything needed referenced and cross-referenced.

*This was the reason the last receptionist ran away; she tried to work on the filing cabinet, and her head exploded.* Whitney smiled at the thought.

"Something funny, little one?"

Whitney jumped and turned to find a very thin, very tall, Black woman standing by her desk. She was dressed in brilliant greens and rich browns like a walking rainforest. Her eyes seemed to glow like fiery amber as she gazed down at Whitney.

A shiver crept over Whitney. It wasn't from fear but something else, power, the same kind that Ravilla emanated.

"Sorry, may I help you?" Whitney snapped out of her silence.

The woman smiled. She started to move around to Whitney's side of the desk. Her movements were graceful and slow. Whitney was fascinated; it was like watching a lion walk. She stopped in front of Whitney. Resisting the urge to back up, Whitney waited.

"I am Unkhabami." The woman's accent was thick, and she had pronounced her name with a click in the middle. She gazed down at Whitney like she expected some kind of recognition.

Whitney only stared at her blankly, mentally trying to pronounce the woman's name.

"I am Unkhabami, High Priestess of the Paka Watu," she repeated, forming her words with such a peculiar enunciation that Whitney found herself staring at the woman's mouth as she spoke.

"Hi," Whitney blurted into the silence, "I'm Whitney…"

"You are Whitney Martindale." The woman spoke her name as if she already knew who Whitney was. Unkhabami peered at her closely, looking her up and down, as if she was looking for something. Finally, she smiled, her eyelids drooped, and her eyebrows moved upward.

"You do not yet know." Unkhabami's smile widened. "You are definitely the one."

"I'm sorry," Whitney frowned. "I'm not sure what you're talking about?"

"You," Unkhabami said slowly as if speaking to a child. "You are Whitney Martindale."

"I am aware of that." Whitney couldn't help it, she rolled her eyes. "What does that have to do with you, and how do you know who I am?"

"I have seen your coming. You will be instrumental in the flow of events very soon." Her smile turned matronly as she cupped Whitney's cheeks in her hands. "Know this, the darkness is coming, but you will not weather it alone."

Whitney opened her mouth to ask her what she was smoking and tell her it was time to quit when Rami walked into the office.

"Bami!" He grinned as he rushed forward to give the woman a hug.

Whitney couldn't help herself; she just stared at them while they exchanged greetings. With the two of them in the room, Whitney felt like a dwarf in a land of giants. Whitney watched Rami usher Unkhabami into his office.

"That is one creepy lady," Whitney muttered with a shiver.

# STIRRINGS

"Unkhabami?" Madraeus rose from behind his desk as the priestess and Rami entered.

"Madraeus, you are well?"

"Yes, and you?" Madraeus bowed.

"I am well." She inclined her head in a small bow.

"Would you care to have a seat?" Madraeus swept a hand toward the armchairs in the corner.

She glided across the room just like the giant jungle cat she could transform into. Sliding into the leather chair, she turned her amber eyes to Madraeus.

Rami hovered beside her. Rami never strayed far from Unkhabami when she visited. Madraeus knew that something had happened between them long ago. He often wondered about their history but would never ask. After all, he was a man who was well-versed in keeping his own secrets.

"To what do we owe the honor of this visit?" Madraeus searched her face. The High Priestess of the Paka Watu rarely left the jungles of the Congo.

"There are stirrings."

"What kind of stirrings?" Rami asked, stepping closer.

Unkhabami glanced at Rami, then back to Madraeus. "I have seen a war coming, unlike anything I have ever known."

Madraeus nodded. Unkhabami, like Mrs. Myers, had the ability to prophesize. Unfortunately, Unkhabami usually foretold massive catastrophes.

"Ancient things are surfacing." The priestess sat forward, her amber eyes glowed with the intensity of what she was saying. "Someone is digging up the Old Sources."

"What Old Sources?" Madraeus asked.

"Dark creatures. Myths. Hidden away, some imprisoned," Unkhabami whispered.

"Imprisoned how?" Rami asked.

"Some by magic, some by ancient machines," the priestess shrugged. "The Hares have guarded them all for centuries."

"The Hares," Madraeus snarled. "Genocidal fanatics." His fangs started to show. He took a deep breath to regain control. "Who's digging?" Madraeus asked quietly, but he was pretty sure he knew the answer.

"It is who you think," Unkhabami confirmed.

"Cecelia is outdoing herself this time," he sighed.

"If she is resurrecting an army..." Rami began.

"There is more," Unkhabami said. "It is not only Cecelia's digging that we must worry about. There have been disappearances as well."

"Disappearances?"

"Yes, fate lines have shifted. There are gaping holes where once there were lives."

"Who has disappeared?" Rami rumbled.

"That is all that I may tell you." Unkhabami held up a hand and shook her head.

"Alright." Madraeus sighed when she refused to say more. "Thank you for telling me. You know that you could have called instead of coming all the way here."

"No, my friend. I had to come in person." She shook her head again. "I had to have a look at her myself."

"Who?"

"Whitney Martindale."

"Why?"

"I will only say this. Keep an eye on her and keep her close. It is very important." She grabbed his hand. "You must not allow her to leave your side."

She continued staring at him until he nodded, then she stood and glided out of the room.

For a long time, Madraeus just stared at the chess set that occupied the table between the chairs. He was so tired of the cat-and-mouse games that Cecelia loved to play. For centuries, he had tried to temper her, to tame her, to fight her. Sometimes he wished he could just kill her, but he couldn't.

And now this. He couldn't allow Cecelia to start a war. On top of that, Unkhabami's warning about Whitney did not bode well either. *What connection did Cecelia's antics have to Whitney?*

Madraeus sighed, then looked up at Rami. "We can't fall behind on this. We had better get someone researching the Old Sources. I'll see if Marcus can track down the," he sneered their name, "Hares."

"I will see if I can find anything about these disappearances," Rami rumbled as he walked to the door, then said over his shoulder, "Do not forget about Mrs. Myers' party."

"Damn," Madraeus shoved to his feet and walked over to his desk. He called into the intercom, "Whitney, would you come to my study, please?"

A moment later, she peeked around the door, then slowly moved over to stand in front of his desk.

"You wanted to see me?"

The scent of her perfume wafted around him, and then all he could think about was pink flannel.

"Mr. Ravilla, I'm sorry about the delivery. I didn't know what to do, so I just made a decision. I'm sorry if it was wrong," she blurted out.

Madraeus frowned. She thought he had called her in here because she was in trouble. Unkhabami's warning about keeping her close flashed through his mind. If Cecelia was planning a war, then keeping a mortal around was the last thing he wanted to do, but Unkhabami had said that it was important. It seemed that he was going to be stuck with Whitney one way or another.

Whitney squirmed under his stare. Madraeus clenched his jaw and got a hold of himself. He had never been one to shy away from his duty just because he knew it would get ugly.

"I am not worried about the delivery."

He wondered if she had seen that the coolers contained a shipment of blood. She didn't act like she had seen anything unusual, so he assumed their secret was still safe, for now.

He cleared his throat and returned his attention to the task at hand. "There is a function tonight."

Whitney groaned.

"It's a birthday party for Mrs. Myers. She has requested your presence."

"Oh!" Whitney lit up. "What time? Where?"

Madraeus held up a hand. "You will be accompanying me—"

"You?" Whitney exclaimed.

"Yes, me!" he snapped. "Is there something wrong with that?"

"No, it's just…" She fidgeted.

"Yes?"

"Are you asking me on a date?"

"No!" he said. "You are going and so am I, and so is Rami."

"Oh, I was gonna say…" she laughed nervously.

"What?" Madraeus frowned at her and crossed his arms, daring her to finish.

"It's not that I wouldn't… I mean… I don't… I just…" She laughed again a little more nervously. "I don't even know your first name," Whitney blurted stupidly.

He stared at her. She was the most confusing woman he had ever met, and that was saying something. "It's Ray," he found himself saying.

Whitney raised an eyebrow.

"Now what?" He couldn't fathom what was wrong now.

"Well…" Whitney shrugged. "I just expected your name to be more…" She gestured around the room.

"More what?"

"I don't know," Whitney shrugged again, "more… um… intimidating, I guess." Madraeus raised an eyebrow. "Sorry! I just meant…" her words faded out. Whitney looked away, and Madraeus sighed.

"My full name is Madraeus Nicoteles Peltrasius Ravilla." His voice was barely a whisper.

Whitney's head shot up. She stared at him with her jaw hanging slack. His accent came out stronger as he said his name.

He hadn't said his full name in ages. He wasn't even sure why he had told her. It made him feel vulnerable. He felt like he had just given her something fragile and now he waited to see if she was going to break it.

"Now that suits you," she slowly smiled.

He let out the breath he had been holding. Why it mattered what she thought of his name he didn't know, but it did.

"Should I call you Madraeus, or Ray? Or would you rather I stick to Mr. Ravilla?"

"Whatever you prefer." He gestured uncomfortably with one hand.

"I like Madraeus," she smiled. "It's fun to say. So, what time do we leave?"

He had trouble processing that his name was fun, and for a moment, he didn't answer. Then he said, "The party is at eight and it is formal attire."

"What?" She searched around for a clock.

"Whitney—" Madraeus began.

"Dude, you could have given me more warning! That gives me less than an hour! What'll I wear? Damn, I hope I have something that isn't completely wrinkled!" She spun around and headed for the door.

"Whitney." He didn't say it loudly, but his tone stopped her dead. She turned as he lifted a large box onto his desk.

"I anticipated your wardrobe needs."

"Oh really," Whitney stomped back across the room. She looked ready to fight until he lifted out the dress from the box. "Oh…"

Madraeus smiled at her sudden silence. "Now, please get dressed. We will wait for you in the lobby," he said, gently replacing the dress and handing her the box.

Whitney grabbed it and fled.

# All Dressed Up

Madraeus paced the length of the lobby again. Then stopped and glared at Whitney's door.

"How long does it take to put on a damn dress?" he growled.

"Sometimes hours," Rami chuckled from the armchair by the elevator.

"You're not helping. How can you just sit there? We're going to be late because that damned woman is taking her time."

He should have known better than to get involved with a mortal. They had no sense of priorities. He was glad that women had faded from his interests; they were too much trouble. He just wished that Whitney hadn't revived his attention.

"Come on, we're leaving without her," he snarled just as her apartment door opened.

Whitney stepped out, holding her coat, and pulled the door shut behind her. Rami surged to his feet.

"Whitney, you look magnificent!" He smiled at her, and she self-consciously smoothed down the deep maroon satin.

She turned toward Madraeus and spread her hands. "Well, what do you think?"

Madraeus grunted. He wasn't going to say that she was an absolute vision. Her dark hair was swept up off her beautifully slender neck, held in place by green-jeweled flower pins that matched her eyes. The maroon dress brought out the bright blush of life that was bursting out of her.

"Look, Bub." She stalked forward and poked him in the chest, "You bought it, so if you don't like it, then it's your own fault. I happened to think it's gorgeous, and if you think you're going to make me feel guilty for taking too long, you can bite me, 'cause you're the one who left it 'til last minute!" With that, she spun on her heel and marched to the elevator.

Madraeus mumbled something about the harpy being back then stalked after her. Rami followed, trying not to smile.

Mrs. Myers' house wasn't a house. It was a mansion. It was three stories with windows everywhere. She lived at the west edge of the city, nestled up against the mountains. The wide driveway circling around a fountain was lined with cars and limos. A set of wide marble stairs led up to the house.

Inside, they followed the noise to the ballroom where two huge crystal chandeliers hung from the inlaid ceiling, making the room sparkle. There was a small stage at the far end with a live mini-orchestra playing. Round tables and chairs were scattered around the edges of the room. A bar was set up along the far side of the ballroom. The whole room glittered with men in tuxedos and women in sparkling evening gowns.

"Close your mouth, Whitney," Madraeus whispered as he stepped up beside her.

Whitney snapped her mouth shut and glared at him. She looked like she was trying to control the urge to kick him in the shin. He smiled at her, daring her to do it. She shifted her weight slightly, and he wondered if she really would kick him, but then Mrs. Myers appeared in front of the trio.

"Whitney?"

"Hi, Mrs. M.!" Whitney turned and gave her a quick hug. "Happy Birthday!"

"Thank you, I almost didn't recognize you. You are absolutely stunning. Wherever did you find that dress?"

"Well, I wish I could take the credit, but I didn't find it." She jerked a thumb over her shoulder toward Madraeus. "He did."

"Oh really?" Mrs. Myers gave her a piercing look. After a moment, she turned it on Madraeus. "Hmm."

He glared back at her, refusing to give the Weaver any ammunition for her meddling.

"What do you mean, hmm?" Whitney challenged. She never got her answer because Rami interrupted by taking Mrs. Myers' hand and bowing gallantly.

"Mrs. Myers," he rumbled, "Happy Birthday."

"Thank you, Rami."

"Apologies for our late arrival." Madraeus bowed slightly to Mrs. Myers. "Happy Birthday."

"Thank you, Ray."

"Nice banner!" Whitney laughed, pointing to the banner proclaiming 'Happy 2,325th Birthday' hanging above the orchestra.

"Yes, well." Mrs. Myers blushed. She turned to Madraeus. "I expect you to keep Whitney out of danger."

Madraeus scowled back at her, insulted that she would think otherwise.

"What do you mean out of danger?" Whitney asked as her gaze slid from Mrs. Myers to Rami to Madraeus.

"She means try not to insult everyone you meet," Madraeus growled.

"Whitney Martindale, you are in a different world tonight." Rami smiled. "Many of the people here are not quite what you think. Try to be careful what you say."

"I doubt it's all that dramatic, but I'll behave." Madraeus looked down at her expectantly. "I promise."

"What's shakin', sugar?" Philtzer said in her ear.

Whitney jumped, spinning to face him. "Don't do that!"

He grinned wolfishly at her.

Whitney rolled her eyes. "I didn't know you'd be here."

"Are you kidding? We're all here!"

"What does that mean?" She frowned at him, then looked at Madraeus.

"You look amazing," Philtzer deftly avoided her question. "You should be dancing!"

"But I was—"

"'Xcuse me, kids!" Grinning, he elbowed Madraeus aside and grabbed her hand, pulling her toward the dance floor. "Pretty girl needs to dance!"

Madraeus growled softly as Philtzer took Whitney away. He turned to find Rami grinning at him before the giant turned to speak to someone standing next to him. Madraeus glared at his back, then looked back toward the dance floor.

"So, you chose her gown?" Mrs. Myers' words sounded like polite conversation, but Madraeus knew better.

"It was the first one off the rack."

"Really? And yet it was a perfect fit." She had managed to keep the irony out of her tone.

Madraeus had to admire her for it, but still, she was up to something. Weavers always were.

"What are you implying?" He slid a glance at her and crossed his arms.

"Nothing at all."

"I don't appreciate being manipulated, Anastasia. You should know better."

"As should you," she snapped, making him glance at her.

"We need to talk."

"About Whitney?" she asked in a chilly tone.

"No. About missing persons." He let his gaze drift over the crowd. "Have you noticed any?"

"Not specifically." Mrs. Myers shrugged. "But you know that our community is ever-changing. We move around all the time."

"This is more specific than just a few people changing locations." Madraeus glanced down at her. "I was led to believe that there were some individuals who have completely vanished."

"Vanished?" She turned to face him. "Have they been killed?"

"I don't know." His eyes returned to the crowd.

"I will see what I can find."

"Thank you. Is Marcus here tonight?"

"No, he couldn't make it." Mrs. Myers looked up to search his face. "What is going on?"

"I was told a war is coming. One unlike anything we've ever seen." He turned and looked down at her.

Her eyes widened, but whatever reply she was going to make was lost to Madraeus when he heard Whitney's laugh. His eyes searched her out on the dance floor. Whitney hung off of Philtzer's shoulder, laughing. Madraeus unconsciously clenched his fists.

As if she felt Madraeus glaring at her, Whitney turned and searched the crowd. Their gazes locked for a moment before Philtzer led her off the floor. Madraeus watched as she hung back while Philtzer moved up to the bar. With effort, he turned his attention back to Mrs. Myers.

"Cecelia's here!" Rami appeared at his elbow. "And she's heading for Whitney."

He spun around. His eyes snapped to the spot where Whitney had been. A tall blonde woman sauntered up to her. He could tell just by the way she was standing with her arms crossed and chin thrust upward that this would not end well.

At that moment, the orchestra announced a break, and the crowd of dancers moved off the floor, obscuring his view. He lost sight of Whitney and Cecelia.

"Get her away from my Whitney!" Mrs. Myers snapped, giving Madraeus a shove.

He didn't need it; he was already moving.

# OLD FRIENDS

Whitney cleared her throat and smoothed her dress as they left the dance floor. She didn't know why Madraeus had to keep glaring at her. She was just having fun. Granted, Philtzer was feisty, and his jokes were the dirtiest she had ever heard, but at least he was fun. She just wished Madraeus would lighten up and quit condemning her for everything she did.

"So, you are the new receptionist," a velvety voice crawled across her skin.

Not liking the contemptuous way the woman had said receptionist, Whitney turned to confront the woman and found herself facing a veritable goddess: tall, blonde, and very well endowed. Her white evening gown, mostly made of translucent layers, seemed to whisper about the secrets they hid as she moved. Languid blue eyes looked her up and down in the same way that Madraeus had that first day.

"I suppose we all must have some sort of job," the woman sneered.

Whitney crossed her arms and glared up at the woman. She had taken enough crap from her boss this week; she wasn't going to let this unknown floozy stand here and insult her too.

Whitney returned her up-and-down appraisal. She had to reevaluate her opinion. This woman was not a goddess. She was a bit manly, more of an Amazonian bully. She was too perfectly constructed. In fact, Whitney was pretty sure that most of her had to be fake.

"Yeah, had to settle for receptionist. I heard the catty bitch position had already been filled."

Fury filled the other woman's eyes, making her face look strangely distorted; then she stopped as if someone was speaking to her, but there was no one around. A moment later, the woman smiled, showing lots of teeth.

"Oh, my little Madraeus must just love having you around. He must think you're so cute!" she said with a little laugh, then shook her head. "No. No. Cute is not the correct word. What is the word?" The woman tilted her head to the side. "Pathetic? Desperate?"

"Excuse me? If you want desperate, just look in the mirror, sister, plastic ain't that fashionable!" Whitney snorted.

"Watch your tongue!" The woman glided forward, stopping just short of stepping on Whitney, and glared down at her. "Someone might rip it out." Then the woman simply turned and walked away.

Whitney watched her disappear into the crowd. Some of the people around her who had witnessed the confrontation started whispering to each other. Everyone was looking at her. She looked around desperately wishing Philtzer would come back, but he was still at the bar. Suddenly, she wanted to be anywhere but here. She needed to be away from all these people. Whitney turned and dashed into the hallway.

"Whitney?" a familiar voice spoke behind her. She spun around.

"Justin?" She gaped. "Why are you here?"

All in one moment, she wanted to scream, laugh, throw herself into his arms, and slap him. Instead, she just stood there as he sauntered forward.

He was in a tuxedo like everyone else, but he looked different somehow. He was paler than he used to be, and there was a wildness about him that hadn't been there before. He motioned to a door down the hall.

"I'd like to talk for a moment."

Still in shock, Whitney let him lead her into the room across the hall. It was a small office with bookshelves, filing cabinets, and a desk. He kept his hand on her arm, but it was not like it used to be. His grip was hard and icy.

"I want to talk about us."

That comment snapped Whitney out of her shock.

"What us? You dumped me with a note!" She jerked her arm away and stepped back. "What happened to your better offer?"

"That wasn't my fault. Someone else left that note."

"Oh, so you let someone else break us up with a note?"

"I didn't let anyone break us up."

"So, you told them to do it?" Whitney shouted. "And what's wrong with your face? Why are you so pale? Are you sick?"

"I was sick before." He shook his head. "We were sick."

"What?"

"It doesn't matter, I'm better now, better than I've ever been, and I can offer you a life you wouldn't believe. You can be better too. I want you with me. We could do things that would blow your mind," he said as he stalked toward her.

"What are you talking about? Are you high?" He certainly seemed to be in an altered state. She wondered if he was drunk, but he wasn't acting like the normal, funny drunk she was used to.

"You don't have to live this mundane existence, Whit." He gestured toward the world at large.

"I kind of like my mundane existence, thanks!" Whitney crossed her arms.

"We're meant to be together. It's okay, I'll take you back."

"Take me back! If you are willing to dump me once, you'll probably do it again."

"No, Whit, you are going to be mine." He smiled, but it didn't reach his eyes. He stepped closer.

"I don't belong to you!"

"You will." He kept backing her up until she was against a filing cabinet.

"You're starting to scare me." Gone was the joking, happy Justin she had spent so much time with. This man was hard, cold, and mean.

She eyed the open door behind him. There was no way to get by him. He had her cornered. He reached out and gripped her shoulders so hard she winced.

"Justin, you're hurting me!" She squirmed, trying to get free, but he held her tighter, pressing her back against the cabinet with his body. His face seemed to change. All his features became sharper. Suddenly, his head dipped, and blinding pain shot through her neck.

Whitney panicked.

She struggled harder. She kicked his legs, but it had no effect. She needed a weapon. Her hands flailed around, trying to find something to hit him with. Nothing came into her grasp. Her vision started to swim. She couldn't get a breath in to scream.

Her knee came in contact with his groin, and he pulled back with a roar. His distorted face was covered in blood. Terror filled Whitney as he lunged for her again. He knocked her back, slamming her against the filing cabinet. Her head was spinning. She couldn't see straight.

With desperate inspiration, she reached up and grabbed one of the jeweled flowers from her hair. It had a five-inch spike on the end of it like a chopstick.

Wildly, she stabbed at him. She must have hit something vital because she heard him scream, then he was gone.

Blood ran down her neck, soaking the front of her dress. She sank to the floor. She tried to put a hand to her throat, but her arm seemed limp. Her eyes drifted closed. She knew she should cry out for help, but all her energy seemed to disappear.

# IT STARTS

Madraeus pushed his way through the crowd as quickly as he could with Rami right on his heels. They were about halfway when his nostrils flared.

*Blood.*

He looked around. He didn't see Whitney or Cecelia anywhere, but werewolves and vampires alike were sniffing the air. The smell of fresh blood filled the room.

Madraeus pushed his way through the crowd faster. From the strength of the scent, there had to be a lot of blood. He had to get to the source before the others or it was going to be a feeding frenzy.

Madraeus dashed through the door to the hallway. The scent was coming from a small office just down the hall. A trail of blood led away from the office, but the source of the scent was still in the room. Cautiously, Madraeus peered into the darkened room. The light from the hall was just enough to pick out the body lying against the wall.

"No!" Recognition had him racing into the room, sliding the last few feet on his knees.

"Whitney!" Gently, he picked her up. She was very pale. Blood covered her neck and chest. Hunger bubbled to life, but Madraeus stamped it down. "Whitney, open your eyes!" he commanded.

Slowly, she drifted back from sleep.

"Whitney?" Rami knelt beside Madraeus.

"Whitney, stay with me!" Madraeus ordered.

"Figures... die in an office," she breathed. Her eyes drifted closed again.

"No! Whitney, stay awake!"

"She is still losing blood! Whatever idiot did this did not close the wound," Rami whispered.

Madraeus leaned forward. He gently held Whitney's head as he bent to her neck. The smell of blood fired his hunger. It was on the floor and all over Whitney. He closed his eyes and shook from the effort of trying to control it. Then the perfume that Whitney wore teased his nose and filled his head, bringing a moment of clarity. Quickly, before he lost control again, he ran his tongue across the bite marks, closing them.

The blood stopped flowing. He held her close for a moment, feeling her life. Her heart still beat but slowly. Her chest rose and fell almost steadily against him.

"Get Myers," Madraeus rasped out.

Rami eyed his still-shaking friend. Then quickly turned away from the couple to face the crowd filling the doorway.

"Get back!" He pushed against them. "Mrs. Myers!"

Madraeus kept holding Whitney tight to his chest. The taste of her was on his tongue: sweet, young, vibrant, and warm.

*Tassste her,* a hissing voice whispered quietly in his head.

He fought against the need to taste her again. He wanted more of that sweetness, that warmth. More than that, he wanted her. He wanted Whitney. He didn't know why. He barely knew her.

*Take her.*

He pulled back to look at her. Stroking her cheek with a blood-covered finger, he watched her eyes flutter as if she was dreaming. She really was beautiful even this close to death. He could save her from dying, but it meant killing her.

*Yesss. Kill her,* the voice hissed again, a little stronger.

*It wouldn't take much,* he thought, leaning forward again.

*Not much at all...*

*Whitney would be gone,* he thought. She would live as he did. A cold existence in the darkness for eternity, but at least she would live.

*Yesss...* He blinked and shook his head, trying to dispel the voice.

"Ray?" Mrs. Myers touched him lightly on the shoulder. "Bring her upstairs."

Slowly, he nodded. He carefully picked up Whitney's limp body and carried her into the hall. It was empty. Rami must have pushed everyone back into the ballroom. Madraeus followed Mrs. Myers up the stairs, holding Whitney close. Holding her was a small comfort against that voice. Hearing it again after so many years disturbed him more than he wanted to admit.

Mrs. Myers led him into a cheerful bedroom decorated with roses. She hurried to the bathroom and grabbed a towel to spread on the bed, then motioned Madraeus to bring Whitney. Madraeus carried her over and laid her down gently.

Dr. Kirkland came through the door behind them carrying his archaic, black doctor's bag.

"You need to go," Mrs. Myers prodded Madraeus gently. When he didn't move, she took his arm and steered him toward the door. "I will tell you what the doctor says."

She closed the door behind him. He turned and headed for the stairs. With every step, the fear that had gripped him lessened. There would be time to feel later, right now, he had work to do. By the time he reached the ballroom door, he was angry.

He flung open the ballroom doors. The room instantly fell dead silent.

"I want to know who did this." Madraeus' voice was deadly quiet. He looked across the faces that stood before him. No one moved.

"I want to know who did this!" His roar echoed off the walls. Several people shifted uneasily. No one wanted to draw attention to themselves by moving. Madraeus was a fair and capable leader, but they all knew he was a dangerous man to cross.

He stood waiting, but no one volunteered any information. Madraeus frowned.

"Philtzer!"

"Yeah, boss?" Instantly, he was in front of Madraeus.

"Take your pack. There is a blood trail, follow it." Philtzer nodded and disappeared out the door with several people on his heels.

"The rest of you, if you don't have any information, go home." Madraeus stood silently as pixies, vampires, werewolves and witches double-timed it to the door. Moments later Rami, Madraeus, and one girl were the only ones left.

She slowly approached, obviously afraid of how her information would be received. Madraeus' expression softened. He remembered this little witch; she had been to see him in the last week. She had a problem with a vampire not paying his bills. He liked her. She was quiet and honest.

"Gloria, you have nothing to fear from me."

"I saw a young man follow her out into the hall. He seemed to know her, but she didn't notice him. I've never seen him before," she said quietly. "I only noticed because he ran into me on the way to the hall."

"What did he look like?" Rami rumbled, making her jump.

"He… he was medium-sized with sandy hair." She looked up at Madraeus. "I hope you find him. I like Whitney. I hope she'll be alright."

"Thank you, Gloria. You should go home now. We will let you know how Whitney fares."

Gloria nodded and fled. He watched her go and then turned and headed back to the little office. Rami followed him.

Anger filled him again at the sight of the carpet covered in Whitney's blood. Madraeus walked toward it; his shoe hit something, skittering it across the floor. He looked down. It was one of Whitney's jeweled flowers from her hair. He picked it up. It was covered in blood. He sniffed. It wasn't Whitney's blood. She must have used it to fight off her attacker.

Madraeus stood in the center of the room and closed his eyes. He let the smells and feeling of the room soak into his consciousness.

He could smell two individuals' blood: Whitney's and her attacker's. It was a new vampire. His blood had no taint of age but was still fresh. The room also smelled of fear… no, not just fear… panic.

He opened his eyes and looked at Rami, who also stood with his eyes closed, scenting the air, but his expression was puzzled.

"What?" Madraeus asked.

"I don't know. There is something familiar about this vampire." Rami shook his head. "No. I don't know." Rami opened his eyes and looked to his friend.

"What do you mean?" Madraeus cocked his head to one side.

"It is like he is familiar but not as a vampire exactly." Rami frowned. "As if I had been around him when he was mortal. Does that make sense?"

"Yes. Try to remember where. I'm going to check on Whitney." He strode from the room. He took several deep breaths to clear his head of the scent of blood. Then, still clutching her flower, he took the stairs two at a time.

# A Little Soul Searching

Mrs. Myers stood in front of the bedroom door. She put her hand on Madraeus' chest to stop him.

"Dr. Kirkland is giving her a transfusion, so I cannot let you go in. You understand?"

He nodded. He could smell the blood through the door already. A shiver of need ran through him. If he went into that room, he wouldn't be able to control his hunger a second time.

"Thank you."

"You may wait in the next room or here in the hall. I will come get you when it is safe," she started to leave and then turned back to him. "Thank you for saving Whitney's life. You did a very good thing tonight. I know how difficult it was for you. I am very proud of you."

Madraeus stared at her silently.  He wondered if she would be so proud if she knew how close he had come to turning Whitney in an attempt to save her life. With a sigh, he threw himself into a chair near the door to wait.

Not more than a minute had passed before he was up and pacing. His mind was racing with possibilities.

*Was it a friend? Did she know this man? Why had he attacked her? Was it a strike against me or Whitney? Was it random because there weren't many mortals at the party, and she was convenient?*

Anger surged again. He was going to kill this man.

*No, that would be too quick. There will be torture,* he thought.

Torture brought Cecelia to mind. He wondered if she had something to do with this. She had been talking to Whitney just before the attack.

*Maybe Cecelia was getting rid of her spy.*

That thought made Madraeus' blood turn to ice. Cecelia had been devious before, and Whitney seemed to be doing her best to drive him insane. He looked at the jeweled flower he had been toying with while he thought. He didn't want to believe it. Sighing, he rubbed a hand over his face and through his hair.

"Ray?" Rami rumbled from behind him.

"What?"

"Philtzer just called. They followed the trail to a car, and then followed the tracks, but lost it when they got to the interstate. Too many scents."

"Damn," Madraeus sighed. "Rami?"

"Hmm"

"Do you think Whitney was attacked because..." Madraeus was hesitant to voice his fears out loud, "because she was an informant for Cecelia and had outlived her usefulness?"

"What? I do not believe it for a minute. Whitney was totally ignorant of our world and still would be if she had not been attacked!" Rami crossed his arms and stared his friend down. "You are seeing betrayals where there are none."

"Then why do you think she was attacked? Coincidence? Convenience?"

"I think it is more complicated than that."

The two friends lapsed into silence. It seemed like hours before the bedroom door opened, and Dr. Kirkland came out with Mrs. Myers. He had been a doctor to the Races for almost three hundred years. He was one of the youngest Weavers.

"Gentlemen, Miss Martindale will be fine. She didn't lose as much blood as I first thought. Although, she will need rest. You are lucky she is a tough lady." He gave Mrs. Myers a quick peck on the cheek. "Call me if you need me."

As he turned to go, Madraeus stopped him.

"Thank you," Madraeus shook his hand.

Dr. Kirkland nodded and headed for the stairs. Madraeus watched him descend. Hesitantly, he walked toward the door almost afraid that Mrs. Myers wouldn't let him in, but she stepped out of his way without a word.

Whitney lay in the middle of the bed. She was no longer covered in blood. Mrs. Myers had removed the blood-stained dress. Tucked up under the white and rose-covered comforter, she slept peacefully.

Every night since he had seen her in her pink pajamas, she had haunted his dreams. Now she would haunt him with guilt. He had told Mrs. Myers he would keep her out of danger and had failed. He should not have let her near his world.

Mrs. Myers sat on the other side of the bed.

"Why did you bring her to me?" he asked quietly without looking at her.

"It was where she needed to be." Mrs. Myers shrugged.

"That is no answer, Weaver," he snapped in irritation.

He was used to Mrs. Myers dodging his questions. It was what Weavers did. They said they were trying to be helpful, but Madraeus knew they were just busybodies playing with people's lives. Myers was the worst. She had been the Oracle of Delphi, telling people what to do with their lives for centuries.

"You needed her," she said quietly.

"I needed her?" He turned incredulous eyes on Mrs. Myers, "Believe me, the last thing I need is a mortal to worry about! You should have known better, woman! Every mortal that gets involved with me..."

He couldn't finish. The words stuck in his throat. He thought about that hissing voice. If he was hearing it again, that could only mean disaster. Cecelia's insanity was affecting him again. He prayed that Cecelia wasn't going to drag them all down with her.

"I am sorry, Ray, but she needs to be with you, and you need to be with her. That is the simple truth."

He frowned at her. The fact that she had brought Whitney into a dangerous situation obviously didn't bother her little plans at all.

"Whitney needs to be safe, and with me is not in any way, shape, or form, safe!"

"You are wrong. After today's incident, the only safe place for her is with you."

"What the hell does that mean?" he shouted, making Whitney stir.

"Justin... no... wait... Justin... help..." She shifted as a dream took hold of her.

"Who is Justin?" he whispered.

"Her ex-boyfriend, the one that just broke up with her."

Madraeus' heart clenched. She was calling for the man she loved, and it wasn't him. A little flame of hope that he didn't know he had faded.

There had been a time when he had relished his power, his immortality. Now he felt like life was his job, and he wasn't allowed to quit. All of life had faded into a pale facsimile of its former self, until Whitney. She was so vibrant and full of more life than anyone he had met in centuries. She was full Technicolor in a world of black and white.

But he could not love her, nor did he want her to love him. That path only led to death of one kind or another. One way he didn't want, and the other she wouldn't want. No, better that she called for her mortal lover.

He stood and paced to the window.

The night had passed so fast. He pulled the curtain aside and stared out at the growing light of dawn. Such a small thing, the sunrise, and yet, for years, he had run from it, hid from it, shunned it. For so many centuries, that simple thing had been the terror of his existence. All so he could keep living an existence that he so often hated.

He tried very hard to remember what sunlight felt like, but he couldn't bring it to mind. All he needed to do was stand at the window a little longer, and he would know again.

The sky began to glow pink. Suddenly, the curtain was pulled in front of him. He looked down. Mrs. Myers was holding the curtain shut.

"Come on, Madraeus, you need rest." She gently turned him away from the window and led him to the door.

He glanced back at the bed. Whitney still slept.

"I will let you know when she wakes." She looked to Rami, who was waiting in the hall. "Rami, you will find rooms in the basement to suit your needs. Go get some sleep."

# YOU'RE A WHAT NOW?

Whitney drifted into wakefulness like she was coming out of a heavy fog. Her head was pounding, and her whole body felt heavy. She didn't want to open her eyes; it would mean she was actually awake, and awake was painful. She didn't think she had drunk *that* much at Mrs. Myers' party.

The party. Something had happened at the party. She couldn't quite remember. Her mind refused to cooperate.

*I was dancing with Philtzer and then... Justin had been there... Justin had... attacked me? No, that's not right.*

She must have been dreaming. Justin had bitten her neck, so it couldn't have been real. She started to turn over to go back to sleep when something on her neck pulled. Stiffly, she fought against the covers and felt around. There was a bandage on her neck where she had been bitten in her dream. Her eyes sprang open.

Panic wedged its way into her mind as she realized that she was not in her own bed. She was in a room elegantly decorated with red roses, and the furniture was white with gold trim.

Whitney struggled to sit up, but for some reason, she felt really weak. Her head spun and throbbed. She put her hands up to steady her head and noticed a bandage wrapped around her arm at the elbow. She frowned at it.

"What the hell happened last night?" she asked aloud. Her voice seemed weak too.

She tried again to sit up. She managed to push herself partway up the pillows. Whitney looked down at herself. She was wearing someone's shirt. So she was at someone else's house, in someone else's bed, wearing someone else's clothes, and bandaged up like she had been in a fight.

"Great," she snorted.

She looked around the room. The curtains were drawn, but there was light coming from a lamp in the corner. Slumped down in a chair next to it, with an open book sliding off of her lap, was Mrs. Myers. A very untidy Mrs. Myers. Whitney had never seen her in anything except pristine suits and dresses, so it came as a shock to see her employer wearing sweatpants and a very fuzzy black sweater.

Whitney hated to wake her up, but she really needed to know what was going on, and she had to go to the bathroom.

Whitney cleared her throat, but that didn't wake her up, so she called, "Mrs. Myers?"

Still no response.

"Damn."

Looking around, she saw a partially open door next to the bed. She hoped it was the bathroom. Slowly and with a lot of effort, she managed to get her feet on the floor.

The world tilted. She reached out for the wall to steady herself. A few steps and then she'd be there, provided that was the bathroom.

It seemed like an eternity before she reached the door. Every step she took, she was more convinced that the room she was headed for was just a closet and not the toilet she was desperate for. However, she kept moving, and soon her bladder was more than happy that she had made the effort.

She leaned on the sink to splash some water on her face and caught a glimpse of herself.

"I look like crap," she moaned.

There were dark circles under her eyes, and her face was pale. She looked at the bandage on her neck; slowly, she peeled it away. There were two ragged holes underneath. Then she noticed something dark in her hair. She pulled at it, and it flaked off in her hand. It looked like dried blood. She pulled off the bandage on her elbow. There was a needle mark there with a small bruise around it.

"What the hell happened last night?"

"Whitney?" Mrs. Myers said from the door, making her jump. "Are you alright?" She came into the room and put an arm around her.

"Mrs. Myers, what...?" she stuttered as she held up her arm like a child with a broken toy.

"I know, dear." Mrs. Myers put a hand to Whitney's cheek. "I know you are confused, and I will explain everything, but right now we need to get you cleaned up a little more. I did what I could last night, but I'm sure a shower will help a lot more. Do you feel up to it?"

Whitney barely nodded. With speedy efficiency, Mrs. Myers started the shower, helped Whitney out of her borrowed shirt, then helped her step into the shower.

"Now you get cleaned up, and I'll be right back with some clothes," she said, then she was gone.

"Great," Whitney groaned, "now one employer has seen me in my pajamas and the other has seen me naked. What a perfect week!"

Whitney leaned against the wall and let the water beat down on her. She felt horribly weak and heavy. She let her head fall forward into the water stream. With growing horror, she watched the water turn red around her feet.

Horror gave her frantic energy. She scrubbed her skin until it was red and then shampooed her hair two times. Exhaustion caught up with her quickly, but she managed to shut off the water and wrap a towel around herself before sinking down to sit on the side of the tub.

"Oh dear," Mrs. Myers exclaimed when she returned.

She quickly helped Whitney dress in sweats and a hooded sweater. Gently, she combed out the mess Whitney's frantic shampooing had left her hair in. Then she helped Whitney to stand and guided her out to the bed. Once she had Whitney tucked in again, she set a tray in front of her with cinnamon toast, strawberries, a big glass of orange juice, and a large cup of coffee.

"Now, you eat that up. The doctor said it would help you get your strength back."

Whitney looked at the tray of food. She wasn't even hungry, but she didn't want to hurt Mrs. Myers' feelings, so she reached for the coffee. After the first sip, her stomach decided it was ravenous, so she picked up the toast.

"Mrs. Myers?" she said between bites. "Can you tell me what happened?"

Mrs. Myers had been standing by the bed, watching her eat. Slowly, she sat down.

"Well, last night at my birthday party, you were attacked. We found you passed out on the floor in a small office off of the hall."

"And these?" Whitney put a hand up to her neck.

"Well..." Mrs. Myers sighed, "I'm sorry, Whitney, but you were bitten by a vampire."

"Excuse me?" She choked on her toast.

"A vampire. You were attacked by one and bitten."

"Yeah, whatever." Whitney let out a nervous laugh. "And how drunk did you get last night?"

"I'm sorry, dear, but it is true," she said.

"You mean it was someone who thought he was a vampire, like he was deranged or something?" Whitney felt a moment of panic as she thought about Justin in her dream, or what she had thought was a dream.

"No. It actually was a real vampire."

Whitney stared at her food but didn't see it. Her mind was searching through her confused memories of the night before: Justin acting different, the chill in his grip, the way his face seemed to change right before he lunged at her, the blood on his face. She shuddered when she thought about him biting her neck.

"No," she said aloud. She couldn't think of Justin that way, and yet the things he'd said-

"Whitney, let me explain. We are members of a group called the Races. Some are born as one of the Races, and some are brought in by other members. There are many of us who live extended lifetimes."

"Wait! What do you mean 'we'? Are you a vampire?" She shifted away just in case, although she still couldn't believe that any of this was real.

"No," Mrs. Myers smiled, "I am a Weaver."

"You're a what now?" Whitney frowned.

# IS THIS A JOKE?

"A Weaver. An Oracle. We've been referred to as mystics or sooth-sayers for centuries, but we preferred to be called Weavers. We see patterns in life's dance and nudge people where they ought to be."

"Oh," Whitney nodded with the air of someone humoring a rather stupid person. "So... good thing you run a temp agency."

"Yes," Mrs. Myers smiled brightly, "I rather thought you would see the connection."

"So, do you see the future?"

"In a way, I see where people will fit so that their lives take the right course."

Whitney thought about this for a long moment. It seemed an awful lot like controlling people's lives and not allowing them to choose their own path, but who was she to argue? She had a sudden picture of the banner at the party.

"Are you really 2,345?"

"2,325, dear. But yes, I am."

"What?"

"I told you that some of us live extended lives." Mrs. Myers shrugged.

"Are you immortal then?"

"Not precisely," her boss replied enigmatically.

Whitney stared at her, shaking her head slightly, then slowly decided to move on from that revelation.

"So? There's weavers and vampires," Whitney said, still skeptical. "What else?"

"Let's see, there are werewolves, pixies, imps, demons, witches—" Mrs. Myers ticked them off on her fingers.

"Werewolves and pixies," Whitney stared at her. "And witches, as in magic witches?"

"What other kind of witches are there?"

"You're serious!" Whitney exclaimed. "About all of this!"

"Well, yes."

"You met a lot of them at the party last night," she said patiently. "Almost everyone there was a member of the Races."

"Really." Whitney thought about the night before. Everyone in the room had looked so normal. Well, except for the group of women who were incredibly tall and looked like supermodels, and that couple whose skin had looked bluish...

Now that she thought about it, there had been something odd about most of the people there. They seemed like regular people, but also, they put off an uncomfortable vibe.

Whitney's eyes narrowed. There had always been a certain oddness to Mrs. Myers, but Whitney had always put it down to age. Suddenly, that thought took on a whole new perspective, considering how old she actually was.

Another scarier thought popped into her head. *These were the same people who had been coming through the InfiniCorp offices all week. Just who am I working for?*

As if reading her thoughts, Mrs. Myers said, "Even Rami, Madraeus, and Philtzer are of the Races."

The stunned silence that followed said more than any denial would have.

"I see you still don't believe me," she sighed.

"Well, it is kinda hard to swallow." Whitney felt guilty that she didn't believe her employer, but she couldn't.

"When Rami comes, I'll have him show you."

"Show me what?" Whitney reared back.

"His fangs."

"He's a vampire!" Whitney shrieked. "But he is so nice!"

Mrs. Myers laughed, "Just because he's a vampire doesn't mean he's evil."

Whitney's jaw dropped open at that statement. Everyone knew that vampires were the evil undead, and now she was being told they were nice. Her brain turned to mush. This was just all too much to take in.

"Well, that is to say, not all of them are evil. Some are real doozies. I mean, they all have their moments, but generally, most of them are nice enough." Mrs. Myers brushed at a piece of lint on her sweater and went on as if this was a normal conversation.

A near-hysterical giggle escaped from Whitney's lips. Mrs. Myers glanced at her.

A tap at the door made Whitney jump. Slowly, the door opened. Rami poked his head in. Cautiously, he came into the room.

Whitney's expression was something to behold. Her eyes were wild and huge, but she was also frowning with one eyebrow up.

"How are you feeling?" he asked gently. The sound of his deep voice startled her.

Whitney's hands shot up to cover her mouth as another slightly hysterical giggle escaped. Rami glanced uncertainly at Mrs. Myers. She gave him a nod of encouragement. He stepped closer.

"Madraeus sends his regrets, but he had an errand to run." That snapped Whitney out of her mushy trance.

"Figures he would abandon me to this lunacy," she mumbled. Then she remembered that Mrs. Myers had listed Rami, Philtzer, *and* Madraeus when she was counting off Race members. He was one of them too.

*He certainly keeps undead hours,* Whitney thought.

"Whitney, do you remember anything about last night?" Rami sat down carefully on the end of the bed.

"Yes and no." Whitney closed her eyes. "Wait a minute, okay?" She opened her eyes again, struggling to keep control of her thoughts.

"Now let me get this straight." She looked at Mrs. Myers. "You're telling me that both of you are some kind of mythical, creepy things that no one knows about, but aren't all bad, just sometimes, and that one of you attacked me?" She looked from one to the other and rolled her eyes. "Well, not *you*, you, but someone like you."

Rami looked to Mrs. Myers.

She slowly nodded. "It is not exactly like that, but yes."

Whitney looked at each of them again. They were both still serious.

"This has to be a joke or dream or something!" She glanced around, feeling more than slightly dizzy. "Are there cameras somewhere? I admit you had me going."

Not believing was so much safer and more comfortable. She didn't want to go back to those few terrifying moments when she actually started to believe them.

"I'm sorry, Whitney, but I think that showing you will be the only way to prove it."

"Wait! You're not going to bite me or something, are you?"

"Of course not," Mrs. Myers sighed. "We are just trying to help you understand."

"I will not hurt you," Rami said sadly as he leaned forward.

Whitney watched as his features sharpened. His eyes transformed from the kind eyes she'd grown to love into feral black orbs.

She now knew how a deer felt when the semi was speeding toward it on the highway. She was frozen with fear. She couldn't tear her gaze away as he opened his mouth, and his top teeth elongated into sharp fangs.

That was all it took for centuries of animal instinct to take over.

She needed to get away. She scrambled backward. Her knees sent the tray on her lap crashing to the floor. In her haste to get away, her head smacked into the headboard. Stars floated in front of her eyes as she sank back into oblivion.

# History Lesson

WHITNEY WOKE AGAIN, MUCH to her unhappiness. Her head hurt even worse than before. It was hard to think around the pounding. Carefully, she opened one eye. Thankfully, the room was still dim. Slowly, so her head wouldn't fall off, she pushed herself up against the pillows. Her vision swam slightly. Her stomach protested the swirling room but started to settle down as her vision refocused.

She caught sight of Madraeus sitting on a chair beside the bed. He was leaning forward with his elbows braced on his knees. His sleeves were rolled up, and his shirt was open at the collar. She had never seen him so rumpled. He was always so pristine and buttoned up that he seemed untouchable, like a rare French painting, but now there was an air of vulnerability. He was watching her silently. She waited for the panic that she had felt earlier to take hold, but nothing came. She wasn't sure if that bothered or reassured her.

"I brought you some of your clothes." His tone was flat. He pointed at the pile of neatly folded clothes on the end of the bed.

"Thank you," she said automatically as she glanced at the pile. Alarm filled her as she realized that the pile contained underwear. Embarrassment flooded her cheeks momentarily, chasing away the paleness. Her eyes flicked to Madraeus.

He was staring at her intently.

She was mortified. First, he saw her dripping wet and in her pajamas; now, he had been digging through her drawers.

*This is the worst job ever!*

"How are you feeling?" he asked quietly.

*Like I've fallen off a cliff, and just run a mile, and then got hit in the head with a baseball bat,* she thought.

"OK," she said instead.

"Hmm," he grunted.

She reached up ruefully and felt the back of her head. She winced when her fingers found a rather large lump had formed there. The memory popped into her head of her conversation with Mrs. Myers and Rami's fangs. She shivered.

"I take it they informed you about the Races."

"Yeah, I didn't believe them until Rami showed me his fangs." She gave another shudder.

"It is never easy to tell mortals about the Races. They tend to get violent or terrified. Then they become unpredictable, and that is dangerous to us. That is why we have a strict policy against letting anyone know about us. It is safer for everyone that way."

Instantly, Whitney wondered if they would let her live now that she knew their secret. Her whole body tensed.

"Are you going to kill me?" Whitney whispered, not sure if she wanted to know or not. She hoped it wouldn't provoke the attack she thought was coming. Then she thought, *Why would he wait until I woke up to kill me? That's just plain mean.*

"No." Madraeus frowned at her.

That one word, spoken quiet and low, relieved her more than she thought possible. She slumped back against the pillows. She wondered how she could so easily believe him, but he had made no threatening gestures or belligerent moves. He was still intimidating, but he had always been intimidating.

"So, you're a... a...?" She got stuck on the word.

"Vampire?"

She nodded slowly.

"Yes." He managed to sound like they were discussing his hair color.

She studied him for a long moment. He simply waited.

She cocked her head to the side and squinted at him, "How... I mean... when did... how is this...?" she fumbled, her curiosity at war with disbelief.

"I was born in Cyrene, Greece in 243 A.D. I was pressed into the Roman Army when I was 19. There was an earthquake in 262." Mechanically, he began to recite his history, but as the memories took hold, he relaxed a little, making it sound more like a story. "It nearly destroyed the city. We worked night and day, rebuilding and finding survivors. There was so much destruction that people regressed; survival was the only thing that mattered, morality became... less important. The city fell into decadence. Sometimes the soldiers were as bad as those they were to protect."

Whitney had never heard him talk so much. Normally, he only barked an order or two then left. She was fascinated by the beauty of his voice; she could listen to it for hours. She watched his face change as he spoke. His eyes glazed over as if he was seeing it all again.

"I was on guard duty one night when I was attacked. I was easy prey standing alone in the dark." Madraeus sighed. "I didn't even see what it was, but by the next morning, I was different." He fell silent, staring at his hands.

He looked so sad and lost that Whitney couldn't help herself; she reached out and covered his hands with hers. His hands were cool to the touch but not cold like Justin's had been. Somehow, it made him seem less scary.

Madraeus stared at her hands wrapped around his. He shot to his feet.

"I have something for you." He moved across the room. He picked up her hairpiece from the table by the door and brought it back to her.

"I found this last night." He handed it to her, avoiding contact with her fingers. "I'm assuming you stabbed your attacker with it. It was covered in blood."

She stared at it and remembered fumbling for a weapon and not finding one, so she had used her hairpiece to stab Justin. She knew it was sharp; she had accidentally stabbed herself in the head with it often enough. It had been an act of desperation. She couldn't believe it had actually worked.

"I cleaned all the blood off of it."

"Thank you," she said softly.

"You want to tell me what happened?" he asked gently.

She wasn't sure if she wanted to tell him about Justin. She wasn't even sure what she herself believed about last night. She looked up at him. She was having trouble reconciling Madraeus the vampire with Madraeus the hard businessman with nice Madraeus, who had gone out of his way to clean her hairpiece.

Absently, she toyed with the jeweled flower. Whitney didn't know where to begin. How could she tell him that between his glaring and that nasty blonde, they had made her desperate to leave? Then there was Justin. If he had attacked her and her attacker had been a vampire, then that meant Justin was a vampire now. But did that mean he dumped her because he was a vampire, and that note was from whoever made him a vampire? Did that mean that he still loved her? He had obviously been looking for her. Or was she convenient, and he used their prior relationship to lower her guard?

*Listen to me just taking vampires in stride*, she thought, almost wanting to laugh.

"Whitney? It was suggested by a witness that the young man who attacked you may have known you." Whitney's eyes widened. "I need to let you know that this young vampire is obviously untutored in our ways. I understand if you want to protect him, but if he is living outside our rules, then he is dangerous and must be stopped."

Whitney stared at him for a long time, absorbing what he said and a whole bunch that he didn't say.

"What makes you think he is untutored?" she asked carefully.

Madraeus sighed, "Long ago, we set up rules to govern the Races for the protection of humans as well as ourselves. The biggest rule is anonymity. Any dealings with humans must leave them unaware of our existence. Vampires who bite humans must do it correctly. It is obvious from the condition we found you in that this vampire doesn't know what he is doing."

"What do you mean 'do it correctly'? Don't you just bite and suck?"

"Technically, yes, we can just 'bite and suck' as you say. A vampire who is starving can kill a human, but the resultant death attracts too much attention."

Whitney stared at him open-mouthed. She was not expecting his blunt explanation.

"In this day and age, it would be too easy to track and expose us. So," Madraeus shrugged, "we have set up a system of... wineries, if you will."

"That is horrible! You harvest people?"

"No," he growled in exasperation. "We have set up blood banks and then bottle the blood for shipment."

"Why not use the bags from blood banks? Why bother bottling it?"

"Bottles look more normal sitting in a refrigerator. Bags would raise questions."

"Oh."

"They supply enough for our needs. Although from time to time we snack," he smiled mischievously.

"So what? We're just a bunch of Twinkies to you?" Whitney snorted.

"Hardly," Madraeus scoffed.

"Don't people notice? Don't they wake up the next day and say, 'Oh look, I have a bite on my neck?'"

"Yes, but most don't think about it, or they dismiss it in favor of the excitement."

"Yeah? No!" Whitney shook her head, "Been there, done that. It's scary, not exciting."

"It's normally not like that. I can show you, then you'll understand." He moved to sit on the edge of the bed beside her.

# And Now the Truth Comes Out

Whitney slid back. "Oh hell no! You are not going to bite me!"

"I'm not going to bite you." His steady gaze made her want to believe him. "I just need you to understand and not be afraid of us."

"You're a little late," Whitney muttered, eying him, but at the same time, feeling curious enough to see where this would lead.

"I won't hurt you, Whitney," he spoke in a low voice that hummed across her skin. As he spoke, he slowly leaned forward.

Whitney froze. Her heart started beating faster, and her breathing became shallow.

Slowly, he reached up and traced a finger gently along her jawline and down her neck. Automatically, she turned her head toward his fingers, unknowingly exposing her neck.

"We are predators, but we only need a little from our prey. We have no need to kill." Madraeus let his fingers linger on the soft, warm skin of her neck.

"But we do enjoy the sensuality and the excitement." The timbre of his voice was weaving a trance around her. He slowly leaned forward. Lightly, his lips brushed her neck. His breath whispered against her skin, sending shivers through her body.

"Most people will defy any fear to court the mystery and the danger of such intimacy with a stranger," he whispered against her skin.

She leaned toward him.

He let out a shuddering sigh. His breath fluttered across her skin again.

With a burst of laughter, Whitney shoved Madraeus away from her. She couldn't help it. At first, his words had done wicked things to her, and she was incapable of resisting; but then, when he started blowing on her neck, it started to tickle and brought her out of her trance. She had tried not to laugh, but she just couldn't stop herself.

Madraeus sat back, staring at her. Whitney took in Madraeus' expression. It was a mixture of desire, anger, and confusion. She felt bad. It must have been a terrible blow to his ego for her to laugh at him. She wanted to make amends and soothe his bruised pride. It was only slowly dawning on her that she might have let him bite her.

"So..." She cleared her throat. "I guess if that is the right way. Then Justin was definitely doing it wrong."

"Wait a minute," Madraeus frowned. "Did you say Justin?"

"Um... yeah?"

"You knew who attacked you, and you didn't tell me!" he shouted, surging to his feet.

Suddenly, she didn't care if his ego was injured.

"Don't yell at me! There is a lot of crazy crap going on, and I'm a little confused about who is on what side."

"Well, now you know. He is trying to kill you, and I'm not!" Madraeus shouted.

"Oh really! You just tried to bite me!"

"I did not!" he protested, "That was a demonstration."

"Demonstration my butt!" Whitney shouted back.

"You had better start telling me everything you know." Madraeus jabbed a finger at her.

"If you're going to be nasty about it, I'm not gonna tell you anything," she snapped.

"Whitney," Madraeus growled.

"What is going on in here?" Mrs. Myers asked from the door. She had her hands braced on her hips.

"He started it!" Whitney jabbed a finger at Madraeus.

"She won't tell me what happened last night!"

"Whitney, calm down. Ray, sit down." Mrs. Myers sighed, shaking her head.

They glared at each other for a moment before finally obeying her command. Madraeus yanked the chair back from the bed, sat down, crossed his arms, and glared at Whitney.

She looked at him, sneered, then turned away, determined to completely ignore him. Mrs. Myers came into the room and sat down on the edge of the bed.

"Whitney, if you know anything about last night, you should tell us, so it doesn't happen to anyone else," she said.

Whitney chewed on her lip for a moment, feeling guilty. She hadn't thought of that.

"It's complicated," she started.

"No, it's not," Madraeus grumbled.

Whitney ignored him, and Mrs. Myers sighed.

"I do know who attacked me. It was Justin," she said reluctantly.

"Justin?" Mrs. Myers gasped.

"Yeah, but I'm confused. I know he dumped me, but maybe it wasn't his fault. He said that he didn't write that note."

"What note?" Madraeus interrupted, but Whitney continued as if he hadn't spoken.

"So, if he didn't mean to break up with me, and it was someone else's idea, then where does that leave me?"

"What note?" he asked again.

"He said," Whitney pointed to Madraeus, "that the vampire that attacked me was untrained or whatever. Maybe he didn't mean to hurt me, and he needs help. What if it was all just an accident?"

Madraeus snorted his disagreement, but the women continued to ignore him.

Whitney searched Mrs. Myers' face, hoping for confirmation. She didn't really think she was still in love with Justin, but she didn't want to just abandon him if he needed her.

"Whitney, I understand that you are feeling confused and over-whelmed by the situation," Mrs. Myers began.

"That's an understatement," Whitney breathed.

"There are many facts that we don't know yet, and although I understand your desire to protect Justin, it would be best if you tell us everything so that we will all make the right decision." Mrs. Myers was using her business lecture tone, and what she was saying made sense, but Whitney was not sure she trusted anyone right now.

"Just tell us, Whitney, so we can take care of this," Madraeus growled.

Whitney sent him a look that could peel paint and then turned back to Mrs. Myers. She started to speak, but Madraeus interrupted her.

"Start with Cecelia."

"What?" she snapped, annoyed by his bullying again.

"Don't be dumb, Cecelia spoke to you last night." Madraeus walked forward and stood glaring at her with his fists balled at his sides.

"What the Hell are you talking about?" she frowned.

"Cecelia is a very tall blonde woman," Mrs. Myers supplied quietly.

"Oh. Well, this big blonde bimbo came up and was being real catty about me being your new receptionist. We both said some other stuff, then I called her a bitch and she got all hissy and left."

"You did what!" Madraeus blurted.

Mrs. Myers gasped softly.

"What?" Whitney looked from one to the other.

"Whitney, Cecelia is a very dangerous vampire." Mrs. Myers' voice was thick with worry.

"Dangerous!" Madraeus shouted, "She makes the Spanish Inquisition look like a comedy show!" He threw his hands in the air and started to pace. "Whatever possessed you to insult her?"

"Hey, I call 'em like I see 'em, and it's not like I knew who she was. You didn't introduce me to anyone. You just gave me dirty looks all night!"

"Dirty looks?" Madraeus spluttered, stalking toward her.

"Madraeus!" Mrs. Myers snapped. "Sit down."

After a moment, he finally complied, although it was with exaggerated surliness.

"I swear it's like having children," Mrs. Myers mumbled. "Go on, Whitney."

"After the bimbo, everyone was staring. I needed some air, so I went into the hallway, and that's when Justin came up behind me. I was totally shocked to see him. He said we needed to talk, and he took me into a little office. Then he started talking about showing me a life I wouldn't believe and that he hadn't meant to leave, but he was so... cold and..." she shuddered at the memory of his face just before he attacked her. It had been like a crazed animal. She glanced at Madraeus. He was frowning at her like usual. He hadn't looked crazed when he was— what would you call what he had been doing? Vamping out?

"I'm sorry, Whitney," Mrs. Myers patted her hand.

"I know he needs to be found because he is hurting people, but can't you help him or something?" Whitney pleaded.

"We will do what we can," Mrs. Myers said carefully, "but I can make no guarantees."

"I need you to make a list of anywhere Justin might go. The more details you can give us, the faster we will find him," Madraeus said.

He waited for her to nod, and then he disappeared out the door. Whitney stared at the door for a long time. She wasn't sure she really trusted Madraeus, but she knew she didn't have a choice.

"Mrs. Myers? What's going to happen to me?"

"Nothing that I know of."

"Are these going to do anything to me?" she asked, running her fingers along the bite marks on her neck.

"No, dear, you were bitten, but you didn't exchange any blood, so you will not turn into a vampire. Actually, you are very lucky. If Madraeus hadn't closed the bites, you would have bled to death."

"What do you mean Madraeus closed them?"

"Vampires are able to close the bites when they are finished, some sort of enzyme. That is why most people never even notice that they have been bitten. They just think it is a scratch or something because the holes heal very quickly."

"Why did he do that? I would think he would be glad to get rid of me," she grumbled.

"You'll find that Madraeus is a very complicated individual," Mrs. Myers said. "Now, you should get some rest. I'll get you something to make that list." She stood and turned to leave.

"Mrs. Myers?" Whitney stopped her. She felt silly for asking, but she needed to know. "Do I still have a job?"

"Of course you do," Mrs. Myers chuckled as she walked out.

"Oh. Yippee," she said without enthusiasm.

# MAN OR MONSTER

Madraeus sighed. It had been a long three days of nothing but failures. Every location on Whitney's list of possible places Justin could be had been meticulously checked, but still, there was no sign of Justin.

The absoluteness of Justin's disappearance seemed to be too convenient. He knew someone was helping Justin. The fact that Cecelia had been in the vicinity was enough to make Madraeus almost positive it was her.

Impatience gnawed at him. He felt out of sorts. Maybe it was just living in someone else's house. He felt exposed.

Nothing had been accomplished by staying at Mrs. Myers' house except that Whitney was recovering. They needed to get back to InfiniCorp. He glanced at his watch as he sprinted up the stairs into the kitchen. It was a little after eight. He should get everyone packing.

He swung the door open and stepped into the darkened kitchen. In the small pool of light coming from above the stove, Whitney stood pouring hot milk from a pan into a mug. At his sudden appearance, she yelped and jumped, pouring the near-scalding liquid on her hand. She dropped the mug, spilling the rest all over the stove.

"Damn!" she hissed, diving for the sink to run cold water over her hand. "You should wear a bell or something!"

"Are you alright?" he asked, moving over to the sink.

"I would be if you'd quit sneaking up on me," she snapped.

"I don't do it intentionally."

"No, I'm sure it's all part of your vampy nature," Whitney mumbled as she pulled her hand out of the water. She tried to examine it in the dim light.

"Let me see," Madraeus said, ignoring her surly attitude. He could see just fine in the dim light, but he didn't want to unsettle her. Although she seemed to be handling her new situation pretty well, he didn't want to push it. He tugged on her hand so she would follow him back to the stove.

Madraeus held her hand out to the light. They both leaned forward to see her burn. Their heads were so close that her hair was tickling his temple. He could feel her gaze.

"You're wearing those pajamas again," he said softly.

"If you don't like them, tough. I haven't got anything else to wear to bed."

"I didn't say I didn't like them." The corners of his mouth twitched. "And as much as I would like to discuss what you are wearing to bed, I think we should put a little burn cream on this to take the heat out."

Whitney blinked at him, then looked at her hand. There was a patch of skin where the milk had first hit her skin that was turning an angry red.

"K." Whitney looked around. "Umm...?"

He pulled out a stool from under the counter. "Sit."

She hopped up on the stool. He turned away and opened drawers and cupboards until he found a first aid kit under the sink.

When he turned back, she was staring at him with wide-eyed wonder. He hesitated a moment before returning with the first aid kit to the counter beside Whitney. Rummaging through it, he found the burn ointment and a really big band-aid. She was still looking at him like he was a wonder of nature when he looked up.

"What?" he asked as he reached out and gently took her hand. Hesitantly, he put one finger on the sleeve of her pajamas and slid it up her wrist. He wasn't sure what was softer: her skin or the pink flannel. He nearly closed his eyes, relishing the chance to run his fingers over her skin even if it was just her hand.

"It must be hard," she murmured.

"What?" he asked as he spread burn ointment across the back of her hand.

"Living so long," she whispered, making his hands freeze.  After a moment, he started moving again.

"Sometimes," he managed to force the word past the lump in his throat.

'Sometimes' was an understatement. There were centuries when it was almost intolerable, others he would regret for all eternity, and now there was just dull, empty monotony.

"Were you...?" she started but stumbled to a halt.

He finished putting the band-aid on her hand and then raised his eyes to hers.

"Was I what?" He leaned on the counter behind her with one hand and waited.

"Nothing." She shook her head and looked away.

"No, ask." He waited, desperate to know what she was going to ask about him.

"I was wondering if... if you had been lonely," she finally asked without looking up.

His world teetered. She was worried about him? Whitney confused him. She sat staring at him with those huge emerald eyes. There was no guile in them. Madraeus savored the purity of her sympathy. He wasn't sure how to deal with her.

He turned away from her scrutiny and moved to the sink, wetting a rag to wipe up the puddle of milk. She hopped off the stool, walked over to pick up the sponge from the edge of the sink, and followed him to the stove.

"I wasn't that lonely," he finally said in a husky whisper, "I had Rami."

"When did you meet him?" she asked as they sopped up the milk.

"At the fall of Antioch in 1098."

"1098!" She gaped at him.

"Yes, 1098," he parroted, then returned to the sink. "It was during the crusades," he said over his shoulder as he rinsed out his rag.

"But didn't you say that you were born in 200 something?" She had stopped wiping up milk and was counting on her fingers.

"243," he confirmed as he came back to the stove and sopped up more milk.

"But what did you do for the first 800 years?"

Madraeus stopped moving again. He thought about the years of panic when he was still in the Roman army, wondering what had happened and trying to hide his affliction, and then the following years in Britannia, where he had gone into seclusion. And then his years with Cecelia. That was a decadent and evil time. He wasn't about to taint her mind with the terrible things he had done. She wouldn't be able to forgive him.

A warm hand on his arm pulled him out of his dark thoughts. He looked down. Whitney was standing beside him. She was too close. She was looking up at him with those big emerald eyes again, filled with... what? Sympathy? Understanding? How could she understand anything about him? Rage filled him and burned away his self-pity. He shook off her hand and strode back to the sink.

Madraeus heard her sigh. Shame washed over him for spurning her sympathy. There was no way that she could have known that what she asked him would cause such a reaction. She had been nothing but nice for once, and he had acted like a child. Perhaps he could redeem himself.

He turned to find her starting a new pan of milk. He stepped up behind her as she slowly stirred. He watched the chocolate swirling.

"Why don't you use a microwave?" he asked, making her jump.

"Stop sneaking up on me!" Whitney spun around and smacked Madraeus in the arm.

"Sorry."

She rolled her eyes and turned back to her pan.

"So? Why don't you use the microwave?"

"My grandmother says that if you heat it in the microwave, it won't work."

"What won't work?" he frowned, leaning forward to stare at the cocoa. His head was bent down so that his lips were right next to her ear.

"It won't help you sleep." Her voice sounded strained.

Madraeus knew that she had been having nightmares. In an attempt at self-torture, he had gone to check on her last night and had heard her cry out.

"Does it work?"

"Sort of." She shrugged. "Grammy used to make it for me almost every night when I was little, after my parents died."

She dipped her finger into the pan to test the temperature and then carefully poured the hot milk into her cup. Whitney scooted away from him and put the pan in the sink.

He stared blindly at the stove. Her comment had made a memory float up from the mire that was his past. It had been from over a millennium ago. He had been a small boy in Cyrene. Concentrating, he tried to bring it forth. He could almost remember his mother. She had been warm and smiling, cuddling him before their hearth. But then the memory was gone.

Madraeus frowned. He looked at Whitney. She had her head cocked to one side, watching him with a fascinated look on her face.

"What?"

"Nothing. You just looked…"

He waited for her to continue, but she didn't finish.

"What?" He crossed his arms and glared at her.

"Wistful."

Madraeus inhaled sharply. He had not realized that she could read his emotions so easily. Scowling he stalked back to the counter. He began slamming things back into the first aid kit.

"Why do you do that? You were actually being human a minute ago, and now you are all 'Grrrr' again." She made little clawing monster motions in the air with her free hand.

"Must I remind you that I am not human," he muttered.

"Yeah, but you were once."

Madraeus flinched. She had a way of getting to him that he didn't understand. He barely knew her, and yet, she had poked and prodded and raked up his forgotten humanity without even knowing it. She had dredged up memories about his life from over a thousand years ago without even trying. Whitney had dug under his skin and left him feeling raw, and he didn't want it. He didn't want to feel at all. Why couldn't she just let him be?

He growled and stalked toward her slowly. She backed up until her back hit the counter. She clutched her cocoa mug to her chest like a shield.

Madraeus stopped in front of her. He was so close that she was forced to bend backward over the counter to avoid touching him. He braced his hands, one on either side of her, on the counter behind her.

"I have been a vampire for one thousand seven hundred and forty-eight years. I was only human for nineteen."

"Doesn't mean you have forgotten how," Whitney rasped out. "You're still a man."

Madraeus leaned in even closer until their noses almost touched.

"And which would you have, Whitney? The man or the monster?"

He watched her eyes widen in surprise. He heard her heartbeat speed up. Her breathing became ragged.

As the silence stretched on, a sudden feeling of guilt took him by surprise. He shouldn't be toying with her like this. It wasn't fair to her. Madraeus eased back and looked away. He stepped back.

Silence hung between them.

"I have decided to move us back into town. You should pack, we are leaving within the hour," he said gruffly, then turned and left.

# BACK TO INFINICORP

For a long time, Whitney just stood at the top of the stairs. She felt so lost. She wanted to go home. She took a deep breath and carried her bag downstairs.

"Whitney?" Mrs. Myers came to the bottom of the stairs and looked up at her. "Are you alright? You look pale."

Not wanting to worry Mrs. Myers with her fears, she just shrugged and looked past her at the chaos being dismantled in the living room.

Mrs. Myers frowned as she turned to watch the last of the boxes being carried out of her house. "When Ray decides something, it doesn't take long for it to go into effect."

Whitney watched them for a moment. She wasn't sure she wanted to be back in town. "Mrs. M? Couldn't I just stay here? I won't be any trouble."

"Oh, Whitney," Mrs. Myers slid her arm around Whitney's shoulder and gave her a reassuring squeeze, "I will be sorry to see you go, but you will be safer in town with him rather than here with just me."

"What do you mean, just you? What about all your staff?" Whitney asked.

"My staff?" Mrs. Myers smiled indulgently, "I am afraid it is only my housekeeper and I who live here?"

"What about all those guys who've been following me everywhere I go? Aren't they your gardening staff?" Whitney felt suddenly confused.

"Heavens no!" Mrs. Myers shook her head. "I have gardeners that come out once a week, but they don't stay. Those men you refer to work for Madraeus."

"For him?"

"Yes, they're his bodyguards. Didn't you know?" Mrs. Myers shook her head at Whitney's dumbfounded expression. She sighed. "Poor Whitney, you still don't understand what you've gotten into. Those men are here to keep Mr. Ravilla, as the head of the council, safe, but they are also here to ensure that nothing happens to you."

"What council?"

"The Council of Races. Our governing body. They work to keep our existence a secret, among other things."

"Is that why they are watching me? To make sure I don't blab?"

"No, they are here to keep you alive."

Whitney blinked. She was flattered but didn't really understand why they would need to.

"We're assuming you were targeted on purpose," Mrs. Myers explained.

Whitney shivered. She still wanted to believe that Justin's attack on her had been an accident, but if they believed that she had been singled out intentionally, that changed everything.

"You don't really think he's going to come after me again, do you?" she asked.

Mrs. Myers hesitated. "I think that there is a real possibility. It will be much safer if you are in town where Madraeus can protect you."

"I don't get it. Justin is just one guy." Whitney shook her head.

Mrs. Myers turned and gazed intently at her. "This is more than just one guy. You need to be very careful, my dear. There are other things at work here that are very dangerous. There is a darkness coming."

"A darkness? Unkhabami said that too," Whitney complained. "I didn't understand what she was talking about either."

"Unkhabami was here?" Mrs. Myers grabbed Whitney's arm. "When?"

"The day of your party. She came to the office."

"Oh, dear, why didn't he tell me?" Mrs. Myers muttered to herself.

"Sorry, who is she?" Whitney was getting tired of being one step behind.

"She is the High Priestess of the Paka Watu," she said absently, looking around the room.

"Paka Watu?" Whitney prompted.

"Yes, were-cats, they're from Africa, she does roughly the same thing that I do," she explained. "Excuse me, Whitney. I must speak to Madraeus." Without waiting for an answer, she hurried off.

"But what does that mean?" she called after her.

"Were-cats, vampires, what next?" Whitney shook her head. Every known truth had gotten together and collectively jumped out the window. She had gone from having a normal life to living in a bad horror film.

She walked toward the front door but was intercepted by Rami.

"I can take that." He reached for her bag.

She gasped and stepped back. Then regretted her reaction. "Sorry." She held her bag out by way of apology.

Rami grinned at her.

"It is going to be alright, Fair Maiden." Rami placed his hand on her shoulder. "I know this is hard for you, but you are doing very well."

"I don't feel like it. I feel like I'm a few books short of a library."

Rami laughed. "Do not feel discouraged. There is a lot to learn. It has only been three days."

"Is that all?" It had felt like a lifetime.

"Come along, children, Madraeus is waiting," Mrs. Myers called as she came in the front door.

"Thanks for everything, Mrs. M." Whitney impulsively hugged Mrs. Myers.

"I'll come see you in a couple of days to see how you are getting on," Mrs. Myers said as she took her arm and walked her to the car.

Madraeus was standing by the car, waiting. A light breeze ruffled his hair. His gaze raked over her.

"You didn't bother to get dressed?"

"It's ten o'clock at night, why should I go through the effort of getting dressed just to get undressed again a few minutes later?"

He glared at her across the top of the car. She glared back at him.

Philtzer bounded past them. "I could help you get undressed!"

"Philtzer!" Mrs. Myers gasped.

He grinned at her, then hopped into the driver's seat.

Madraeus turned to open the front passenger door.

"Shotgun!" Thomas, his bodyguard, grinned as he slid past him into the front seat.

Madraeus scowled and slammed the door shut. He yanked the back door open and got in. Rami opened the other door for Whitney and slid in after her, sandwiching her in the middle.

There wasn't a lot of room in the back seat, especially once Rami got in. Whitney tried to scoot over to give him more room. Madraeus grunted and shifted away from her.

"I don't have cooties, vamp boy," she grumbled under her breath.

Philtzer snorted. Thomas glanced at Philtzer with a grin. Rami tried to cover his laugh but went into a coughing fit. Madraeus glared at both of them, then reached over and whacked Rami on the back. Whitney leaned forward to avoid an elbow in the head.

"Ahem, thank you." Rami grinned as tears sparkled in his eyes.

Madraeus turned to the window and ignored them all for the rest of the ride back into town. Whitney sat back and crossed her arms, trying not to notice any of them.

Halfway back to town, Whitney began to regret the pajamas. She had only thought about the effort it would take to change; she hadn't thought about walking from the car to the elevator. Now, the fact that she was going to be in downtown Denver in her pajamas made her panic. Desperately, she hoped that there would be no one in the parking garage.

She need not have worried. As soon as she got out of the car, she was surrounded. She couldn't see past the wall of muscle, much less anyone seeing through it to notice her pajamas. Madraeus led the way. Philtzer, Thomas, and two other men she had never seen walked on either side of her, and Rami brought up the rear. They all packed into the elevator and rode silently up to Madraeus' floor. As soon as they reached the lobby, Whitney bounded out of the elevator to her door. She couldn't wait to get behind closed doors and away from everyone.

"Wait!" Madraeus' voice stopped her dead.

"What?"

"Please, step back, Whitney," Madraeus commanded. "Thomas, Hamilton, check the apartment."

"Are you kidding me?" She moved back as Thomas stepped up and took her keys from her.

He unlocked her door, and the two men disappeared inside. She looked back at Madraeus and Rami.

"I'm taking no chances." Madraeus crossed his arms and waited for Thomas.

"This is insane!" Whitney muttered as she glanced at the other men. None of them had moved, and every one of them wore the same intent, serious expression.

"All clear, Boss." Thomas returned and handed the keys to Whitney.

She snatched them with a snort and shook her head. She stepped past the two men and glanced back at Madraeus before shutting the door. "Goodnight."

# WEREWOLFISM 101



After a nightmare-filled, sleepless night, she awoke to her grandmother calling for an explanation of her three-day absence.

"I just don't understand why you're staying at this job. It just seems a little odd to me that you live at work. He has you keeping such strange hours; then he drags you off on business without one word of warning!"

Whitney made another mark on the scratch paper lying on her desk. So far, Grammy had managed to insert this particular comment three times already into the conversation.

Whitney couldn't bring herself to confess where she had really been. There was no way that she could tell her grandmother that she had been attacked by a vampire ex-boyfriend and that her boss had saved her life by not sucking her blood. It just didn't seem sane.

"I don't know what to tell you, Grammy. It's just the job." She had felt terrible about lying, but it seemed to be the only choice.

"But three days? You couldn't call me in three days?"

"I'm sorry, Grammy, we were busy."

"Are you sure you're not getting in over your head?"

"No," Whitney blinked back the tears that threatened her lies. "This really is a good job, Grammy. I have to go to work now. Love you."

Whitney sighed.

Although she wanted desperately to talk to someone about all this, she just didn't think that her grandmother was the right one for the job. There was no way she'd believe any of it. Whitney barely believed it herself. If she hadn't seen Rami's fangs, she probably still wouldn't. And if it had scared the Hell out of her, imagine the trauma knowing would cause her grandmother.

Whitney had thought about it long and hard. She was pretty sure that the only reason she had been able to cope with her new knowledge was because she had already spent time with Rami first. Knowing he was a really nice guy allayed a lot of her fears.

The giant was frightening enough at first impression. If Whitney had learned that he was a vampire the first day she had met him, she probably would have run screaming from the room. Although, she was ready to do that anyway when she thought about going back to work. Now that she knew that vampires and werewolves were the clients that came through her door every day, she was a little apprehensive about sitting in that office all by herself.

She knew that Rami was there if she needed him, but he was still one of Them. Whitney felt very much alone, but fear of Madraeus coming to find her and drag her into work was enough to make her swallow her fear and cross the hall.

To her surprise, she spent the whole morning receiving well-wishers and courtesy calls from concerned clients. It seemed like every member of the Races that she had met so far had called to see how she was doing. She hadn't realized she had met so many people since starting work here.

It had been an exhausting and humbling morning. Now, all she wanted to do was to get through a cup of coffee and a snack before she had to see anyone else or answer the phone again.

She was just indulging in the first chocolate chip cookie when she looked up to find Philtzer sitting on the corner of her desk. She jumped when she saw him, sloshing coffee onto the desk.

"What is it with you people? You're always popping up with no warning," she accused as she wiped up the liquid.

"It's all part of the fun." Philtzer grinned at her and reached over to steal a cookie from her stack.

"Hey! I earned those!" She tried to grab it back but wasn't fast enough.

"Really? What else would you do for a cookie?" he asked, waggling his eyebrows at her.

She couldn't help but smile.

"Alright, so out with it," she picked up a cookie and waved it at him before taking a bite, "what are you?"

"Me? I'm devastatingly handsome."

"No." She wasn't going to be deflected. "I mean, Mrs. Myers is a Weaver, Rami is a vampire, what are you?" She looked at him with squinty eyes.

Philtzer grinned again and leaned close to her, then whispered, "A werewolf."

"What?" She snorted, "You are not."

"I am so," he protested.

"But you're so..." She struggled for a description that wouldn't inflate his already huge ego.

"What? Cute?" He preened.

"Right," she hedged, "aren't werewolves supposed to be all scary and tear out everyone's throat?"

"That's a total misconception. See what Hollywood movies do?" He shook his head. "We are actually quite pleasant and fun-loving. Like puppies!"

Whitney stared at him. "Puppies?"

"Ish," he shrugged. Philtzer popped another cookie in his mouth.

"So, you would never tear anyone's throat out?"

"I didn't say that."

"You're so full of it." She rolled her eyes.

Philtzer seemed so normal, not like Rami or Madraeus or even Unkhabami, who exuded a kind of power. Then again, he was kind of weird.

"What, you need proof?" he asked, hopping off the desk. Before she could say no, he started to transform. Whitney scrambled out of her chair and backed across the room into the corner.

It wasn't like the movies at all. There wasn't any of that slow-motion bone cracking and howling. He was just standing there one minute, and things started to blur around him. Then he was suddenly standing before her as a wolf. Not a movie monster but an honest-to-goodness wolf. He was a rather large black wolf with pale blue eyes that were regarding her curiously. He looked slightly comical with Philtzer's clothes hanging off his furry form. He sat down on his haunches and started to wag his tail.

Whitney gave a little hysterical hiccup and took a tentative step forward. "Philtzer?"

The wolf bobbed his head as if he were nodding.

"You can understand me?"

The wolf nodded again.

She gave another little laugh. "Okay, this is freaking me out. Can you change back?"

The wolf whined, and the area around him shimmered and blurred again, and then Philtzer was standing in front of her, straightening his clothes.

"Believe me now? Or do you want me to do it again?" He grinned with a mischievous twinkle in his eyes.

"No, that's okay." Whitney felt her way to her chair and sat down. "That was really fast."

"Yep." He sat back down on her desk again and stole another cookie. "If we changed slowly, we would be vulnerable: neither man nor wolf with no defense."

"Oh." She had no idea how to respond to that. Something else popped into her head: "What about your clothes?"

"Normally, if we know we are going to change, we undress," he grinned at her, "I could do it again and get undressed first if you want."

"No! That's okay!" She held up her hands. "I'm done!" She shot out of her chair and into Rami's office.

He looked up from his desk, which was covered in papers and stacks of ancient books. "Whitney, are you alright? You look a little pale."

"I... Can I go home?" she blurted out. "Philtzer just demonstrated Werewolfism 101, and I need to lie down now."

Rami's eyebrows rose as he glanced over her shoulder to a grinning Philtzer.

"Of course you can go. Did you need someone to come with you?" he asked.

"I think... I... I'm not sure, all this has thrown me for a loop." She bit her lip and then offered, "Maybe I'll just take some filing and go home."

"Alright," Rami watched her retreat from his office.

He stood and followed her out. She picked up a filing box, filled it from the Dreaded File Cabinet, and then carried it out the door. He turned his attention to Philtzer. He was sitting on the corner of the desk finishing off Whitney's cookies.

"Werewolfism 101?"

"Well, she asked." Philtzer grinned.

"I do not think she asked to be upset."

"No, but she's a good sport about it." He shrugged.

"Do not let your antics go overboard. She is still just human."

"I know," Philtzer looked toward her apartment, and for once, he was serious. "She's tougher than she looks."

"Yes," Rami sighed, "I am afraid that may get tested."

# JUST ACT NORMAL

WHITNEY CLOSED HER APARTMENT door behind her, clutching the box filled with files to her chest. In her mind, she watched Philtzer change into a werewolf again. She shivered.

"Work. I just need to keep my mind off it."

She sighed and sat down to work on the filing. Unfortunately, the Dreaded Filing Project was mind-numbing at best. She flipped through the files, but her brain kept replaying the night of the party, Justin's face, Rami's fangs, Philtzer, and a million other scenes from the past few days. She pushed the files away and sat back. She just needed to get her brain sorted.

All the events of the last two weeks kept rolling around in her head. Everyone here treated the idea of vampires and werewolves as normal and commonplace. They were all so offhanded about it. When she was with them, she could almost see it as normal.

But on her own, it all seemed ridiculous. Their existence alone was too hard to comprehend. To think that a vampire had attacked her was unreal. She reached up to touch the ragged scabs on her neck and knew that it was very, very real.

"I can't do this." She stood and paced.

She couldn't just 'unknow' about the Races. She had to learn to live with the knowledge. She stopped at the window and stared out at the skyscrapers, trying to remember what her life had been like before she knew that monsters were real. It seemed like a dream.

"Information. That's what I need. Facts."

Whitney got up and went over to her computer. She started searching for information on vampires and werewolves. She printed out the few things she found that sounded a little like the people she was involved with. However, nothing really fit. There was too much weird stuff and not enough actual information. It was all legend. She felt silly looking up myths and fairy tales.

"Alright, new tactic."

She did a search on her boss. One address and the InfiniCorp information came up. She tried several of the other people she had met, but most of them she only knew by one name like Rami and Philtzer.

"Well, that was a bust." Whitney sat back and sighed.

Looking across the room, she let her eyes roam over her family photos.

She had always told her grandmother everything. She wasn't going to be able to lie forever. She let her imagination play out the scene. The first take involved her grandmother having a heart attack from fear. She pushed that one aside and tried again. Her second take had her grandmother whacking Madraeus with her cane and chewing him out for involving her baby girl in the workings of evil.

"Okay, that one's funny."

It was all a moot point anyway. Madraeus would never let her tell anyone, but she hated keeping secrets. She was terrible at it. Christmas time was torture for her because she couldn't keep her mouth shut about the presents she bought for people. This was going to be so much harder.

She walked over and picked up a book from the coffee table. She wanted to stop thinking about all this. As she tried to concentrate on the words, a cloud passed over the sun, darkening the room. She frowned; there just weren't enough windows in this place.

"It's like it was built by vampires," she mumbled absently but faltered when she realized what she was saying.

Whitney made a sound that was part whine and part laugh. She threw down her book, got up, and stomped into the bedroom.

She changed quickly into workout clothes, grabbed her earbuds, and headed for the door. There was obviously no way that she was going to get away from her demons while staying in the apartment. So maybe if she was surrounded by normal reality, then she could relax.

Whitney headed down to the lobby and hailed a cab. It took only a few minutes to get to the gym, and only a few more to check in and get out on the floor. She plugged in her earbuds and started making the rounds on the machines. It had been a while since she had worked out and already felt the burn. Unfortunately, it wasn't affecting her thoughts.

There were a few other people in the gym. A couple of guys kept coming over and using machines right next to her. It was annoying. She wasn't here to flirt. She had enough trouble with guys right now. Especially ones with sharp teeth.

Finally, she saw one of the treadmills open up, so she hopped up to grab it before someone else did. Hopefully, that would discourage her admirers.

The treadmills faced the sidewalk so members had something to watch while they ran, or there was a TV up by the ceiling. She tried watching the TV for a while, but it was on the news channel, and she really didn't feel like watching the pompous commentators. They only talked about trifling things like the latest trend in fashion or the newest movie.

*Why don't you talk about the fact that monsters are walking around waiting to bite you?* she mentally screamed at the TV.

She turned her attention to the windows. She watched people walking by. Several of them looked in the window straight at her, but none of them stopped or showed any interest in her. She watched them closely for signs that any of them might be from the Races. Then she felt silly; she had no idea what traits she was looking for.

She wondered how many people out there had run-ins with members of the Races and never knew it. She wondered how many there were worldwide. Madraeus would know. She shook herself. She didn't want to think of him.

Her two admirers joined her on the treadmills. The hair on the back of her neck prickled. She glanced at them warily and received only cocky smiles in return.

This was stupid; she was getting paranoid. They were just guys bent on getting lucky. Whitney refocused on her treadmill. She was going to feel normal if it killed her.

# UNINVITED

Madraeus knocked on Whitney's kitchen door. Rami had just told him that Philtzer had transformed in front of her. He had scarcely gotten up. He was hungry. He was grumpy, and this was the first thing that they mentioned.

"Why can't anyone ever say, 'Good evening, did you sleep well? Nothing going on today, you can go back to bed'?"

He knocked again. He probably should have stopped to feed before coming to check on Whitney. It would have at least improved his mood a little.

Madraeus frowned at the door. She should have answered by now. He put a hand against the door and closed his eyes. He opened his senses and searched the other side of the door for any sign of Whitney. He heard nothing.

Growling under his breath, he reached into his pocket and pulled out the key. He had started carrying it all the time now. He could imagine Whitney's response to that, but it was for her own good.

He opened the door slowly and moved into her kitchen. There was no sign of Whitney. He moved more quickly through the other rooms, finding the same results. He pulled out his cell phone and called her. He heard the answering ring tone from Whitney's phone coming from the desk. He walked over to find it happily vibrating and chiming its way across a pile of papers.

"Damn it!" He stormed back toward his study. Rami stepped out into the hall.

"Whitney is gone," Madraeus snapped.

"Gone, gone? Or temporarily gone?" Rami asked calmly.

"Her stuff is still here."

"Where do you think she went?" Rami asked as they walked back to his office.

"I don't know!" Madraeus snarled. "No one knows what goes on in that head of hers. She's not a prisoner, but I would prefer that she not go out alone until this thing with Justin," he spat out the name, "is resolved."

"I agree." Rami nodded as he picked up the phone. He dialed a number and waited only a moment before it was answered. "Philtzer?" Rami rumbled, "Whitney is gone. You scared her. You find her."

Madraeus glanced at the clock. It was almost seven. He had better eat if he wanted to be in any shape to deal with his errant receptionist.

***

An hour later, Madraeus sat at his desk, drumming his fingers. He sat up, listening. He was sure that he had heard something. Once again, he strode down the hall to Whitney's door. He could hear her singing through the door. Relief flooded through him, followed closely by a new wave of anger.

This time, he didn't even knock. Within seconds, he was through the door.

Whitney's singing was coming from the bathroom. He was tempted to burst into the bathroom and start demanding explanations, but common sense won out. Madraeus sat down on the couch with his arms folded across his chest and glared at the bathroom door, waiting.

Finally, he heard the water turn off, but he had to wait another fifteen minutes before she emerged, wearing nothing but a towel.

She yelped when she saw him sitting on her couch.

"Where the Hell have you been?" he said without preamble.

Her embarrassed pink blush turned into red anger.

"Who do you think you are?" she snapped. "You have no right to come in here uninvited!" She stomped past him to her bedroom.

He was up in an instant following her.

"I have every right to be in here! I own the place!" he growled at her.

She slammed the bedroom door in his face. He threw it open again.

"Do you mind?" she snarled.

"Not at all."

"What? You're going to watch me get dressed?"

"Don't tempt me," he warned. "Where have you been?"

"What makes you think that it's any of your business?" she huffed, wrapping her arms around herself to hold the towel in place.

"Everything you do is my business!" he shouted.

"Since when?" she shouted back.

"Since one of my people tried to kill you! Although at this point, I'm thinking about finishing the job myself!"

Whitney stared at him with her mouth open.

Madraeus took in Whitney's stunned expression and tried to rein in his temper. There was no one in the world who could make him lose control faster than this silly woman.

At that same moment, he realized how nearly naked she really was. Her towel was barely long enough to reach mid-thigh. As his gaze traveled the length of her legs down to her bare feet, he knew he was in trouble. There was no way he would be able to talk to Whitney rationally with his mind wandering around her bare legs. With more effort than he should have needed, he turned and walked into the living room.

"Get dressed," he growled, slamming the door behind him. He heard something hit the door after it closed.

He fidgeted and paced across the room. He paced back again. He tried to go over what he was going to say to Whitney in his head, but the image of her legs kept intruding.

"Pink flannel, now legs?" he mumbled.

One of his pacing routes took him by the desk. The pile of papers he had seen earlier caught his attention. Moving closer, he scanned the top page. Picking up the pile, he sat down and skimmed through them. Madraeus smirked.

"What a load of nonsense," he murmured.

Just then, the bedroom door opened, and Whitney came into the room.

Madraeus looked up. He let his eyes drift over her. She had dressed in a pair of sweats and a tank top. Her wet hair was dripping slightly onto her shoulders. He felt his emotions stir to life again.

She watched him warily.

"Do you actually believe this nonsense?" he asked, holding up the pile of papers.

"No," she snapped. "I was just trying to understand. I'm just trying to get all this into some logical order. It's like fitting a square peg into a round hole. No matter how big I make the hole, the peg still won't fit right!" She sighed, "I was just looking for information."

He let the papers drop to the desk again. Madraeus stood and walked toward her slowly. She backed up a little, then decided to hold her ground. He made a slow circle around her, breathing in the intoxicating scents that floated around her, then stopped behind her.

"If you want to know something," he whispered against her ear, making her shiver, "ask." Then he moved away.

"Oh yeah, like you'd answer?" she snorted.

He turned and spread his arms wide. "I am the one true source," he said with more than a little derision.

"Really." She eyed him. "You would tell me anything?"

Madraeus dropped his arms and stared at her intently, "Will you tell me where you were?"

Whitney bit her lip and stared at him.

He waited. It occurred to him that either she was purposely hiding where she went from him, or she was just not telling him out of spite. Half of him was desperate to believe she was just doing it to annoy him. The other half was terrified that she had betrayed him.

Finally, she looked him straight in the eye and confessed.

"I went to the gym. Too much weird stuff has been going on. I needed some normal."

He watched her for a moment, trying to decide if she was telling him the truth. She looked innocent enough.

"We have a workout room here. You are free to use it anytime you want," he offered.

"I thought that you didn't want anyone in your place," Whitney cocked her head, watching him.

"Normally." He shrugged.

"Do I get to ask questions now?"

# VAMPIRISM 101

"Anything you want," he said solemnly as he moved to the couch.

Madraeus sat down with his back to the corner and his arm resting on the back of the couch. He crossed his legs and waited as Whitney padded over to settle into the other corner.

"Okay." She tucked her bare feet under her and flicked the wet hair off her neck. "Anything I want? No limits?" She bit her lip.

Madraeus nodded, amused by her enthusiasm.

"Oh man, where to begin? Okay, let's start with the super obvious. Coffin?"

"No and yes."

Whitney rolled her eyes. "Oh, come on, you have to give better answers than that, or I'll go back to the Internet!"

"No, I don't sleep in one; yes, I have used one."

"When?"

"For a few fake funerals, and they are very handy for travel," he said honestly. Seeing Whitney's confusion, he elaborated. "When we need to travel long distances unexpectedly and are not sure of arriving when or where we want."

"When? You mean like daylight?" She shook her head. "Can you go out in daylight?"

"No."

"You are really good at short answers." Whitney waited, blinking at him.

He was quite enjoying making Whitney work for her information.

She sighed, "Okay, what happens when you go out in sunlight?"

"Poof." Madraeus made a little explosive motion with his fingers.

"Poof? Like up in smoke and ashes?" Whitney frowned.

Madraeus nodded.

"Why?"

"I don't know." He had always wondered that himself.

"Why not?"

Madraeus frowned, "Do you know the answers to all things?"

"No."

"Neither do I."

Whitney thought for a moment. "So how come Rami could come with me to my old apartment? It was still daylight."

"Rami is different."

"Why? He is a vampire, right?"

"Yes, but," Madraeus shrugged, "he tolerates light better than other vampires. I'm not sure why, but he can go out in dim light, like when it is extremely cloudy. He refuses to tell me how. He just grins at me," Madraeus snorted. He suspected it had something to do with Unkhabami, but Rami would never say.

"Hmm." Whitney scratched at the edge of the couch cushion. "Where do vampires come from?"

"Some believe that we are demons sent to prey on humankind, or we are damned souls. To others, we're just victims in the night. Some believe that we are descended from Judas who was cursed by God never to see the light again. Rami has his own theory about being keepers of history. Take your pick."

"You don't really know?"

"Do you know where humans really come from?"

"Touché," she admitted. "Do you think you are cursed?"

Madraeus shrugged. "Some centuries yes, some no."

Whitney frowned.

"Does garlic freak vampires out?"

"No, otherwise Italy would be vampire-free," Madraeus smiled.

"Do crosses keep you away?"

"Not the cross itself, but the faith behind it can affect us, although not how you think," he amended.

"Then how does it affect you?" Whitney sighed when he wouldn't elaborate.

"We were human once. How does the apparent abandonment of your God and Faith affect you?"

Whitney was quiet for a moment.

"So, you can go into churches?"

"Yes."

"Can you enter a house you haven't been invited into?"

"Yes," Madraeus smiled wickedly, "but it's illegal."

Whitney rolled her eyes.

"Heightened senses?" she tried.

"Our sense of smell, hearing, and eyesight are better than a human's," Madraeus acknowledged.

"Ridiculously super strength and speed?"

"It is not like in the movies, but we are stronger than humans and a little faster. We have much greater stamina."

"So, what about the whole idea of human blood versus animal blood in the strength department?" She cocked her head to one side.

"Well," Madraeus was slow to answer because he didn't want to frighten her. "Animal blood is more pure because of the diet they consume, and human blood tastes so much richer and sweeter for the same reason, but they are both sufficient for consumption. I haven't seen that either one is more powerful, it really comes down to taste preference."

"And what is your taste preference?"

Madraeus smiled slowly, "I have a sweet tooth."

Whitney shivered.

"Hypnotic stares?"

"You tell me?" Madraeus raised an eyebrow and gazed at her intently.

Whitney swallowed.

"Hypnotic stares. Check." She shook herself. "Wooden stakes through the heart?"

Madraeus sighed. "Whitney anything would die if you put a stake through its heart."

"So?" She threw her hands up. "How do you kill a vampire?"

"Planning my demise?"

Whitney heaved a sigh, "If you don't start answering questions."

"Fine." He tilted his head back and stared at the ceiling. "The most effective ways to kill a vampire, number one: sunlight: poof. Number two: beheading, very effective on all species. Number three: stake through the heart." He sounded like someone giving instructions on an infomercial.

"Number four: fire, as in whole body on fire. Five: starvation."

"That's horrible," Whitney said in disgust.

"Why?" Madraeus was surprised at her reaction.

"You are so," she searched for the word, "cavalier about it. This is how we die, one, two, three," she said in her best imitation of his voice.

"So? You are the same way. Mortals are indifferent about shootings and stabbings. You don't get excited about how you could die. Why should I?"

"I guess."

Madraeus watched her bite her lip again. He waited for her to come up with something else to ask. It was impressive how much she had come up with. He was confident that Hollywood movies supplied most of her facts and that was okay, to a point.

Whitney glanced up at him. A look of determination had crept into her eyes. He waited for her next question, but she reached out with one hand instead. Slowly, she stretched out her hand as if she was afraid he would move. Madraeus watched her movements with fascination. Carefully, she wrapped her fingers around his wrist. A jolt shot up his arm. Her fingers were so warm. His throat went dry.

"What are you doing?" he whispered.

"Shh!" She closed her eyes as if listening for something.

Madraeus let his gaze trace her face. He almost smiled at the concentration he saw there.

"What are you listening for?" he whispered.

"I was trying to see if you had a heartbeat."

Madraeus rolled his eyes and grabbed her hand.

Her eyes snapped open.

He gave a tug pulling her forward until she was practically kneeling in his lap. He put her hand flat against his chest.

Whitney's mouth fell open as she stared at her hand. She flexed it experimentally, spreading her fingers slightly.

His heart sped up and his breath quickened. Slowly, she raised her eyes to his.

"Yes, Whitney, I have a heart, and it beats. It pumps blood through my body just... like... yours," he whispered slowly, enunciating the last three words.

They stared at each other for a long time. Then finally, Whitney sat back against the couch, pulling her hand away. Madraeus resisted the urge to feel the spot on his chest where her hand had been.

The silence stretched and finally broke.

"I need to get back to work," he murmured as he stood. Whitney nodded.

"Whitney?"

"Hmm?" She looked up at him.

"The threat from Justin is still very real. Please take your cell phone with you if you leave, although I would really prefer it if you took someone with you."

He wanted to demand that she follow his safety rules, but he just couldn't bring himself to command it. Something had changed in the last few minutes. A deep sense of sadness had come over him as he realized he had taken a step that he couldn't back away from.

"I'll try," Whitney whispered as Madraeus turned and left the apartment.

# GIRLS' NIGHT

"THAT WASN'T AS FUN as I thought it would be," she grumbled, staring at the spot on the couch where Madraeus had been sitting.

Unfortunately, things now made less sense than before. She'd hoped for some resolution or guidelines or something, but now she just felt sad. She had assumed that vampires were the evil undead with no soul or heart, but he wasn't. He was just a man.

*Well, maybe not just,* she thought, lying her head back and staring at the ceiling.

She didn't want to think about Madraeus being just like her. She was definitely in deeper water than she had first thought.

Suddenly, her phone rang. Not the Ravilla Leash, as she called it, but her personal phone. "Hello?"

"Hey girl, we haven't seen you in a while!" Kaylee's voice chirped. She had almost forgotten she had normal friends.

"Yeah, I know." She didn't want to explain why. Fortunately, Kaylee had never been one to care.

"Well, we're going out tonight. You wanna come? Girls' night!" she screamed happily.

"Maybe." She was really tired from her workout, but then again, maybe it would get her mind off her new life.

"Just say yes, I know you have been hiding since the Justin thing."

"Justin thing?" Whitney's mind raced. *How did she know about Justin's attack?*

"Yeah, we heard you two broke up. You need to get out and get on with your life!"

"Oh." Whitney rubbed her forehead, feeling stupid. "The break-up. Right."

"Just come out with us and you'll forget all about it."

"Um... I don't know." Whitney thought about Madraeus' warning.

"Great, text me the address and we'll come pick you up. Be right there!"

Before Whitney could protest, the call ended. She sighed as she texted her new address.

"So much for crawling into bed," she groaned as she dragged herself off the couch to change.

In the time it took for her friends to drive downtown, Whitney had changed into a short black dress with boots. Whitney's phone vibrated as she picked it up. It was Kaylee. They were downstairs waiting.

She picked up the Ravilla Leash and cringed.

Madraeus had asked her to take someone along if she left, but if she brought along one of his bodyguards, she would have to explain his presence to her friends. That would lead to explaining other things she wasn't allowed to talk about.

Her phone vibrated again.

If she didn't go down, they would come up, and then there would be even more questions. She thought about telling Madraeus she was going. She sighed.

"He's gonna be pissed at me either way." She grabbed her jean jacket and headed for the elevator. "Better to ask forgiveness than be denied action."

"Dude, how did you get this gig?" Kaylee asked, looking up at the skyscraper Whitney had walked out of.

"Just lucky, I guess." Whitney shrugged. She had no intention of going into any details.

"Where's everyone else?" she asked as they drove toward the area in lower downtown Denver known as LoDo.

"They're gonna meet us there," Kaylee said as she looked for a parking place.

Her friends all worked for Mrs. Myers. As Whitney listened to Kaylee rattle on about the latest gossip from their group of friends, she felt an odd sense of surrealism. She felt like there was normal reality on one side and the reality that contained monsters on the other. She was literally on the fence and could see both sides at the same time; it was like having double vision.

Kaylee finally found a parking spot. It was a block away from the club Kaylee wanted to go to. As they walked toward the club, Whitney saw that Lisa, Emma, and Ashley were already waiting for them by the door. Kaylee and Whitney got in line with them. They could hear the music pulsing from inside.

When it was their turn, Whitney fished her license out of her jacket pocket. She had learned a long time ago not to carry a purse. Take your ID and a limited amount of money, keep them in your pocket, and you never get into trouble. The bouncer was a tall and very muscular Mexican. Whitney thought that he looked vaguely familiar, but she wasn't sure.

"Good evening, ladies!" He smiled as he checked their IDs and stamped their hands. His movements were quick and efficient.

Whitney held out her ID. He took it from her automatically, just like he had the others, but then he paused. Wondering at his hesitation, Whitney held out her hand to be stamped.

"Ms. Martindale?" He held her hand a moment while he stamped it. "You let me know if there is anything I can do to make your visit to The Loop more enjoyable. I am Esteban Hernandez." He smiled wickedly at her as he motioned her into the club.

"Okay," Whitney eyed him, "thanks?" She wasn't sure what to make of him singling her out. As she turned to go, he winked at her.

"What was that all about?" Lisa asked. Whitney shrugged. She was here to be normal and not think about strange things happening.

"I think he liked you," Emma grinned.

"Oh, shut up!" Whitney rolled her eyes and pushed the other girls down the hall and into the club. Just inside the inner door they stopped.

It was completely packed. The music blasted. The bass pounded inside her chest. Lights and mirrors flashed everywhere. It smelled like sweat, booze, and a thousand perfumes. It was absolute party heaven.

Whitney grinned. *Yes, this is what I need, normal and carefree.*

She followed her friends as Kaylee plowed a path through the crowd to the bar. Kaylee believed that the best way to spend any night was with a drink in each hand.

Immediately, they were surrounded by a crowd of guys. As usual, Kaylee and Emma basked in the attention.

Whenever she went out with Kaylee and Emma, she rarely had to pay for anything. Just being associated with them guaranteed that guys would buy all her drinks and anything else she wanted in the hopes of scoring brownie points with Kaylee or Emma. She just rode the gravy train with Lisa and Ashley.

Emma handed her a drink absently while she spoke with her nearest admirer. Whitney slowly sipped as she scanned the room. Whitney smiled. Ashley was dancing with some guy already, but she didn't see Lisa anywhere.

"Where's Lisa?" Even leaning close to Emma, she still had to shout to be heard over the music.

With a quick glance around as she drank, Emma shrugged. "Bathroom?" Emma guessed and then turned her attention back to her fan club.

Whitney rolled her eyes. Emma and Kaylee excluded Lisa whenever they had the chance. It was always Whitney's job to include her.

Sighing, she made her way around the edge of the dance floor to the hallway that led to the bathrooms. It was dark, but at least when she turned the corner, the music faded a little. She shook her head and popped her ears. It wouldn't surprise her if she was a little deaf in the morning.

Whitney pushed open the bathroom door and looked around. The fluorescent lights turned everything a sickly green color. She blinked trying to get her eyes used to the sudden brightness.

"Lisa?" she called but got no answer.

An eerie feeling crept up her spine. Slowly, she bent down and looked under the stalls, but there was no one there. Shaking her head at her flighty horror-film moment, she went into one of the stalls. She had just shut the door when her Ravilla Leash rang.

"Seriously?" she groaned.

It was bad enough that he had seen her half-naked twice now; she wasn't going to talk to her boss while she was peeing. A girl had to draw the line somewhere.

Before she was out of the stall, two text messages came in.

"Dude, impatient much?" she grumbled as she washed her hands. Finally, she picked up her Leash and looked at her text messages. One was from Rami and the other was from Madraeus. Out of spite, she opened the one from Rami first.

"Get out! Justin at Loop!"

Her heart stopped. She didn't even bother to open the one from Madraeus. She just ran for the door.

# GUESS WHAT?

MADRAEUS SAT DOWN AT his desk and scrubbed his hands over his face. He felt every bit of his 1,767 years.

He had made a terrible mistake. He had fallen for Whitney completely and hopelessly. He hadn't meant for it to happen, but this afternoon, when she had felt his heartbeat, somewhere inside, he had taken that step without conscious thought.

He didn't know what to do now. Attachment made him vulnerable. Admission alone put him in a precariously dangerous position. If Cecelia were to find out, she would not hesitate to seek out and destroy Whitney.

He knew his desire to protect her would one day come into conflict with his duty. He had no doubt about that. What had him worried was which he would choose, Whitney or his duty.

"Ray?" Rami asked again.

He hadn't heard Rami come in.

"Sorry, what?" Madraeus raised his eyes to Rami.

"Ray, are you going catatonic, or did you want to accomplish something tonight?"

He said nothing; he couldn't summon the energy to respond.

"Are you alright, my friend?" Rami asked, coming further into the study. "It is not like you to be so quiet."

"I'm tired," Madraeus sighed. "Did you need something?"

"I said I have a list of missing persons if you want to see it, or would you rather I come back later?"

He really didn't want to talk to anyone right now, but life went on even if he didn't want to participate. "No. Go ahead, what did you find?"

Rami brought the list over to his desk. It was a thick stack of paper.

"This is the list of missing persons reported in the last month. It covers North America."

"This is a big list," Madraeus said, leafing through the pages. "How many are from the Races?"

"Some, but we should check with Marcus since we generally don't report to the police if someone does disappear."

Madraeus nodded and handed the list back to Rami. "So basically, this gets us nowhere."

"Pretty much."

Madraeus sat back, steepling his fingers and tapping them on his lips pensively. "I take it Unkhabami wasn't forthcoming with anything more."

"Not pertaining to this," Rami grinned.

"Did she say anything useful about anything?" Madraeus dropped his hands.

"She said I was incredibly handsome." Rami's grin widened.

"Great," Madraeus snorted. "What about the Old Sources? Anyone found anything yet?"

"No." Rami's grin disappeared. "Every time we think we've found something, it turns into a dead end. They've gone searching for an obscure book or a text only to find that it had gone missing. There are some Sources we've actually found the location of, and when we get there, it's empty. Cecelia is miles ahead of us at this point."

Madraeus wondered how many sources she had already freed. With the power of the Old Sources behind her, Cecelia would overwhelm the mortal world quickly. Nothing would be able to stop her.

"I wish I would have seen this coming. I should have studied our histories better," Rami rumbled.

"We've never had the time or resources. Our lives have been consumed with managing the Races in the here and now." Madraeus shook his head. "Don't blame yourself. We just need to find a solution."

"Of course." Rami nodded with a sigh. "You are right."

"Try Myers. See if she can track down what Unkhabami was sensing."

"Boss! Guess what?" Philtzer burst into the room, grinning.

Madraeus waited. He never had to ask. Philtzer could never wait to tell him news.

"Some of my pack just caught Justin's scent."

"Where?" Madraeus shot out of his chair.

"Commons Park. Headed this way. He is following Cherry Creek toward downtown." He held up his cell phone. "They're hot on his heels."

"Keep in contact," Madraeus said as he came around the desk and motioned Philtzer and Rami to the door. "We will trap him in between us. Maybe we can finish this once and for all."

The elevator ride was spent with Philtzer getting updates and Rami calling in teams.

"There are only about ten of us close enough; most are in other areas of the city," Rami grunted as the doors opened.

"It'll do." Madraeus nodded.

As one, they started to run. They were only about twenty blocks from the park. It was faster to run than to try and drive. This was a hunt, and traffic would only slow them down.

"This would be a lot easier if I was a wolf," Philtzer complained as they ran.

"Yes, but then you could not use your phone," Rami laughed. "Who knows what message your little doggie paws would write!"

Madraeus smiled. The exhilaration of running at night through the city on the way to a fight had overpowered his melancholy mood. Now, there was only the hunt. They dodged down alleys and across streets. Anticipation was speeding them on. He would soon have his revenge.

As they closed in on LoDo, they slowed. There were a lot of humans out tonight. Suddenly, Philtzer stopped and frowned at his phone. He dialed a number and waited.

"What do you mean you lost him?" he shouted into the phone.

Rami and Madraeus backtracked to where Philtzer had stopped. He put it on speaker.

"I don't know!" The other person sounded like they were running. "He was there one minute, crossing the tracks, then a train came, and he was suddenly gone! We are retracing our steps, trying to pick up his trail again."

Rami and Madraeus looked at each other.

"We are only a couple blocks away, be there in a minute," Philtzer said, then snapped his phone shut.

They started running again.

"Are you freakin' kidding me? They lost him at a train!" Philtzer complained.

Just then, Rami's phone chimed. Without breaking stride, he pulled it out and answered.

"Yes?"

"Rami, my friend! You will never guess who is here at The Loop," Esteban Hernandez cooed.

"Justin?" Rami hissed.

"Give the man a prize." Esteban laughed, "Guess who else?"

"Who?"

"Whitney Martindale."

"Keep them apart! We are almost there!" Rami growled. "Damn! Damn!"

"What's wrong?" Madraeus didn't like the panic that was in Rami's voice.

"Justin is at The Loop." Rami frantically texted as he spoke.

"So?" Madraeus didn't see this as a need for panic, maybe triumph, but surely not panic.

"So is Whitney."

Madraeus stumbled.

"Whitney? What the hell is she doing there!"

He pulled out his phone and called her. There was no answer.

This was a disaster. Madraeus sprinted faster. He could see some of his people coming down the side street. When they burst out of the alley across from The Loop, they all slowed to a walk.

"Philtzer, take your men to the back," Madraeus growled as he headed for the front entrance with Rami on his heels.

# DID YA MISS ME?

Right before Whitney grabbed the handle, the bathroom door swung inward, and Justin sauntered into the women's bathroom.

"Hi, Whit. Did you miss me?" Justin smiled viciously.

Whitney skittered backward. He looked just as cold and cruel as he had at Mrs. Myers' party. She stared at him.

She couldn't find her voice. Although she had no trouble mouthing off to Madraeus the vampire, Justin the vampire scared the crap out of her. She wondered absently why it wasn't the other way around, given her history with Justin.

"Nothing to say?"

She snapped out of her wayward thoughts and focused on Justin.

"I'm surprised. I've never known you to be speechless."

When she still didn't answer, he smiled and wandered toward the sinks.

"You know, Whit, I thought that we could start over now that you know what I am. I was a little worried that you wouldn't be able to handle the idea of vampires, but you have taken it remarkably well."

"What do you want?" she managed to rasp out.

Immediately, Justin grinned. Whitney could see his fangs clearly.

"That's better." He moved a little closer, and she backed up again. He cocked his head to the side and frowned. "Whit, you act like you're scared of me."

"Duh!" His innocent act made her mad. "You bit me!"

"Well," Justin smiled sheepishly at her, "you can't fault me for that. You looked absolutely delicious that night. You can't blame me for wanting you."

Whitney wasn't going to let him charm his way around her.

"What do you want, Justin?" she repeated.

"You," he stepped toward her, "I want you, Whitney. I can make you like me. You don't have to work for that stuffy ass. You could live forever with me."

Whitney's head started to shake before she started to speak, "No. No way, you're sick. Justin, they can help you."

"Help me? With what?" he snapped. "I'm a God."

In that moment, Whitney realized: Justin was gone. He couldn't be helped. Becoming a vampire had made him insane. Fear and despair crushed her chest

"Justin, I think—" the door burst open, cutting her off.

"Whitney?" Lisa said as she came in the door, but the sight of Justin shocked her into silence.

"Lisa! Get out of here!" Whitney cried.

Lisa started to speak, but then her gaze focused on Justin's fangs. Her eyes bulged. With a feral growl, Justin lunged at Lisa.

She shrieked and spun toward the door, but it was too late.

Justin tackled her. They slammed into the door. Within seconds, he had ripped Lisa's throat open.

Carelessly, Justin dropped her limp body and turned back to Whitney. Blood was smeared across his chin and shirt. He smiled at her nonchalantly as if nothing had happened.

"Now, where were we?" He hopped over Lisa's body like she was a log. "Oh yeah, you were going to come with me."

He held out his hand, but Whitney shook her head. Her gaze flicked to Lisa's body behind him.

He snarled, "It's with me or not at all."

"Go to Hell!"

Justin let out an exaggerated sigh. "Well, if that's the way you want it." He shifted into a crouch.

A chill spread through her, and she started to shake. Justin was going to kill her. She didn't even have a weapon. As if reading her mind, he made an exaggerated effort of looking at her hair.

"What? No hidden daggers this time?" Slowly, he began to stalk her.

"Stay away from me!" She backed up. He was between her and the door. *Why did bathrooms have to have only one exit?* She thought desperately.

***

Esteban spotted Rami and Madraeus as they pushed past the crowd at the door. He threaded his way through the crowd until he was next to them.

"There are too many people here," Rami complained.

"Where is she?" Madraeus demanded.

"I don't know. I was keeping track of her, but there was a fight. When I looked back, she was gone." Esteban shrugged. He stepped back under the force of the murderous look Madraeus shot at him.

"She was with her friends over there." He pointed to a table in the corner.

Rami started forward, plowing his way through the crowd. Madraeus and Esteban followed in his wake. It was like Moses and the Red Sea. People scrambled to get out of the giant's way.

They were halfway across the dance floor when a scream pierced the air. All three vampires turned toward the sound. It had come from the back of the club where the bathrooms were. More screams rent the air; this time, they were louder than the music, and it caught everyone's attention. A tide of curious, drunken clubbers wanting to be the first to see what caused the scream swept them along toward the back of the club.

When the first intrepid curiosity-seekers reached the source of the screams, pandemonium erupted, starting a backlash of panic. It swept backward through the crowd. People started pushing and shoving, trying to get away from the back hallway.

"What just happened?" Madraeus shouted as terrified clubbers crashed into them, trying to get away.

"I don't know," Rami rumbled.

Madraeus wrestled down his desire to start throwing people out of the way. They fought against the crowd, but they couldn't get through; even Rami was being forced back.

Through the crowd, Madraeus saw two of the other bouncers converging on the hallway. Esteban pushed his way toward the wall.

Madraeus and Rami followed. If they couldn't go forward, they would go around, but the panicked clubbers delayed their progress.

Estaban reached the hall first and slipped around the corner.

The door of the women's restroom was propped open by the crumpled body of a woman. There was blood on the floor, and several people were lying unconscious and bloody against the wall across from the door.

A loud crash reverberated inside the bathroom. Esteban stepped inside and almost tripped over the body of a girl who was sprawled just inside the door.

Justin had Whitney cornered. She was wielding the trash can like a club. Trash and broken bits of the mirror were strewn all over the floor. There was blood everywhere.

Justin spun around. His face was covered with blood. His fangs were out, and his hands were curled into claws.

Without warning, Justin lunged.

Esteban caught him in midair as the other bouncers entered the room. They jumped forward and tried to get a hold on him but couldn't. Justin twisted, punched, and kicked as he grappled with Esteban. Snarling, he tried to get his teeth into anything that he could. He managed to bite Esteban on the arm.

Esteban howled in pain and anger. He grabbed Justin by the hair and threw him across the room. Justin bounced off the wall, then jumped up and shot out the door, bowling over the bouncers in the process.

Esteban scrambled after him, but Justin was already gone.

Police were shouting from the front door. They were trying to get the crowd under control. Esteban glanced around for Madraeus and Rami. He saw them shoving their way toward the bathrooms

"Did you get him?" Esteban shouted.

"He didn't come this way!" Rami shook his head. "He must have gone out the back!"

Esteban looked past Rami to where the police were flooding into the room.

"You have to get out of here." Esteban took Madraeus by the elbow and steered him toward the back door.

"What about Whitney?" Madraeus shook off Esteban's arm and started back toward the bathroom.

"I'll take care of her. You're wasting time! Go before the police see you, or you'll never get out of here!" Esteban grabbed his arm again, but Madraeus still resisted.

"Esteban is right, my friend, we will lose his trail if we waste time answering police questions," Rami snarled.

"Go before they notice." Esteban clapped Rami on the shoulder and disappeared back into the bathroom.

Rami pulled Madraeus out the back door and into the alley.

# OH, GOODIE POLICE

As soon as she was sure Justin wasn't coming back, Whitney let the trash can clatter to the floor. She leaned back against the wall and slowly slid to the floor. Her entire body started to shake, and her teeth started to chatter.

All but one of the bouncers had followed Esteban out the door. The last one came over to her and squatted down in front of her.

"Are you alright?" he asked gently.

Although she wasn't all right at all, she looked up at him and nodded. She let her gaze slide past him to Lisa's body.

*Poor Lisa, she didn't have a chance. This is all my fault!* she thought. *If I hadn't gone out with them, Justin never would have come here!*

Esteban came back into the room and motioned to Jerry, his fellow bouncer. He left Whitney and stepped over to the door with Esteban.

"This is now a crime scene. The police are trying to get everyone organized so they can find the witnesses. We need to help with crowd control. The paramedics are on their way," Esteban explained.

"What about her?" Jerry jerked his thumb toward Whitney.

"I'll try and get her out of the bathroom." More than happy to let Esteban deal with a distraught female, Jerry hurried out into the main room.

Esteban moved over to Whitney. "Hey? How are you doing?"

Whitney just kept staring at Lisa's body.

"Okay, stupid question," he conceded. "Look, the police are going to be in here any minute, and you need to get your story straight."

Whitney finally looked at him.

Esteban smiled. "You need to tell them that Justin surprised you, then started freaking out and attacking people."

"That's kinda what happened." Whitney's expression clouded. Her brain wasn't catching up with the action.

"Good, then it will be easy to stick close to the truth, just be sure you don't spill our secret," he warned.

"Secret?" Whitney echoed, then suddenly caught on. "Oh. Are you a—?"

"Vamp? Yep," Esteban nodded.

Relief flooded through her; she wasn't alone in this. She immediately grabbed for the lifeline he represented. "What should I do?"

Before he could answer, the paramedics came through the door. She shot a look at Esteban.

"Just tell them what I said," he whispered. "I'll try and stay with you for as long as I can."

"K," she whimpered as he helped her off the floor. She followed the paramedic out the door, trying not to look at Lisa's body or any of the other victims lying in the hall.

***

Whitney was exhausted. She felt like she had been up for days. Her head felt like it weighed a thousand pounds. After the paramedics had pronounced her unhurt, the police had brought her to the Denver police station to take her statement. True to his word, Esteban had come with her.

One of the officers escorted her to his desk, typed up her personal information, then started asking questions. He was trying to get a timeline out of her.

She wasn't sure if the officer had noticed or not, but the more questions he asked, the more nervous she felt. She glanced over at Esteban. He was sitting three desks away, answering questions from a different officer. She wished desperately that she could be as cool and calm as he appeared. He was even laughing with the cop.

Whitney wasn't sure how long she'd been there until Esteban stopped by her chair.

"How are you holding up?" He stared at her intently.

"I'm still going." She smiled in what she hoped was a reassuring way.

Esteban nodded. "I know that you have been through a tough night, but it's almost dawn, so hopefully you can get out of here soon."

"Are you leaving?" she asked, panicking at the thought of being alone.

"Yeah, gotta get home," Esteban winked at her, "I have a rare skin condition that keeps me out of the sun."

"Lucky you." She let out a short, unenthusiastic laugh.

"Don't worry, Whitney, everything will be okay." He gave her shoulder a squeeze and then swaggered toward the door.

Whitney watched him go, feeling like her lifeline was being reeled in without her attached.

"Miss Martindale?" the officer asked, drawing her attention back to him.

"Yeah? Sorry."

"Will you come with me?' he asked.

"Uh, sure, where are we going?" she asked.

"I just need you to wait in another room for a few minutes," he said over his shoulder as he led the way out of the main room.

Reluctantly, Whitney followed him. He led her into a room with a table, four chairs, and a two-way mirror on the wall.

"Great, I'm in an episode of *Dragnet*," she groaned and plopped down in one of the chairs.

Fortunately, she didn't have to wait long for her new interrogator. The door opened only a few minutes later to admit an older man with graying hair and a drooping mustache. He wasn't in a uniform, but he was carrying a file and two cups of coffee. He smiled at her self-consciously and sat down across from her.

"Morning, Miss Martindale, I'm Detective Sanders," he said as he arranged his paperwork and got settled into his chair.

"Morning," Whitney echoed half-heartedly.

He shuffled his papers again and pushed one of the cups toward her.

"I thought you could use a pick-me-up," he smiled.

"Thanks." She sighed as she reached for the cup. However, Whitney's gratitude was short-lived after nearly gagging on the so-called coffee.

*No wonder cops are grumpy if their coffee tastes like this.*

"So? What can you tell me about last night?" he asked as he rearranged his papers again, pulled out a pair of reading glasses, and slipped them on.

"I told the other officer everything already." She was tired, and she didn't feel like starting over.

"I know, but I would like to hear it again. It helps me get a handle on things better than reading it." He smiled at her again, then took a drink of coffee.

Whitney was surprised that he didn't grimace at the taste. He just kept looking at her expectantly. He didn't seem like the kind of man to be dissuaded from his purpose, so she resigned herself to telling the whole story again.

Taking a deep breath, she started to retell the 'edited for non-vampire aware' version of the night from the time that Kaylee picked her up until the police came to The Loop.

"So, you went to the club to meet Justin and your friends?" Detective Sanders asked absently as he made notes.

"No," Whitney sighed. "I went with my friends to the club. I had no idea that Justin would be there."

"And you said that," he searched the pages for the name, "Lisa, was dead when you got into the bathroom."

"No," Whitney sighed again. "She came in after Justin, and he jumped her."

"You didn't try to help her?" Detective Sanders looked at her over his reading glasses.

"I didn't have time!" She leaned forward, flopping her hands onto the table palm up in a helpless gesture. "I yelled for her to run, but it was too late." She felt the tears starting again, and she blinked a few times.

"And this Justin, you broke up with him?"

"No!" She slumped back in her chair and stared at the detective. He just couldn't get anything right that she had told him. "Justin dumped me with a note. It was a surprise to me."

"And had you had any contact with Justin from the time you broke up until last night?"

Panic hit Whitney. She didn't know how to answer that question without giving information away about the first time he attacked her. Her poor, exhausted brain couldn't come up with an answer. She was just too tired and stressed out to come up with a decent lie. Desperately, she wished that Esteban hadn't gone home.

"Miss Martindale?" Detective Sanders prompted when she didn't answer. She decided to pull the pity card.

"Sorry, what? I didn't hear what you asked. I'm just so tired." Whitney rubbed her hands over her face in an over-exaggerated effort to wake herself up, then smiled sheepishly, "I've been up for almost 24 hours, and with everything that's happened, my brain is a little fuzzy."

"I understand. I just have a few more questions," he smiled back.

Whitney cursed silently; he had obviously seen the pity card before and didn't care.

"Fine," Whitney sighed.

"Had you seen Justin since breaking up with him?"

"I guess maybe once." Whitney tried to answer vaguely.

"And when was that?"

"A few days ago, I guess." Uncertainty was thick in her tone.

"And was he upset then?"

"Maybe a little." Upset was an understatement considering he had tried to kill her. Whitney was beginning to like understatements. "I wasn't exactly nice to him."

"Did you argue?"

"Wouldn't you if you saw an ex that had dumped you with a note?" Whitney snorted.

Detective Sanders smiled indulgently and nodded. "I probably would."

"Has he ever shown any violent tendencies in the past?"

"No." Finally, she could answer honestly.

"Any idea why he would start attacking people now?" he asked as he looked over his glasses again.

It took everything she had, but she looked him straight in the eye and shook her head. "Not sure."

Detective Sanders searched her face for a moment, looked down at his notes, and wrote something down.

*What is he writing?*

Her nerves were stretched to the breaking point. She couldn't tell if he believed her or if he was suspicious. She had tried not to squirm as she lied.

*When is this interview going to be over?*

"Any idea where he could be now?"

"No. I don't know." At least that was the truth.

The detective looked at her intently again. She tried to sit still under his scrutiny, but she was becoming more nervous by the minute. She wondered if he could tell. Detective Sanders shifted and started gathering his paperwork.

"All right, Miss Martindale, I think that is all I need for right now." He stood, picked up his stack of papers, and smiled. "If you would give me a couple of minutes, we can get you out of here."

"Okay." Whitney was shocked that he was done asking questions so suddenly, but she wasn't going to complain. She watched him slip out the door.

# HOME PLEASE?

Whitney waited, and waited, and waited. Sitting still was making her extremely sleepy. She finally rested her head on the table, pillowed on her arms. She couldn't tell if her headache was from lack of sleep, a hangover setting in, or maybe from stress.

All she knew was that she wanted to go home. Not home with Madraeus and Rami, but home to Grammy's. She wanted to be safe and normal. However, she knew that if she went home, she would be facing a bunch of questions from her grandmother that she couldn't answer.

When she left here, it was going to be a barrage of questions no matter where she went. For a moment, she almost wished that Justin had succeeded in killing her.

She raised her head and looked at the clock above the door. It was almost seven.

"Where the hell did that damn detective go?" She was tempted to just get up and leave, but she wasn't sure if she would get into more trouble by just walking out. With a whimper, she flopped her head back onto the table.

"Miss Martindale?" Detective Sanders shook her shoulder. "Miss Martindale?"

Slowly, Whitney sat up and looked around.

"You can go now, Miss Martindale, I'm sorry we kept you so long," he said quietly.

Her eyes searched out the clock. It was almost eight.

"Did I fall asleep?" she yawned.

"Yes."

"Oh! Sorry!" Whitney flushed with embarrassment.

"That's alright. You ready to go?"

"Yes, please!" She nodded and followed him out the door and back down the corridor.

Whitney squinted at the bright light coming in the windows. The main room was a mass of noise and movement. Day shift had taken over. Whitney's head pounded harder. Detective Sanders escorted her to the front door.

"I may have some more questions for you later, but for now, you should go home and get some sleep," he said, holding the door for her.

"Thank you." Whitney gave him a weak smile and then walked out into the chilly morning air.

She walked away from the police station without looking back. She could feel Detective Sanders watching her, and she didn't want to appear nervous. She walked to the corner and looked around for a taxi. Before she could flag one down, the rumble of a motorcycle engine drew her attention.

Sitting across the street from her was Philtzer on his bike. He shoved his sunglasses up on his head and motioned her over.

Relief flooded through her. She hadn't expected anyone to come get her. Whitney gave a quick glance around and trotted across the street.

"Hey, babe!" Philtzer called out as she got closer.

"Hey," she smiled tiredly.

He got off his bike and opened his arms. She walked straight into them. Tears started to pool in her eyes, but she wouldn't let them fall, not here in the middle of the street.

Philtzer held her tight for a moment, then pulled back and searched her face. She knew he must have seen the tears, but he didn't mention them.

"Man, you look like crap!" He grinned.

"Thanks." She gave a halfhearted laugh. "You always know just what to say. Did you find Justin?"

"Nah, bastard slipped through our fingers again! I'm beginning to think this guy's a magician. One minute he is there and the next he is gone. It's getting on my nerves," he grumbled.

"How did he get past you?"

"There were too many people running out of the back. He shot out of there like a rocket and disappeared around the corner. He was gone before we could get through the crowd. I'm betting he had someone waiting for him in a car. That's the only way he could have disappeared so fast."

"You think he has an accomplice?" Whitney shivered.

"Don't worry, Whit. We're gonna find him. My pack is searching every alley and street around the Loop, trying to pick up his scent."

Philtzer flicked a glance over her shoulder toward the police station.

"Is that Detective still watching?" Whitney asked.

"Old dude with a mustache?"

"Yeah." Whitney wanted to turn and look, but she didn't dare.

"Yep." Philtzer looked down at Whitney and grinned. "Wanna give him a good show? I could give you a good kissing."

"Oh God no!" Her cheeks flamed red.

"Come on, it'll be fun."

"I cannot handle that right now, thank you." Whitney shook her head.

"Spoilsport. Come on, I'll take you home." He turned to get back on his bike.

"Do we have to?" she asked, pulling on the helmet he handed her.

"Yeah," he sighed, buckling his helmet. "Sorry, honey, but Madraeus is climbing the walls, and he'd kill me if I took you anywhere else."

Whitney nodded, resigned to her fate. Carefully, she sat on the back of Philtzer's bike. She had to hike her skirt up embarrassingly high. It was one of those racing bikes, so she had to practically lay on his back to hold on.

"You couldn't bring a car?" she complained.

"No way!" he laughed. "This is more fun!"

She started to protest, but as he sped away from the curb, all she could think of was holding on for dear life. He sped down alleys as shortcuts, and when he couldn't find an alley, he darted through traffic like a bumblebee. By the time they were in the parking garage, she was shaking and praying for a quick death. His driving was not something that she wanted to experience ever again.

Whitney got off Philtzer's bike the moment he stopped, and collapsed as soon as her feet touched the ground.

"You okay?" Philtzer chuckled as he wrapped an arm around her waist and hauled her to her feet.

"No!" Whitney snapped as he guided her into the elevator.

"Come on, you'll live."

"Is he really mad?" she asked as the elevator glided upwards.

"I don't think mad is quite the right term."

"Do I have to see him now? Can't I get some sleep first?"

"Whit..." Philtzer hesitated.

"Please?" Whitney begged. "I haven't slept in forever, and I don't think I can handle him yelling at me."

As the doors opened, Philtzer searched her face. He sighed, "Madraeus said bring you back, he didn't say directly to him."

Whitney visibly relaxed.

"Alright, I'll go tell him you are here and safe. And I'll try to get him to leave you alone to sleep, but I make no promises." He tapped her on the end of the nose.

"Thank you," she whispered and turned toward her door.

Philtzer watched her go inside, then turned to face his fate. With dragging feet, he walked to Madraeus' study.

# TIME FOR BED

MADRAEUS PACED THE LENGTH of his study again. He glanced at the clock. Philtzer should be back by now.

*What's taking so long?*

Just one more frustration. Failing to find anything about the Old Sources was frustrating him. Unkhabami's vague reference to disappearances was frustrating him. Everything about this situation with Justin was frustrating him.

He threw himself into his chair. He watched Rami as he napped in the armchair across the room and drummed his fingers on the desk.

For being such a new vampire, this kid was incredibly adept at avoiding capture. Madraeus knew he had an accomplice, and he was almost certain that it was Cecelia. But why would Cecelia bother helping Justin if she had bigger plans in mind? It didn't make sense.

If Cecelia was searching out the Old Sources, then she would have more important matters to attend to than this thing between Justin and Whitney. It was all too convenient that Whitney had come to work for InfiniCorp right when Justin had been turned. There had to be more to this mess than was first apparent.

He glanced at the clock again.

*Where the hell are Philtzer and Whitney?*

Madraeus heard the door swing open and surged to his feet. Dread filled him when he saw Philtzer was alone. He tried not to look down the hall past him.

"Where's Whitney?"

"She's fine." Philtzer held up his hand in a placating gesture.

"Where?" Madraeus frowned.

Rami sat up, eying Madraeus silently.

"Now, boss, you gotta understand that she has been through a really tough night," Philtzer spoke low and slow.

"Where?" Madraeus asked again.

"She's gone to lie down."

As Philtzer said it, Madraeus made to move past him, but Philtzer stepped in front of him.

"I think you should let her be. She is not prepared to handle a confrontation right now."

"Get out of my way!" Madraeus snarled.

"Ray, maybe you should let her be for a while," Rami said quietly.

Madraeus didn't say anything for a moment. He just stared at Philtzer.

"Move," he hissed.

Philtzer stood between his boss and Whitney only a moment longer and then shifted aside slowly. Madraeus pushed past him and stalked down the hall.

***

Whitney was standing in front of the bathroom mirror staring at her reflection when she caught sight of him in the mirror and screamed, jumping sideways. She fell against the toilet and sat down abruptly.

Her breath came in short gasps, and her teeth started to chatter as she stared accusingly up at him.

Madraeus stared back. Philtzer had warned him, but he hadn't been prepared to find her so ragged. Her hair was frazzled, and her eye makeup had smeared. Her cheeks were pale, and there was blood on her clothes. Rami was right; he should have let her be for a while. He wanted to turn around and go, but he couldn't just leave her like this.

"What did you tell the police?" He knew the question would make her mad, and maybe anger would pull her out of her shock. He was right; Whitney glared back.

"The police?" she hissed. "Not 'hi Whitney' or 'you okay Whitney'? Oh no! You want to know about the police!" she shrieked.

Madraeus flinched; perhaps he had miscalculated.

"I told them there was a massive lair of vampires and were-wolves holed up in downtown Denver!" she snarled. "What do you think I told them?" She shoved herself up.

"Whitney—" Madraeus reached for her, hoping to calm her down, but she shoved his hands away.

"No!" she shouted. "How can you only care about yourself? My friend is dead!" Her voice became strangled, and she started to shake all over. Tears started streaming down her face, and she swiped at them with her hand.

"I can't do this right now," she rasped past the lump in her throat. "Please, will you go away? Please?" She wrapped her arms around herself and squeezed her eyes shut.

"Whitney—" He tried again to reach for her.

"Stop! Why can't you just go?" Whitney shoved at him. "Why do you have to control everything? I just wanted to be normal for a night!" She shoved at him again.

Madraeus' arms shot out, trying to get a hold of her. Whitney struggled, shoving against his attempts to catch her.

"Why did you drag me into this?"

He reared back to avoid her flailing fists. She was dissolving into hysterics.

"She died because of you... I killed her!" she sobbed as she hit him again.

Eventually, Madraeus managed to get ahold of her shoulders. She struggled, but he held tight, pulling her into his chest. He wrapped his arms around her and waited. She struggled a little more, then suddenly all the fight went out of her. She sobbed uncontrollably. He held her upright when her knees buckled. An ache shot through his chest. He would have given anything just then to spare her this pain.

"Shh." He stroked her hair. "It's not your fault." He murmured, "I'm sorry. I should have kept you out of my world." He laid his cheek on the top of her head. With one hand, he kept stroking her hair and rubbed her back with the other. "I should have kept you safe."

She continued to cry, but slowly she sobbed less and less until she was crying silently. After a while, she was only sniffling periodically. He turned his head and pressed a gentle kiss on the top of her head.

Weakly, she pushed against him.

Reluctantly, he let her go.

She grabbed a tissue and wiped her eyes and nose, but she refused to look at him.

"I'm sorry," she croaked. She sounded utterly defeated.

"Don't be," he whispered bitterly. "You didn't deserve any of this."

"No, it is my fault." Finally, she looked up at him with red-rimmed eyes and shook her head. Her lip quivered with the threat of more tears.

"This was Justin's fault!" Madraeus stepped forward and cupped her face with his hands. "He hurt those people. You can't blame yourself for what he did."

"But it was me he came looking for. If I hadn't been there, he wouldn't have been either," she said sadly. Her voice was raw from crying.

"Whitney," he sighed, "the truth is, he is looking for you. Eventually, if he couldn't find you, he would start with those closest to you and force you out of hiding by hurting them."

Her eyes widened as the implications sank in. He hated to scare her more, but she needed to understand.

"It is not your fault that he is after you. It is his choice. You have no control over that. So don't blame yourself, alright?"

He let his hand slide down her neck. His fingers grazed Justin's bite marks. The reminder burned into him, filling him with a determination so strong it hurt. He huffed out his breath in a rush, trying to get a handle on his anger.

"Now, you need to clean up so we can get you to bed." The thought of taking her to bed flared up to consume him. He jerked his hand back.

She blinked at him in confusion.

Quickly, he turned away. He reached over to start the shower while he tried to banish his desire. After a moment, he turned back to find her watching him warily. He gestured toward the shower and then stalked past her, closing the door behind him.

He paced the length of the apartment. He had to keep her safe somehow, not just from Justin, but from himself as well. His path took him through the kitchen, giving him a sudden idea.

***

Madraeus sat on the chair in the corner of her bedroom with his legs crossed, absently stirring the steaming cup he held in his lap. He looked up as Whitney peered around the bedroom door. His eyes traveled the length of her. Once again, she was standing in front of him, half-naked, wearing only a towel. Tears started to cloud her eyes.

Madraeus pointed at the bed where he had laid out a t-shirt and pajama pants. She looked back at Madraeus. She inched toward the bed without taking her eyes off Madraeus.

"You gonna turn around?" she asked as she picked up the clothes.

The ghost of a smile tugged at the corner of his mouth as he watched her silently, but he turned his face away. When he didn't hear any movement, he reassured her. "I won't look."

After a moment he heard her rustling around and he smiled. There was a time, long ago, when he wouldn't have cared how a woman felt. If he wanted to watch, he would have watched.

*She's really gotten to me,* he thought.

When the rustling stopped, he turned back to her. Slowly, he stood. Whitney looked ready to fall down. He handed her the cup he had been stirring. She looked at it in confusion.

"It's cocoa, heated on the stove, just like your grandmother said," he explained.

Carefully she took the cup from him and started to drink. Whitney shook her head.

"What?" he asked.

"I don't know," she whispered. "I just don't understand you."

"What is there to understand?" He shrugged.

They stared at each other silently as she drank the last of her cocoa. He took the empty cup from her and gestured toward the bed. "Sleep."

Wordlessly, she climbed into bed. Her exhausted body didn't want to wait anymore. Her eyes started to close on their own. He pulled the covers up around her.

"Thank you," she murmured as she drifted off to sleep.

Madraeus stood holding the empty cup and watched her. She was here, but was she safe? He heaved a sigh. Whitney would never be safe until she was removed from his life. Now, more than ever, he knew that any future with Whitney was doomed. He crushed down the part of him that wanted to crawl into bed with her and left the room. There was work to be done.

# TIME TO GO

RETURNING TO HIS STUDY, he found Rami dozing and Philtzer sitting on his desk

The young wolf was playing with a letter opener. When he saw Madraeus, he jumped down and glared at him. Rami sat up, yawning, and raised his eyebrows.

"She's sleeping," he answered Rami's silent question.

"Did you fight?" Philtzer asked quietly, looking down at the letter opener. Madraeus wondered if he was planning on using it on him.

"A little, but she is fine. I want a guard outside her apartment door. I want no chances."

After a moment, Philtzer nodded, set down the letter opener, then wandered out the door. Madraeus glanced over at Rami as the giant stood and stretched.

"What? No accusations from you?"

The giant said nothing, but his face transformed into one of his knowing grins.

"I hate it when you do that." Madraeus shook his head.

Rami's grin widened. Madraeus sighed and leaned on the desk. "We have to assume that the police will start investigating us."

"Did Whitney tell them anything?" Rami's grin disappeared.

"I don't know. She wasn't very coherent. You can bet they are going to be watching her looking for Justin, and that means they will be watching us too.

"Any way we can hide this incident?"

"Not this time. It's gotten too big. Too many people have seen. Their forensics teams are going to have a field day. Even if we could get at the evidence, this kind of carnage doesn't just go away." Madraeus scrubbed his face with both hands. "We need to be ready to move."

Rami sighed eloquently.

"I know," Madraeus agreed. "I don't want to either."

"I have had a location in mind for some time now. I will start transferring funds and making preparations."

"Do it quietly. Like I said, they will be watching us all, and I don't want it to be obvious."

"I know the drill." Rami nodded, then sighed again. "Too bad, I liked it here."

"Me too," Madraeus murmured as Rami left.

He sank down into his chair and pulled out his phone.

"Marcus?"

"Yeah?" his cheerful voice asked. "How are you, Madraeus?"

"I've been better."

"So I hear."

"Really? What have you heard?"

Marcus chuckled, "Everything."

"Thanks, that's helpful," Madraeus groaned. The man always knew something or someone who knew something.

"Rough business last night."

He could hear Marcus typing.

"Yeah. I think it might get bad."

"I'll start pulling info and covering tracks. I have some info on the Hares too," Marcus offered, "but no locations. They're better at hiding than we are."

"That's because they're cowards," Madraeus snarled.

"Or just smart enough to stay out of our crosshairs," he chuckled again. "I've sent a courier with all the info."

"Thanks. You find anything on Cecelia yet?"

"Not sure."

"What? What do you mean, not sure? You always know something."

"Yeah, but something is different this time." Marcus hedged, "I can't really explain."

"Why not?"

"I've been looking for her, but I keep hitting walls. Whatever she is doing, she's hiding really well."

"Great. Look, we have another issue. Unkhabami said—"

"Unkhabami was here?" Marcus' voice shook a little.

"Yeah, a few days ago, why?"

"Nothing, it just never turns out good when she's involved."

"Hmm." Madraeus tried to be non-committal. "She believes that people are going missing."

"Our people or normal people?"

"I don't know. Can you just see what you can find?" Madraeus rubbed his forehead.

"Yeah, I'll add it to my list. Talk to you later."

Madraeus flipped the phone shut and tossed it onto the desk. He let his head fall into his hands.

He was so tired of mysteries and secrets. He was beginning to wonder why he even bothered anymore. Maybe he should just step aside and let the two worlds collide.

He glanced at the clock. It was almost noon. No wonder he was so tired; he hadn't eaten or slept since the day before.

He retrieved a bottle from the kitchen, downed about half of it, and then wandered back into the study.

He stared at the pile of papers on his desk. He didn't want to work. He didn't want to worry about it. Without thinking, he found himself walking toward Whitney's door. He told himself that he was just going to check on her, that's all.

She was sleeping peacefully. She hadn't even moved. In that moment, he knew that he would never sleep unless he held her. But at the same time, if he crawled in next to her, he would never be able to sleep again without her.

All of his past experience had taught him to guard against the future. But as he watched her sleep, he knew there would be no future, and for once, he wanted to seize the day. He wanted to take what he wanted like he used to. At least he would have the memory to keep him warm after she was gone.

With a tired but rebellious sigh, Madraeus kicked off his shoes and crawled in next to Whitney. She was sleeping on her side, so he curled around her, pulling her into the protective curve of his body. He finally felt peaceful enough to sleep.

***

Madraeus woke with a start. For a moment, the unfamiliar surroundings startled him, but then the warm body he was curled around reminded him. Absolute contentment filled him. This is where he wanted to be for the rest of his life. Smiling, he turned on his side, buried his face in her hair, and inhaled deeply.

Unfortunately, the reason he woke intruded again. A phone was ringing in the other room. Reality followed. He didn't want the noise to wake Whitney, so he carefully got up.

It was Whitney's personal phone, not the one he had given her. For a moment, he messed with it, trying to put it on silent mode, but eventually gave up. There was a long list of text messages and missed calls, but he wasn't going to wake her. Pocketing her phone, he padded back to her room. Lightly, he brushed a kiss on her forehead and tucked the blankets back around her, then put on his shoes and left. It was early evening already. He had only slept a few hours, but he felt better than he had in days.

Rami was sitting at Madraeus' desk in the study, sorting through a stack of papers. When he heard Madraeus come in, he smiled.

"Feel better?"

Madraeus grunted. Rami's smile spread into a self-satisfied grin.

"How are preparations coming?" he asked as he poured himself a glass of blood from the bottle sitting next to Rami.

"Good. Slow, but good." Rami's smile faded. "Lady Douglas called. The council is asking for a report on the incident at The Loop. She wants to know why it is on the front page of *The Post*."

"I knew that was coming," Madraeus sighed. He may be the head of the council, but he still had to answer to the rest of the members. If he worked too much on his own, they would start questioning his motives.

"She has faith in you. She just needs reassurance," the giant murmured.

"If only it were that easy." Madraeus shook his head. "Between Justin and Cecelia, it just keeps getting worse, and I keep falling further behind."

"Do not fear, my friend, he will surface again." Rami rested a hand on Madraeus' shoulder. "And we will find Cecelia soon."

"By then, it may be too late."

"Do not be so quick to fix your future in darkness and despair; it may yet turn out all right."

"I don't even dare hope," Madraeus sighed. "Perhaps-" Whitney's phone rang again, cutting him off.

"What is that?" Rami frowned.

Madraeus pulled it out of his pocket and tossed it onto the desk while he took another drink.

"Whitney's personal phone. I couldn't get it to be silent, so I took it with me so it wouldn't wake her."

Rami glanced at the clock. "She is not awake now?"

"Nope." Madraeus grinned. "I found some sleeping pills in her kitchen when I was making her cocoa."

"You drugged her? That is your solution?" Rami raised an accusing eyebrow.

"It was the only way I could think of to make sure she slept and didn't run off again," Madraeus shrugged. "Nothing else has worked. Every time I think she understands that she is in danger, she takes off again. I just want her to be safe."

"I want her to be safe too, my friend, but beware of pushing her away with questionable actions," Rami warned.

# PRINCIPAL'S OFFICE

Whitney woke up groggy and stiff again. Everything ached. She wondered what time it was. The clock said four, but was it morning or night? For the first time in a long time, she had slept without waking up with nightmares.

She stretched and rolled over onto the opposite pillow. Whitney buried her face in its softness. She sighed. It smelled really good. It smelled like... Madraeus?

Instantly, Whitney sat up. She thought back over the events of the last day. She remembered Madraeus putting her to bed. She didn't remember him leaving. She couldn't remember anything.

Scooting across the bed, she grabbed the curtain and pulled it aside. Light flooded in and blinded her. Obviously, it was four in the afternoon.

She should be at work! She pushed the curtain closed again and dashed through the apartment. She rushed to the bathroom and dug through the clothes she had left on the floor. Her cell phones weren't in her pocket.

"Oh crap." In a frenzy, she pulled off her shirt to get dressed and caught the smell of Madraeus' cologne on her shirt. "Oh crap. Crap. Crap!"

Less than an hour later, she cautiously poked her head through the door of Madraeus' study. She hoped that no one would see her. She wanted to gauge Madraeus' mood before she had to talk to him. She jumped when her ring-tone screeched through the silence in the study.

"Damn it." Madraeus slapped a folder onto the phone, hoping to muffle it, but it only started to vibrate across the desk with the folder on top.

"Why do you have my phone?" she blurted, forgetting her desire not to be noticed.

"Ah, Whitney!" Rami grinned.

They were standing on either side of the desk. It was covered in papers and more old books. There were even a few stacked on the floor next to the desk.

"Don't worry, you can have the damned thing back. It won't shut up," Madraeus growled as she stepped forward to pick it up. "I took it so it wouldn't wake you up. It's been going off non-stop."

She stared at him. She had no idea what had happened last night, or if she should mention it. He glared at her, but his expression was shielded.

"Really?" She frowned as she looked at the list of text messages.

"Have a seat." Madraeus gestured to the chairs that surrounded the chess set as he turned back to his work.

"I should really go get something to eat. I just didn't know if I was supposed to be at work." She edged toward the door.

"No. Sit," Madraeus said without looking up from the file he was reading.

"What do you mean, no? What? I can't get something to eat?" Whitney crossed her arms.

Madraeus sighed and let the file drop to the desk. He turned and looked at her.

"I meant no work. Sit, and we will get you something to eat." He looked tired, but there was an ominous edge to his tone.

"Oh," she mumbled and shuffled over to the chairs.

Madraeus pressed the intercom and spoke into it, "Mrs. Myers? She's up and would like breakfast."

"Be right there," Mrs. Myers' voice called over the speaker.

Whitney sank into the cushions of the chair. She felt like she was in the principal's office. She was relatively certain that Madraeus' bad mood had to do with her—it usually did—so she was going to try to be as quiet as possible, and maybe he would forget she was even there.

She watched Rami and Madraeus for a while. They were talking, but it was too quiet for her to hear what they were saying. She hoped it wasn't about her. She gave up trying to eavesdrop and turned her attention to her phone.

She began the painstaking process of reading her texts. There seemed to be a million of them. She didn't know why there were so many. Then she noticed the time stamp; there were some from Saturday and a few from Sunday.

*Sunday? Isn't today Saturday?*

Whitney went back to the main screen to check the date. It was Sunday!

*What happened to Saturday?*

She glanced up at Rami and Madraeus. Had they let her sleep through almost two days? How could she have slept that long? Groaning, she sent out a general reply to everyone. Whitney told everyone that she was alright and had spent the rest of Friday night talking to the police, then gone home to sleep. She hoped that would keep everyone happy for a while.

She then turned to her voicemail. Just as she had started listening to the first message, her phone started to go off. People were texting her back. She cringed as her ring-tone blasted into the quiet study. Slowly, Madraeus turned his attention to her, which was exactly what she was trying to avoid.

"Sorry! Sorry!" She hastened to turn the sound off.

Madraeus frowned and turned back to the desk.

Whitney looked back down at her phone. Everyone had replied that they were relieved that she was okay, but now a new question had come up. Was she going to Lisa's funeral?

*Of course I am.* Whitney glanced at Madraeus. *Maybe.*

She wondered if he would let her go. Sighing, she tried her voicemail again. There was one from Mrs. Myers and one from her grandmother. Both contained the same kind of sentiment.

Whitney sighed again. There was no sense in calling Mrs. Myers. She would see her in a minute, but her grandmother was a different matter. She still didn't know what to say to her. Reluctantly, she called Grammy.

"Hi, Grammy," Whitney said when she answered.

At the sound of her voice, Madraeus and Rami both looked at her. She cringed and slid down in the chair, turning away from them, trying to speak quietly.

"Whitney! Where have you been? Why didn't you answer your phone? Are you alright?" It took several tries, but Whitney finally stopped her.

"Grammy! I'm okay, honestly! I've been sleeping."

"Sleeping? I've been worried sick, and you're sleeping?"

"Sorry, Grammy, I don't know why I slept so long."

"Well, I guess I can forgive you after what happened, and then to have to stay all night with the police."

"How did you know about that?"

"Well, it wasn't from you!" her grandmother snapped. "I had a visit from the police."

"What!" Whitney sat up and glanced at Madraeus. He was glaring at her again. She turned away.

"Yeah, imagine my surprise when the police knocked on my door Saturday morning asking about you and Justin!"

Whitney cringed.

"Not that my own granddaughter could have called me and told me about something so important. Oh no, I get the story from a perfect stranger and then you wait a whole day to call me!"

Guilt flooded Whitney. She had gone from the police straight to bed. *When did I have time?*

"Grammy, I'm sorry, it's just that... things have been complicated." Maybe it was something in Whitney's voice, but her grandmother changed tactics.

"Maybe it's time you came home for a while. You are dealing with a lot, and you need to be somewhere safe."

Whitney squeezed her eyes shut. Her grandmother was more right than she could know. Although Whitney was pretty sure she wouldn't be safe anywhere for a long time.

"Um... I don't know that I can right now."

"What do you mean you don't know if you can? What's stopping you? And don't you dare say work." Her grandmother knew her too well.

Whitney sighed and bit her lip. She glanced at Madraeus and cringed again. He had come around the desk and was watching her with his arms crossed over his chest. He was waiting for her reply. Suddenly, she realized that he had heard the entire conversation.

*Stupid vampire hearing!*

"Ah, Grammy, I gotta go. I'll call you later."

"Whitney Elizabeth Martindale, don't you dare hang up on me!"

"Sorry, Grammy, I'll come see you soon." Whitney snapped the phone shut with a grimace.

Reluctantly, she raised her eyes to Madraeus. His expression was frustratingly unreadable. Fortunately, or unfortunately, Mrs. Myers came in at that moment carrying a tray.

# WOMEN ALWAYS WIN

With an over-bright smile, Myers sat the tray down in Whitney's lap. Whitney looked down at the simple breakfast of toast and oatmeal.

"Sorry, it's not much," she cast an accusing glare at Madraeus, "I'm sure you're extremely hungry after sleeping so long."

"I'm sure that she needed the rest." Madraeus glared back at Mrs. Myers.

"She didn't need that much rest!" Mrs. Myers snapped.

"After the events of the past couple of days, that much rest is exactly what she needed!" Madraeus growled.

Whitney glanced from Mrs. Myers to Madraeus. The looks being passed between them were downright menacing. Something was going on. Whitney glanced at Rami. He was watching them both as if he were watching an overfull balloon just waiting for the explosion. Suddenly, Madraeus and Mrs. Myers noticed her scrutiny.

With a dignified sniff, Mrs. Myers turned her attention to Whitney. "You should eat, dear."

Whitney smiled half-heartedly. Slowly, she picked up a piece of toast and took a bite. She wasn't really hungry anymore. Her stomach was too full of butterflies.

"Now, Whitney, since you are *so well rested*," she flung another glance at Madraeus, "maybe you could tell us about what happened?"

The toast turned to dust in her mouth. With an effort, she swallowed.

"Well, um…" Carefully avoiding Madraeus' eyes, she began to recount her evening out. She stumbled over a couple of spots, choking to a stop when she had to tell them about Lisa's death. Mrs. Myers handed her a tissue, and after a moment, she went on.

She stopped her story at the point where Philtzer had brought her home. Her recollection of what happened after she returned home was a little vague. She remembered fighting with Madraeus, but the rest was a little fuzzy.

She glanced at him. He was still watching her intently. She was desperate to ask him what had happened, why her shirt and pillow had smelled like him, but she just couldn't do it. Whitney looked away and found Mrs. Myers gaping at her.

"What?" Whitney squeaked, afraid that her thoughts were written on her face.

"I… I just can't believe that you fended off a vampire with a trash can." She sounded awed.

Whitney relaxed a little. "It was all I had."

"Why didn't you take someone with you?" Madraeus asked.

"Well…" she had been dreading that question, "I was gonna, but then I would've had to explain them to my friends, and they would have started asking questions that I couldn't answer. It's not like you gave me a script to follow when I have to answer questions. I did take my phone!" she added defensively.

"From now on, you do not leave the building without an escort," Madraeus stated.

"Um… that's not going to work for me," she blurted, then winced when he scowled.

"Oh really?" Madraeus raised an eyebrow.

"I already told you that it would raise questions."

"Then don't go anywhere," Madraeus shrugged.

"I can't do that!" Whitney glanced at Mrs. Myers. "I have to go see my grandmother, and I need to go to Lisa's funeral."

"Out of the question." Madraeus shook his head.

"Not out of the question." Whitney started to stand but remembered the tray and stopped.

"Haven't you learned your lesson?" Madraeus shoved away from the desk. "Every time you leave here something bad happens!"

"My grandmother is getting worried! I haven't seen her in weeks!" Whitney gasped. "She is gonna come looking for me if I don't go see her. Then what?"

"Let her."

"Ray," Rami rumbled a warning.

"If you go see her, what will you say?" Madraeus challenged. "What will you tell her?"

"I…" Whitney had no idea. She glanced between Rami and Mrs. Myers. "I don't know, something."

"Well, you had better be more prepared than that."

"Can I tell her the truth?" Whitney asked.

"No." Madraeus crossed his arms.

"Well, why don't you tell me what to say? What do you usually tell people? Normal people?"

Madraeus snorted.

Mrs. Myers laid a hand on Whitney's arm, "We don't tell them anything, dear; this situation doesn't normally come up. If you remember how much trouble you had believing me, you will understand."

"Well, I'll think of something," Whitney said stubbornly.

"It doesn't matter. You are not going." Madraeus turned and walked around his desk to sit down.

"You can't keep me here," she muttered.

"Watch me," Madraeus growled quietly.

"I'm not your prisoner."

"You could be."

Whitney glared at him.

"Ray, enough!" Rami sighed. "It is like watching toddlers."

"You are not going to the funeral either," he added, ignoring Rami.

"Yes, I am," Whitney countered.

"No, you are not," Madraeus said slowly, trying to keep a rein on his anger.

"Yes, I am." She mimicked his slow enunciation.

"No, you are—" Madraeus started again but was interrupted by Mrs. Myers.

"Ray, I must agree with Whitney. She will go to the funeral."

With just a blink, he turned his icy stare on Mrs. Myers. "And why is that?"

"She will go because it was her friend," Mrs. Myers said without inflection, but Whitney felt like she had been punched in the stomach, "and because the police will be there watching. If she doesn't show up at her friend's funeral, they will wonder why."

Every time Mrs. Myers said 'friend' a new wave of guilt hit Whitney.

Madraeus sat a moment, glaring at the two of them.

"Very well," Madraeus sighed. "She will attend the funeral."

Whitney started at his sudden acquiescence.

"Mrs. Myers, you will be there." He looked to her for confirmation.

"Yes," she nodded.

"Good, you will stay with Whitney at all times. I don't care if it is only to the bathroom; you do not leave her alone. Philtzer will be there as will Thomas and a few others."

Whitney snorted, "It's going to be daylight, I doubt Justin will show."

"Then you will be able to come home without incident for once," he said smoothly, gaining him another of her juvenile facial expressions. "Until then, you will stay here," he continued, ignoring her childish display.

"Uh, no, I'm going to see my grandmother."

"Whitney—"

"No, before you start throwing commands around, listen. It is still light out, so I'm safe. I'll even take someone with me. Mrs. Myers?" She looked to the older lady for a volunteer.

"Of course, I'll come," she agreed and then looked at Madraeus, daring him to disagree.

He looked at Mrs. Myers and then at Rami. He turned his gaze to Whitney. Whitney was determined to go whether he agreed or not. There was no way he was going to win this one.

"Fine," he sighed, "but you will take Philtzer or Thomas with you also. You best get going before the sun goes down," Madraeus said before turning back to the pile of papers on his desk.

# WHAT CAN I SAY?

"Do you have any ideas about what I should say?" Whitney asked Mrs. Myers on the way to her grandmother's house. She had already discarded as many ideas as she had come up with about what to tell her.

"It just depends on the situation."

"Great, thanks for the help!"

"I'm sure we'll think of something." Mrs. Myers squeezed Whitney's hand as they walked up the path.

Despite her reassurances to Madraeus, Whitney didn't feel safe. She kept glancing around, wondering if Justin was hiding behind a tree or in some doorway. She jumped at every sound and flinched every time she caught movement out of the corner of her eye.

When her grandmother enveloped her in a huge hug as soon as she walked through the door, it almost reduced her to tears.

"Elizabeth Martindale, meet Mrs. Myers from Orchard Employment. Mrs. Myers, this is my Grammy." Whitney pulled the older lady forward in an effort to avoid breaking down.

"Ah, Mrs. Myers, I've heard a lot about you."

"Nice to meet you." Mrs. Myers smiled broadly and shook Elizabeth Martindale's hand.

They hadn't even sat down before her grandmother started in on the interrogation.

"Tell me about that rat, Justin. Why did he attack you? I always knew he was no good. Do the police have any news?"

"Grammy, please." Whitney couldn't get a word in. "I'll tell you the whole thing."

Whitney told her grandmother everything that she could. But she could tell that her grandmother knew she had left bits out of her story. That disappointed look she always gave Whitney when she knew that she was lying was hard to miss. She felt awful about it, but there was no choice. She had been warned that the truth was out of the question.

"Why don't you just come back home, Whitney? Is that job so special? You can find another one."

"Mr. Ravilla is a very good employer, Mrs. Martindale. He is in the middle of a delicate business deal that Whitney was instrumental in bringing about. The business couldn't go on without her at the moment."

*Way to spin it, Mrs. M!* Whitney thought as she stared at her boss.

"Hmm." Elizabeth Martindale eyed Mrs. Myers.

Whitney knew that her grandmother had not believed a word of it, but her good manners wouldn't let her argue with company.

"It's not the job, Grammy, it's Justin."

"Exactly, I don't like you being out there by yourself. Are you sure you're safe from Justin living alone in the middle of the city?"

"Yes, Grammy, with all the building security, it is very safe." At least she got to answer that one honestly.

"I'm not convinced. I would prefer it if you came home." Elizabeth pursed her lips and rapped her cane against the floor.

"Grammy, I'm safer there than here. What if Justin showed up here? I don't want you to get hurt. At least in town, I'm surrounded by security and even some bodyguards."

"Bodyguards!"

*Oops, wrong thing to say!* Whitney thought.

"Is your job that dangerous?"

"Mr. Ravilla has engaged extra help during this crisis. He wants to keep everyone safe, as well." Mrs. Myers jumped in. "Speaking of which, I see the sun is starting to leave us behind. I need to get home before dark," Mrs. Myers smiled sheepishly. "These old eyes don't drive too well at night anymore."

"Hmm." Grammy looked Mrs. Myers up and down.

"I'll call you soon, Grammy, love you!" Whitney hugged her tight before they left.

"Be careful, baby girl!" her grandmother whispered as she let go.

On the way back to the office, Whitney watched the sun sinking. It felt like a prison door shutting. When they got back, she was ushered into her apartment by Mrs. Myers and Thomas. He took up guarding her door, and Mrs. Myers left with a promise to see her tomorrow before the funeral.

Whitney felt restless. She didn't want to be home alone, but she wasn't willing to brave Thomas to go anywhere else. TV couldn't keep her interest. After channel surfing, she realized that all those made-up shows that were supposed to pump you up with the action just didn't cut it after you had lived it.

It was depressing.

She tackled the Dreaded Filing Project. She was only partially through sorting and still had the labeling and cross-referencing to go, but at least it occupied her brain so she wouldn't think too much.

A little while later, Whitney sat on the floor in the middle of a million piles of papers spread out around her. She sighed and looked around miserably. Today was not really topping her list of good days.

There was a knock on her kitchen door. Whitney froze and then mentally smacked herself. It was highly unlikely that Justin would knock at the kitchen door, she was just being paranoid.

"Whitney?" Rami rumbled from the other side of the kitchen door.

She hurried to the kitchen and opened the door.

"I thought I would visit the prisoner." He bowed slightly and grinned.

She smiled back and motioned him in. Rami preceded her into the living room and whistled.

"What happened in here?" he asked, surveying the piles of papers.

"This," she spread her arms out, "is the Dreaded Filing Project."

Rami chuckled. "I thought I kept reasonably good files."

"Well, maybe you do, but this is a mess. I think that my predecessors were filing-cabinet challenged," Whitney snorted.

"Apparently." Rami glanced around, "Are these the files from the cabinets in your office?"

"Yep," Whitney sighed as she sat down in the middle of her paper fort. "What I want to know is why you people don't use the computer. This would be so much more efficient if you had it all logged where a search engine could get at it."

"It would indeed," Rami nodded.

"So why not get it all digitized?"

"Whitney, my dear, the computer system is a wondrous thing. All of InfiniCorp's investment business is on the computer, but what you are filing is not public business," Rami explained.

"Not public?" Whitney frowned. "You mean that all these files are from the Races?"

Rami nodded.

"But there are invoices here from a dozen different divisions, travel, shipping, real estate, even butcher shops!"

Whitney looked around her again. She suddenly felt very naïve.

"You are telling me that all these businesses are run by the Races through InfiniCorp?"

"I told you we take care of our own," Rami smiled.

"I thought you meant watching each other's backs. This is like the supernatural mob running fronts for all its shady deals," she protested.

"Shady? We are not doing anything shady." Rami grinned. "All of these businesses are legitimate."

"Then why is it all on paper and not in the computer with the rest of InfiniCorp's dealings?"

"Paper invoices," Rami was suddenly serious, "cannot be traced by outside sources. They can only be accessed by those who know of their existence. If all of the information contained in those files were entered into a computer, then all of our movements could be traced and tracked. It is for our safety that we stay out of the cyber-world and its search engines and hackers."

Whitney searched his face for a moment, then looked around at the piles. What he said made sense. Even a normal person's name goes through a ton of computers each day. This way was much harder to track.

"But someone could still track you down if they got a hold of the paper copies."

"Yes, but they would have to know about them and then get past our security to get them." Rami grinned like he knew something that she didn't.

"What happens if someone who knows about the files tells someone they shouldn't, and then someone comes after them?"

"We have precautions set in place to prevent anything from happening."

"Precautions?" She raised her eyebrows. "That sounds kinda scary."

Rami gave her one of his knowing grins.

"I hate when you do that," she frowned.

Rami laughed out loud. "I get that a lot. Now, let me see if I can help you sort out this mess."

"K, here." She handed him a pile of papers then grabbed a new stack.

# AWKWARD

After a few minutes of silent sorting, Whitney looked up. "So... Rami?"

"Yes?" Rami kept sorting papers.

"If you don't mind me asking, who are you?" She shrugged. "I mean, where are you from?"

Rami grinned, "I do not mind, little Whitney. My name is Rashid ibn Ahmed al-Rahim al-Makhrami."

"Wow," she smiled, "good thing you shortened it."

"Yes." Rami returned her smile. "I was an apprentice baker in the city of Antioch."

"You were a baker?" Whitney gaped.

"Why is that so hard to believe?" he challenged but only received a shrug from her.

"So how did you become a vampire?" It was getting easier to use the word vampire now.

"The city was under siege, and we were low on food. Some of us volunteered to help smuggle food into the city through a hidden way not yet blocked by the Crusaders." He continued to sort papers while he spoke.

"We had been out of the city several times, but one night we were caught. Soldiers came out of the night and slaughtered men and animals alike. I had fallen under a packhorse that had been cut down. They must have thought me dead and left, but a shadow came out of the dark." He paused and shuffled the papers in his hands.

Whitney stared up at him in awe. She had assumed he had been a soldier like Madraeus, but he was just an ordinary man.

"After that, I was not really alive, nor was I dead. I did not know what had happened or what to believe. I quickly learned to stay in during the daylight hours. For days, I hid in caves near the city. Finally, I managed to return to my family inside the city. The hunger that plagued me was not unlike my fellow starving citizens, so I tried to ignore it as they did, but I soon had to... accommodate my needs." He shrugged. "Nearly eight months later, treachery breached the city walls and that led to massacre. It was anarchy. Soldiers, citizens, Christians, Muslims. It did not matter; they were all trying to kill one another. The city was flooded with mayhem and death. My family tried to hide some of the children in our bakery. I stood at the door and learned what I was capable of." His voice rumbled to a stop.

Whitney felt tears stinging her eyes.

Rami looked up at her and smiled, "That is when I met my friend, Madraeus. He burst into the bakery near dawn. He was running from the sun. It was a tense moment. He nearly killed me, but once he saw what I was protecting, he joined me at the door. Together, we kept out the mob."

He fell silent and then looked pensive.

"I believe that, in that act, he found the first chance for the redemption he sought when he joined the crusades," Rami said.

"What do you mean?"

"Like many of the Christian knights, he joined the crusades because the Church promised absolution from all sins if they took the Holy Land. He hoped to rid himself of his curse by finding absolution from God," Rami explained, then shook his head. "Unfortunately, the crusades were not a Holy cause. It only increased his guilt."

"That's so sad!"

"Yes, but we have made our own way since then." Rami tapped her on the end of the nose. "We traveled the world and learned many things."

Whitney bit her lip and stared at the pile of paper in her hands. These men were extraordinary. She felt like such a wimp compared to them. She resolved to be stronger. She would work harder and make a difference like they had.

"Now, let us forget sad things and work on boring things." Rami bopped her on the head with the stack of papers in his hand and grinned.

***

Hours later, piles of paper covered most of the floor. Several glasses and cups, along with a half-eaten bowl of popcorn, were sitting in the middle of the coffee table.

"Seriously? You want meat-flavored ice cream?" Whitney gagged.

"Absolutely! Meat-flavored anything is good!" Philtzer replied.

They were sitting on the floor in front of the couch.

"I'm a confirmed carnivore, baby, and I say all food should taste like meat, even popcorn. Dude, they even have meat-flavored water and mints now!"

"Ugh!" she groaned and threw the handful of popcorn she was going to eat back into the bowl. "Now I've lost my appetite."

As she sat back, she caught sight of Madraeus standing in the kitchen watching them and stopped.

"Ah, hi?" She gestured at the paper mess. "Come to join the fun?"

"Yes, Ray, come join us!" Rami chuckled. "Come enjoy some mindless filing!"

"Thank you, but no." He shook his head.

"Oh, come on, ya big chicken," Philtzer taunted as he shoved himself up onto the couch.

"Philtzer, what are you doing here?"

"Got drafted," Philtzer shrugged.

"Drafted?" Madraeus glanced at the papers littering the floor.

"I called him. I think there may be a clue to Cecelia's movements in Whitney's Dreaded Filing Project."

"Really?" Madraeus shot a look of warning at Rami as if he didn't want her to know their secrets.

"Yep. Regular shipments that end suddenly or massive shipments out of the blue," she answered smugly.

"Interesting."

"Wanna help now?" Philtzer almost sounded like he was begging.

"Actually, I came to check," Madraeus glanced at Whitney, "that you were going to get some sleep before the funeral in the morning."

"Oh, I should, I guess," Whitney said, glancing around for the clock. "It is getting late."

"That's our cue, Rami." Philtzer grinned, hopping off the couch as if he couldn't wait to get away from the filing.

"Thank you for an interesting evening and all the work you have done," Rami rumbled before following Philtzer out, leaving Whitney and Madraeus alone.

For a moment, an awkward silence stretched, then Madraeus gestured to the papers as he stepped closer. "Seems you may have solved our mystery."

"I'm trying." Whitney shrugged as she picked up the bowl of popcorn and gathered the empty glasses. "We kinda got side-tracked when Philtzer showed up."

"He doesn't like filing." Madraeus smiled as she walked past him into the kitchen.

"Neither do I." Whitney set the glasses in the sink.

Silence stretched between them again.

"Well, I will go and let you get to sleep."

He made it almost to the kitchen door when she stopped him. "Madraeus?"

"Yes?" He turned back warily.

"I just wanted to say," she slowly stepped closer to him, "thank you for letting me see Grammy. It didn't really go like I wanted, but," she gestured helplessly, "I really did need to see her."

He nodded, but said nothing, all the while only staring at her.

"About last night?" She took another step closer.

"Philtzer warned me to leave you alone. I should have listened."

"I'm sorry I freaked out."

He slowly raised his hand, then hesitated. After a moment, he reached out and gently cupped the side of her face. His thumb brushed against her soft cheek.

"I just want you safe," he whispered fiercely.

She stared at him, thrilled and terrified by the protective pos-session in his tone.

He let his fingers slide down the side of her neck. He felt the marks left by Justin's teeth. He lifted her hair out of the way and brushed his fingers across the marks. He ran his fingers lightly along the tiny scars, making her shiver. Her heart started racing, but she didn't move.

"I should go," he breathed and fled the room. "Goodnight, Whitney."

"But..." Whitney started, but he was already gone.

Complicated, Mrs. Myers had called him, but that didn't even begin to describe Madraeus. She let out a little whimper and then slowly walked to her bedroom. Sleep seemed like a dream, and all she ever had anymore was nightmares.

# WHAT A LOVELY FUNERAL

Whitney stood quietly beside Mrs. Myers. She barely listened to the preacher as he said a final blessing at the grave site. This was all such a mess. Her friends were all here, sniffling and crying, their red, puffy eyes hidden behind sunglasses. Whitney also had her sunglasses on, but they hid dry eyes.

Her friends were shaken and grief-stricken that one of their own could be taken so violently. Whitney watched them as they wrapped their arms around one another, trying to give comfort. It seemed so fake. Most of them had never really liked Lisa. They had included Lisa with their group out of convenience. It was Whitney who had tried to involve her. It was Whitney who had spent the most time talking to her, who knew the most about her, but she wasn't the one crying.

If she hadn't been so shocked and ashamed at her own thoughts, she would have laughed at them. Maybe she just dealt with grief in a different way, but she just couldn't bring herself to cry. She knew she should be crying. She had been the cause of Lisa's death, and yet, she stood here dry-eyed.

She glanced at Mrs. Myers. The lady could have been a statue, not a muscle moved to show any emotion. Whitney knew that Mrs. Myers had been fond of Lisa. She wasn't crying either.

Perhaps death was so commonplace to the Races that one more human passing had no effect. Whitney hoped she wasn't becoming immune to violence and death. She didn't want to be unemotional. She glanced at Mrs. Myers again.

*Would any of them cry if it were me?* That thought almost made her cry.

She turned her attention back to the preacher. He was dry-eyed too, but he had an excuse, he didn't know Lisa personally. Funerals and death probably didn't affect him anymore either. She didn't know if that would suck or be a blessing.

Then it was over, and everyone was drifting away toward their cars. Whitney watched her friends walk away together. She didn't even want to see them. She didn't want to speak to them and have to explain what had happened. She just wanted to go home, but she couldn't go there either.

Tears started to well up in her eyes when she realized that Justin had succeeded. She was just dying slower than expected, a little piece at a time. All the lies were ripping a gulf between her and her grandmother and poisoning her friendships. It was just a matter of time before she was going to be cut off from everything. Maybe that was what he wanted. If she was cut off from everyone, then he would be her only option.

*I'll never turn to him*, she thought fiercely. *This is his fault, and he needs to be stopped.*

She reached up to wipe the tears from her cheeks and realized that Mrs. Myers was still standing with her. Whitney gave her a token smile, and together they walked toward her car. Whitney glanced around. Everyone else was starting to drive away. They would all be going to Lisa's parents' house for the reception. She didn't want to go, but she had to face everyone sometime.

There were only a couple of cars left. One belonged to Mrs. Myers, and the other one, Philtzer and Thomas had come in. The third car was parked down the lane a little. It was a lot like Rami's car: black with heavily tinted windows. She wondered if it was Rami or if it was someone else who needed the extra protection from the sun.

A chill went up her spine.

Whitney stared for a moment, trying to see who was driving, but she couldn't tell; it was too far away.

When she failed to get in the car, Mrs. Myers poked her head back out.

"Something wrong, dear?"

"Yeah," Whitney said. "You recognize that car?"

Mrs. Myers followed her gaze.

"No." Mrs. Myers shook her head.

"Me neither," she frowned. "Can you tell Philtzer?"

"Yes." Mrs. Myers disappeared back into the car. Whitney was going to stay and keep an eye on the car, but a movement at the corner of her eye made her curse.

"Mrs. Myers! Tell Philtzer to hold on!"

"Why? What's wrong?" Mrs. Myers' head appeared again.

"Detective Sanders is standing over there by that tree."

Sanders inclined his head, acknowledging that she had seen him. Whitney slid into the car.

"If Philtzer goes to check out the car I was staring at, Sanders will know something's up." She glanced over her shoulder out the back window. The detective was still watching.

"Just tell Philtzer to follow them, not us."

"Ray won't like that," Mrs. Myers warned.

Whitney rolled her eyes. "He isn't here. If that is Justin, and we don't do something, he will be just as mad."

An angry Madraeus was something that she was getting used to. She didn't want to let this chance slip away.

Whitney watched out the back window as they drove away. She was right, Detective Sanders was already suspicious. He hadn't moved, but his attention was on the remaining cars. He started to write something in a notebook. She listened as Mrs. Myers spoke to Philtzer.

"Whitney thinks it might be Justin."

"Here, let me talk to him." She rudely grabbed the phone from Mrs. Myers.

"Dude, Detective Sanders is watching you guys. He knows I saw him, and he saw me looking at the other car. I think he is suspicious. You might want to leave before he decides to come looking."

"Right. I see him. We'll follow you and see if your mystery car follows," Philtzer said.

Whitney flopped back down in her seat as they turned a corner. She couldn't see the cars or Detective Sanders anymore. She handed Mrs. Myers her phone back.

"Sorry, I grabbed it. I was kinda in a hurry."

"That's alright, dear," Mrs. Myers smiled. "You seem to be taking to this life like a duck to water."

"Yeah," Whitney snorted, "too bad it's Duck Season."

"Indeed."

They rode in silence to Lisa's family home. It was just a normal house on a normal little street. It was a lot like her grandmother's house. Whitney shivered at the thought.

Cars lined the streets in every direction. She followed Mrs. Myers up the steps. She felt like she was going to her own execution.

The house was filled with people. Some she knew, others she had never seen before. Mrs. Myers moved off to speak to one of her clients, the man Lisa had been working for, leaving Whitney alone.

Whitney drifted through the crowd, listening to bits of conversation as she passed. They were all speaking about Lisa's murder. Everyone was looking for the latest news, any bit of information they could find. They all wanted to know why a friend had turned on her, and how could someone she knew and liked turn out to be so violent.

The more Whitney heard, the more she wanted to leave. She looked around for Mrs. Myers. She wondered if maybe she should just go wait in the car. She turned back toward the door and walked right into Kaylee.

"Whitney! How are you? I'm glad you came. What happened with the police? Have they found Justin? How did you get away from him?"

Whitney glanced around. Kaylee's questions were getting the attention of the people around them. Suddenly, she was being bombarded with questions from everyone standing within earshot.

"Were you there?"

"What happened?"

"Did he try to attack you too?"

"What are the police doing?"

"Why haven't they arrested him yet?"

Questions were coming so fast. As soon as she opened her mouth to answer, another was thrown at her. Whitney felt like she was drowning. Then she heard it, a damning sentence that hushed everyone abruptly.

"The guy who attacked Lisa was Whitney's ex-boyfriend," Kaylee blurted.

Whitney winced.

After a moment, a whole new set of questions came at her. This time, however, they were not curious. They were angry. They started to grab her arms.

"Were you fighting?"

"Did you make him angry enough that he killed Lisa?"

"Did Lisa just get in the way, or did you use her to get away?"

"Why were you dating a psycho?"

"Why did he kill Lisa and not you?"

Whitney flinched. Every statement was a knife stabbing her conscience.

"Look, I'm sorry—" she started, only to be pulled away by someone else, "Please. I don't know why—" She frantically looked for Mrs. Myers.

Someone slapped her cheek.

Whitney stared in shock at the small lady standing in front of her. It was Lisa's mother.

"How dare you!" she hissed. "How dare you come to my home after what you've done!" She stepped toward Whitney, making her back up across the room. "You and your boyfriend problems have murdered my little girl!" she spat. "Get out of my home!" She pushed Whitney toward the door.

"I'm sorry!" Whitney protested. "Lisa was my friend!"

"Get out!" the woman shrieked. "Get out!"

Whitney flinched and, without another word, turned and ran out the door.

# WHAT A BIG WOLF YOU HAVE!

Sᴎᴇ ᴅɪᴅɴ'ᴛ sᴛᴏᴘ ᴡʜᴇɴ she reached the sidewalk. She just kept running. Tears poured down her cheeks. She ran and ran, down one block, and then another, and another.

She stumbled to a stop and fell to her knees. She couldn't breathe. She gagged and vomited. Shaking, she dragged herself up and stumbled into an alley. Out of sight, she slid down the wall beside a dumpster. She hugged her knees to her chest.

The scene at the house replayed itself in her mind. They were right, it was her fault. Her boyfriend problems had killed Lisa.

*How many more people would get hurt or die because of me?*

Whitney jumped at the sound of her phone ringing. She dug it out of her pocket and looked at the number. She didn't recognize it, but she answered it anyway. "Hello?"

"I was wondering how far you were gonna run."

"Justin?" Whitney shoved herself up off the ground.

"That must have been some party," he laughed.

"Where are you?" Whitney looked around. She couldn't see anyone. She walked to the end of the alley and scanned the street. Across from her was the black car from the cemetery. Whitney shivered.

"Close enough to see you shaking." He laughed again. "Really, Whit, do I scare you that much?"

"Can't you leave me alone?" She tried hard to keep her voice steady.

"Oh, come on, and miss all the fun?"

"Dammit, Justin! You're killing people!"

"So?"

"You have to stop this!"

"You're right. Tell you what. No one else has to die, just walk across the street and get in the car."

Whitney's heart banged against her ribs. Terror gripped her legs.

"Come on, Whitney, I'll stop if you just come with me."

"Will you?" she managed to ask.

"Whitney!" he snapped impatiently. "Walk across the street! Get in the car!"

Ravilla's Leash rang in her pocket.

It was like being doused with cold water.

It was suddenly clear. Justin was a vampire. It was the middle of the afternoon.

He was demanding that she come to his car like a sacrifice, and she had almost fallen for it! All she had to do was answer her other phone and help would come. She reached for her phone and flipped it open.

"Don't answer that!" Justin growled.

"Whitney, where the hell are you?" Philtzer demanded.

"Don't tell him, Whitney! You're going to lose the chance to protect your grandmother."

She hesitated.

"Walk across the street and get in the car."

"Whitney!" Philtzer tried again.

She didn't know what to do. She couldn't give in to Justin, but she needed to keep him here until Philtzer arrived; but if she told Philtzer where she was, Justin would leave or worse.

"Whit, we are driving up 10th. If you can hear me, just wait, we're coming!"

Whitney glanced down the street to the corner, and with relief, she saw that she was indeed on 10th. All she had to do was wait.

"Whitney, if you don't come with me now, you'll regret it," he warned.

Suddenly, she was tired of his threats.

"No, Justin, you'll regret it. I know you can't come out in the sun," Whitney taunted.

She jumped when the front door popped open, and a rough-looking guy stepped out. The man paused, waiting for a passing car to go by.

"You aren't the only one with werewolf friends," Justin purred.

"Crap!" Whitney turned and sprinted back up the street the way she had come. She hoped that traffic would delay him and give her a head start.

*This is what I get for being a smart ass*, she thought.

Whitney ran as fast as she could. Her legs protested. They weren't used to this much exercise in such a short amount of time.

"Philtzer! Drive faster!" she puffed into the phone. "He's got a wolf!"

Whitney glanced back to see where her pursuer was. Terror gripped her anew when she realized that he was gaining ground on all fours. He had changed into wolf form in order to catch up.

*No fair! This can't be happening! Philtzer must be on the wrong street! I'm going to die!*

She urged her aching legs to go faster. She could hear the wolf growling behind her. He was closer.

Philtzer's car came into view. Relief almost made her stumble. Whitney dodged to her right between two parked cars into the street. She kept running and waved her arms.

They screeched to a halt. Both doors flew open. Philtzer and Thomas launched themselves toward Whitney. She shot past them and slammed into the side of the car. Her momentum had been too great to stop gracefully. She spun around, crouching against the side of the car.

Justin's wolf had leaped on top of the parked car that she had dodged past. He stood growling and watching them.

Her two saviors took up fighting stances in front of her, facing the wolf.

Whitney stared wide-eyed at their backs. Both men were shimmering slightly. Whitney remembered Philtzer shimmering like that just before he changed into wolf form. They were getting ready to change. Whitney glanced around. Several people on the sidewalks had stopped to watch their little drama. Philtzer's car was blocking the street and starting to cause a small traffic jam.

"No! No! No!" Whitney puffed. They couldn't have a more public scene if they tried. Madraeus would kill her.

"Philtzer! The crowd!" Whitney hissed.

Her warning must have been heard by Justin's wolf too because his head shot up. He seemed to be staring at something behind Whitney. Then just as quickly, he was gone, loping down the street. Whitney crumpled to the pavement in relief.

Philtzer and Thomas turned toward her.

"Get in!" Thomas growled.

Quickly, Philtzer grabbed Whitney and pushed her into the backseat just before Thomas sped away.

Whitney put her head on her knees. Now that it was over, and her adrenaline wasn't pumping, she felt sick.

"It's alright," Philtzer rubbed her back. "You're safe. We gotcha."

Whitney couldn't even raise her head. She knew that he was wrong. She was nowhere near safe.

Sooner than Whitney would have liked, the car pulled into the parking garage below InfiniCorp's offices. As soon as the car stopped, it was surrounded. Whitney was once again escorted to the elevator, corralled by a wall of muscle. She felt like a stray sheep being brought home by a pack of herd dogs.

She almost giggled at the thought, considering most of the men were wolves. In the elevator, Whitney glanced at Philtzer. He was watching the floor numbers change as they ascended.

"Are you mad at me?" she whispered.

Philtzer looked at her in surprise. "Me? Why would I be mad?"

Whitney rolled her eyes. "Come on, I got in trouble again and almost forced you to expose yourselves."

"I don't mind exposing myself," he grinned, eliciting a collective chuckle from the other men.

"I'm serious. You aren't mad?"

"Babe! We live for this stuff!" Philtzer exclaimed.

Whitney eyed him disbelievingly.

"Listen, we love the thrill of the hunt. And the prospect of a fight with that mangy mutt? Bring it on, sister!" Philtzer punched Thomas in the arm. "Am I right?"

"Yeah," Thomas grinned. The others murmured agreement.

"Look, Whitney, I'm not saying you weren't stupid to run off like that."

"Thanks." Whitney rolled her eyes.

"But us wolves and even the vamps deal with this kinda thing a lot. We're predators. We hunt and we protect our territory." He shrugged. "It's the law of the jungle, man."

Whitney looked around. Hamilton, Thomas, and Cody were all nodding.

"I'm still sorry though,' she said quietly as the doors opened.

"Don't worry about us, worry about yourself!" He grinned as he pushed her forward. "You have to go tell the boss."

# THAT DIDN'T TAKE LONG

WHITNEY TRIED TO PUT on the brakes, but Philtzer propelled her forward anyway. She managed to stop completely by bracing her hands on the door frame to the study. She couldn't make herself go any further. Philtzer grabbed her shoulders and steered her into the room.

"Come on, he won't bite," he chuckled.

Madraeus was standing behind his desk with both hands braced on it. His fierce expression made Philtzer stop.

"Then again, maybe he will," he muttered under his breath. Whitney immediately started to backpedal.

"Oh no you don't. Sit!" Madraeus snapped, indicating the chair with a quick nod.

Whitney stopped, then bit by bit, came forward. Slowly, she sat down in the chair in front of his desk. It was the same chair that she had interviewed in. She felt no less nervous now.

"Four hours. That's it." Madraeus stared down at her. "You've only been gone four hours. And yet you managed to find trouble. What is it with you?" He threw up his hands. "Do you put up a sign or something?" he shouted. "Do you call them up before you leave so they can come find you easier?"

"No!" Whitney gaped. "How dare you? This is not my fault!"

"Isn't it?" he challenged.

"No! I'm not doing all this on purpose!" She jumped out of her chair. "I never asked to be dragged into all this craziness! Yes, I may have been stupid enough to go to that nightclub and stupid enough to run away today, but I don't plan it out first!" She slammed her fists onto the desk. "How was I supposed to know he'd have a werewolf? I thought daylight would be safe!"

"I didn't!" Madraeus growled.

"Oh yeah, you're so smart!" Whitney tilted her head back and forth with each word.

"Well, if you had done as I asked and stayed here, you wouldn't have gotten into trouble to start with!"

"Yes, I would have!" Whitney protested. "Just a different kind."

"What are you talking about?" Madraeus growled.

"That detective was at the funeral just like we said he would be."

Madraeus stared at her for a moment. Philtzer saw his chance and stepped up.

"She's right, Boss. He was there and he was real interested in watching Whitney. He followed us to the reception too."

"What?" Whitney turned to Philtzer. She had been so wrapped up in her own anguish she hadn't noticed the detective.

"Oh yeah, he showed up right after we did. Did a double take on our car too," Philtzer nodded.

"Do you think he followed us?" Whitney asked Philtzer.

"Hard to say," he shrugged. "We got there, then he got there and went in. You shot out of there, and we took off after you."

Whitney's heart started to pound. She wondered if he might have followed her again and seen the confrontation with the wolf.

"You better sit down and tell me everything," Madraeus sighed.

Whitney could barely sit still as Philtzer recounted the events at the funeral and afterward. Mrs. Myers had joined them not long after Philtzer had started talking. Madraeus listened patiently to Philtzer's report.

He then asked Mrs. Myers' view of the events. Whitney jumped up and started pacing. She was completely mortified as Mrs. Myers retold Whitney's interrogation by Lisa's family and the resultant expulsion from the house at the hands of Lisa's mother. She started to chew on the nail of her index finger.

Glancing at Madraeus, she found him watching her as Mrs. Myers spoke.

"Did the detective follow Whitney?" he asked.

Whitney looked at Mrs. Myers, waiting for her answer.

"I'm not sure." Mrs. Myers hesitated. "As soon as Philtzer left, I went to my car so we could look for Whitney."

Whitney cringed, feeling guilty for causing so much trouble for everyone.

Madraeus looked at her again. He met her unhappy gaze and motioned her forward.

"Tell me what happened after you left the house," he prompted.

"I took off down the street." She shrugged. "I didn't have a plan; I just wanted to get away. When I stopped running, my phone rang. It was Justin. He said if I came over and got in his car, then no one else had to die. I almost went. Then Philtzer called, and I remembered that vampires couldn't come out in the sunlight. I would've blindly walked right into his trap." Whitney gave a short laugh.

"I knew all I had to do was wait for Philtzer, but he threatened Grammy, and I kinda spouted off that I knew he couldn't get out of the car." Whitney couldn't look at Madraeus.

"That's when the wolf got out and chased me. I saw these guys," she gestured at Philtzer, "and dove for their car. I warned Philtzer not to change 'cause a bunch of people were watching. The wolf took off, and so did we." She finished with a rush, then looked up at him.

Madraeus sat staring at her for a couple of minutes. Uncomfortable, she shifted behind Mrs. Myer's chair. She couldn't tell what he was thinking, and it was unnerving.

He looked at Philtzer, "Did you know the wolf?"

"Nope." Philtzer shook his head.

Madraeus took a deep breath and let it out slowly.

"I think—" he started but was interrupted by the intercom buzzing.

"Mr. Ravilla?" Rami was manning the front office while Whitney was at the funeral. His use of 'Mr. Ravilla' meant there was a mortal in the office.

"Yes?"

"There is a Detective Sanders here to see Ms. Martindale."

Whitney's eyes widened. "What's he want?" she whispered.

"Alright, she will be right out," he answered without taking his eyes from Whitney.

"I don't want to go out there!" she squeaked.

"Tough, you have no choice." Madraeus came around the desk and took her by the arm and propelled her to the door. "Don't worry, I'll be there too."

"Oh thanks! That makes me feel all better." Whitney rolled her eyes. "What am I supposed to say?"

"As little as possible," he offered before opening the door.

# MORE QUESTIONS

Detective Sanders was sitting in one of the wooden chairs in the front office. He stood when Whitney and Madraeus walked in.

"Ms. Martindale?"

"Detective Sanders, may I introduce you to my employer, Mr. Ravilla?" Whitney pulled out the professional armor.

"Mr. Ravilla." Sanders extended a hand.

Madraeus shook it. "Detective, how can we help you today?"

"Well, I came to speak to Ms. Martindale for a moment, if you don't mind."

"Of course." But when he didn't leave, the detective eyed Madraeus curiously.

Whitney noticed the way that Detective Sanders' gaze was switching back and forth between her and Madraeus. She glanced at her boss. He was staring down the detective with one of his menacing looks. Whitney stifled the urge to elbow him and stepped forward.

"We can talk in the lobby if you like," she offered, guiding him back out the door.

"Alright," he agreed. Once they were near the elevator, he turned to her and took a notebook out of his pocket. "How are you doing, Ms. Martindale?"

"Okay, I guess." Whitney shrugged. She wasn't sure what he was up to.

"That's good, I was wondering because you must have been pretty frightened earlier."

"Earlier?" Whitney shook her head. It wasn't hard to play dumb; she had no idea what he was talking about.

"Yes, when you were chased by that dog," Detective Sanders offered.

"Oh yeah, that was a really big dog!" She quickly agreed now that she had caught on.

"Where did that thing come from, huh? Not often you see an animal that big running loose," he said absently as he thumbed through his little notebook.

"Yeah. I don't know. That was kinda freaky."

"Speaking of freaky, do you know anything about another attack that happened last night?" he asked, looking up suddenly.

"Last night?"

"Yeah, couple of guys got their throats ripped out," he shrugged.

"Oh!" Whitney covered her mouth. "That's horrible!"

"I only ask because it reminded me of the wound that your friend Lisa died from."

Whitney blinked a couple of times then stuttered, "You... you don't think that Justin attacked those guys, do you?"

"I was hoping you would tell me." He planted his feet and crossed his arms.

"I honestly have no idea." Whitney shook her head.

He watched her for a moment and then nodded. "Alright, so who were those guys who picked you up today? They were really something, facing down all those teeth."

"Oh, they work for my boss. They are trained to do that kind of thing," she shrugged. Glad to be on a different conversation.

"Your boss must lead an interesting life if he needs men like that."

"I guess." Whitney shrugged.

"Why were you out there anyway?" he asked suddenly. "Didn't you go to the funeral reception?"

*This is it. He's trying to trip me up.*

If she lied and said that she was on her way there or something, and he had already seen her there, she would be caught. But if he had been there and heard the accusations or even seen Lisa's mother slap her, then she would have to explain that too. Saying a quick prayer that she wouldn't screw this up, she plunged ahead.

"No, I went to the reception."

"But you didn't stay?" He watched her intently.

"Well, I got a little upset." She shrugged and looked at her toes.

"Being slapped and accused like that would be upsetting."

Whitney looked up at him.

*So, you were there*, she thought, reevaluating her earlier opinion that he was flighty. *He's playing up the 'bungling idiot' role.*

"They accused you of using Lisa to get away from Justin; that must've been pretty rough?" He nodded and then suddenly asked, "Is that what you did?"

"What? No!" Whitney stared at him in disbelief. "It happened just like I told you that night. She came in the door, I yelled for her to run, and then Justin jumped her."

"Is everything alright out here?" Madraeus asked from the doorway. He was leaning against the frame with his arms crossed.

"Everything is fine, but this is a private discussion." Detective Sanders glared at him.

Madraeus looked from Whitney to the detective and back again. "You seem to be upsetting Ms. Martindale."

"I have certain questions to ask, and they are not your concern."

"Well, Ms. Martindale is my concern," he said.

Sanders puffed up at the warning tone in Madraeus' voice. The detective waited for him to leave, but when he showed no signs of moving, he sighed and turned to Whitney.

"Did you see Justin at any time during or after the funeral?"

"No," Whitney looked him straight in the eye to answer. She had not *seen* him, only talked to him.

"Has he contacted you at all?" *Crap.* Whitney quickly racked her brain for a good way to answer.

"Why would he contact her?"

*Madraeus to the rescue!*

Detective Sanders sighed in annoyance at his continuing interruptions. "There seems to be a connection between these two, and I am hoping that he will try to get in contact somehow. Then we can catch him. If Ms. Martindale really is just an innocent victim, then she should have no problem helping us." He turned an accusing eye on Whitney. He had neatly trapped her: help or become Justin's accomplice.

"Hey, I have no problem helping catch him," she held up her hands, looking properly intimidated, "but you know everything that I can tell you." She was secretly proud of that evasion: *can* tell, not *would* tell.

Detective Sanders scanned her face, looking for any sign of deception.

"Alright," he sighed and put his notebook away. "If you hear anything..." He reached over and pushed the elevator button.

"I will definitely call you." Whitney nodded, trying to look extremely compliant.

"Right. Watch out for those dogs, eh?" he said as the doors opened. He stepped in and turned to watch them as the doors closed.

Whitney let out the breath she had been holding. She jumped when she felt Madraeus' hand on her back.

"Nicely done," he murmured. "Alright, Whitney, you can go back to work."

Whitney blinked. "Just like that? Whitney, go to work?"

"Yes or no?" he prompted when she didn't move.

"Ah, I guess, yes?" she stuttered, following him into the office.

Philtzer, Rami, and Mrs. Myers were waiting.

"Philtzer, you have office duty today." He looked pointedly at the young werewolf. "She is not to be left alone. Ever."

"Right-o, Boss." Philtzer gave a little salute.

"Mrs. Myers, unless there is something else, I think you can leave us."

It sounded rude, but Mrs. Myers didn't seem to notice. She merely nodded and stood.

"Where are you going?" Whitney blurted when Madraeus crossed the room to the door leading to his apartment.

He turned back and sighed, "I am going back to bed."

"Bed?" Whitney gaped.

"Yes, Whitney, bed. Unlike you, I am not a day person."

"Oh," Whitney gave a little embarrassed laugh, "but what about the other attack he mentioned?"

"Hmm," Madraeus flicked a glance at Rami then left the room, leaving her feeling frustrated and lost.

# COME AND GET ME

Whitney sat behind the desk and tossed the wadded-up ball of paper back at Philtzer across the room.

She had spent the afternoon trying to work on the Dreaded Filing Project, and poor Philtzer had been drafted again. She'd made him help carry all the files from her apartment back to her office and then to help her sort them as well. Granted, he wasn't doing much sorting with his feet braced up on the desk and his preoccupation with the paper ball.

She couldn't keep her jumbled mind on sorting either. She felt trapped. She wanted to stop and go home, back to life where people were people and crazy maniacs were the police's problem.

But then again, she couldn't imagine going back. Her eyes had been opened to so many things. She had become a very small fish in a very big pond filled with hungry sharks: blood-sucking, undead sharks and hairy wolf sharks.

She threw down the papers she was holding. "How do you stand this?"

"What?" He threw the ball at her head. She deflected it, scowling. He jumped up and retrieved it from the floor under a chair.

"Dealing with this life! How did you come to terms with becoming a werewolf?"

Philtzer tossed it in the air as he wandered back to his chair. "Becoming a werewolf? I was born a werewolf, baby."

"Born a werewolf? I thought you had to get bitten by another one."

Philtzer shook his head in mock sadness. "Have we been watching movies again?"

She threw up her hands. "See? This is what I'm talking about! Before I got bit in the neck, I couldn't even comprehend how other people could live in mansions and own sports cars, now I'm sitting here trying to deal with myths and monsters and... stalkers from Hell!"

The paper ball smacked her right between the eyes, halting her rant.

"You should lay off the caffeine." Philtzer nodded sagely.

"Shut up."

"Look, Whit," he took pity on her and leaned forward in his chair, bracing his elbows on his knees, "the world hasn't changed. This world has always been full of things that you and I couldn't possibly understand. Just because you didn't know about stuff, doesn't mean it didn't exist. Quit trying so hard to fit it into some little box on a shelf. Take it on faith, girl! You're just experiencing culture shock. We may not be what you consider normal. We may not be what's in the movies, but oh," he grinned with true pleasure, "we are life! I feel privileged to know that I live in a world where magic and myths exist. The real question is how do you deal with your life? Living every day not knowing that anything more is out there. How can you stand the boredom?"

Whitney stared at him. She felt like she had been punched in the chest.

"It's all perspective, baby!" he said, sitting back and propping his feet up once more.

He was right; she had been looking at it all wrong. She had been trying to stuff their world back into her box, but it was really her job to step up and move into theirs.

She picked up the paper ball from the desk and stared at it. Culture shock was the best explanation. It was like traveling but never leaving home. She could do this. All she had to do was readjust her thinking.

She tossed the ball at him. "Thanks, Philtzer."

"For what? Being awesome?" He grinned as he caught the ball.

"Yeah, that." She rolled her eyes.

"No problem!" He tossed the ball up and did an overhand serve.

Whitney tried to block it but missed and had to dig it out of the trash can. She threw it back at him and started sorting papers again. Things were still rumbling around in her head, but she just kept reminding herself it was culture shock.

After a few minutes, she stopped and frowned as a thought occurred to her. "You know what I don't get?"

"Yeah. But what were *you* gonna say?" Philtzer grinned as he tossed the ball at her.

"You're nasty!" she cried. "What I was going to say was, why did Justin want me to come to his car when the wolf could have come after me at any time?"

"I don't know." Philtzer shrugged. "Maybe he's lazy."

Whitney winged the ball at him again but missed.

"No, I don't think it's that." She chewed on her lip. "Something doesn't fit right."

"What difference does it make? You didn't go; that's what's important."

"I almost did."

Philtzer smacked her in the forehead with the ball.

She gave him a dirty look. "Ha. Ha. Very funny," she said as she crawled under the desk after the ball.

"I just don't understand why he's so single-mindedly trying to get me. I couldn't possibly be that great of a girlfriend that he would try this hard to get me back. He left me once and tried to kill me twice. Why does he keep coming for me?"

He wolf-whistled at her back end sticking out from under the desk. "I think it's for your cookies."

"Oh, shut up!" She rolled her eyes as she crawled out from under the desk. "What about the other attack?  Do you think Justin's been ripping out random people's throats?"

"Maybe." Philtzer shrugged. "He is a rogue vampire."

"If Justin has werewolf friends, then he's not limited by day or night. He could come after me whenever he wanted. So why drag it out?"

"Maybe his momma never taught him not to play with his food."

"Really?" She glared at him. "That has to be the worst joke you've told yet."

"Oh no." Philtzer shook his head. "I've said worse."

"Do you think Madraeus will check out that attack? He didn't seem too interested. He barely even reacted to the news that Justin had a werewolf with him," she said. Whitney toyed with the paper ball, pulling at the loose edges.

"Thomas and Hamilton are already checking it out." Philtzer shrugged.

"Really?" She didn't think that Madraeus had cared that much.

"Yep. Stuff like this is like a big flashing 'come get me, I'm a newbie' sign."

Whitney sat up. "Come and get me?" She suddenly had a ridiculous idea.

*He wants to play cat and mouse? Fine. If my life is gonna be a bad horror film, why not turn it into a ridiculous cartoon? In the cartoons, mice always won anyway.*

She grinned at Philtzer.

"What?"

She threw the paper wad at him and, for once, hit him. Her grin widened. "I've got an idea."

"I don't like the sound of that."

"No, probably not, but you're gonna help."

"Ha! That's what you think!"

"Come on, you live for this stuff, remember?"

"Ah, crap."

# BAIT?

Madraeus rolled onto his back. It was well after sundown, however, he felt no desire to get up.

All he could think about was how close he had come to losing Whitney again. The woman was a walking magnet for disaster, and he was just one more victim. As soon as this Justin problem was taken care of, she had to go, no matter what his heart might say.

Madraeus sighed. He had better get up. The Justin problem had gotten more complicated with the news that he had werewolf conspirators. If there was more than one of them gunning for Whitney, then they would need to change tactics in order to bring this to an end, especially if the police were watching Whitney so closely.

They were going to have to go on the offensive: maybe set up a trap to catch Justin instead of waiting for him to find Whitney. It was not a road that he wanted to go down, but there seemed to be little choice. He opened his eyes and stared at the ceiling.

"Morning! Or evening, I guess it should be," Whitney chirped.

Madraeus sat up like a shot, gaping at the woman sitting in his favorite chair at the end of his bed.

"What the Hell are you doing in my room?"

"Rami let me in," Whitney said, trying not to look at his bare chest.

"Oh, did he?" Madraeus was going to murder him.

"Yeah, it was well past closing time, and Philtzer didn't want me to wait at home alone, so Rami told him to bring me over here. You have a nice place by the way, very classy."

"But why are you in my room?" He tried to stay calm while wishing too hard that she might have come for personal reasons.

"Well, I have an idea about how to catch Justin, and I knew that you would want to hear about it right away. When you didn't get up at sundown, I thought that I would wait; but then it just kept getting later, so I thought that I would come and wake you."

"You decided to sneak into the room of a vampire and wake him?" he snorted, trying to get his intense disappointment under control that she was only here for business.

"When you put it that way, it sounds dumb," she smirked.

"So, what is this idea that couldn't wait?" Madraeus sighed and rubbed his face with both hands.

"I want to set a trap for him and use myself as bait."

Madraeus let his hands fall from his face and stared at her. He blinked a few times and replayed what she had said in his mind. Finally convinced that she had indeed said that she was going to be bait, he shook his head. He had thought about setting a trap not moments before, and it had sounded like a good idea, but not when she said it.

"No."

"What do you mean 'no'? You haven't even heard the plan?"

"No." He slipped out of bed and stalked toward the door.

"Come on, it's a great idea. You're not even listening!"

She followed him as he padded barefoot out to the kitchen. He grabbed a bottle from the fridge and popped the cork.

"At least hear me out before you reject it!" She persisted as he drank half the bottle in one go.

She bounced up and down impatiently, watching him drink. He turned and started back toward the bedroom, pausing beside her. He leaned in so close they were nose to nose.

"No."

"Grr!" She stamped in frustration, then turned and followed him. Just as she got to the door, he shut it in her face. He stalked to the closet and pulled out a shirt.

"It's not like there's a choice," she yelled through the door. "I've already called Justin."

He yanked the door open. Whitney jumped back.

"You what?" he snapped. He started toward her, carrying his shirt in one hand. "You called Justin!"

She backed away from him. There was a couch in the middle of the room. She maneuvered so that it was between them while she explained.

"Yeah, you gave me the idea." She rounded the couch.

"Do you have some sort of death wish?"

"No!" she protested. "I just want to get this over with. I'm sick of hiding. I'm sick of being scared. I'm sick of the police."

"So, what? You're just going to sacrifice yourself?" He shouted, stalking after her.

"No!" She moved around the couch again. "I told you. I have a plan. I already told Rami all about it, and he agreed."

"Rami agreed to this?" Madraeus choked.

"Yeah, and if you would listen, you will see it's a good idea too." Whitney watched him, waiting.

"I don't believe this." Madraeus threw his arms up. "You are the most..." he gestured wildly in frustration, "...insane, obnoxious, idiotic woman I have ever met!"

Whitney flinched.

"I should just let him have you," he muttered under his breath as he shrugged into his shirt.

He jerked the collar into place as he stomped back to his room to retrieve the bottle of blood. She watched him stalk across the room and then stop. He took a long drink from the bottle and stared at the ceiling.

Finally, he sighed. "What is this amazing plan?"

"I called Justin and told him that I want it all to stop and that I'm willing to meet him. I told him I would be at City Park around ten by the picnic benches near the kids' playground. There's lots of cover there, so it should be easy to ambush him." She knelt on the couch and leaned her elbows on the back as she finished.

Madraeus turned away and walked to the kitchen.

"Philtzer took his wolves to the park hours ago before I even called Justin, so they will already be in place if anyone is watching. They won't see what's coming."

He drank a little more and then set the bottle down on the counter carefully, knowing that if he didn't, he would smash it against the wall.

"See? It's all been taken care of," she reassured him. "I'll be visible the whole time, and when he shows up: BOOM! All done."

Madraeus started to shake his head. He had almost lost her three times already. He couldn't just let her walk up to Justin. She was so naive. There was no way she could survive if something went wrong tonight.

"No. I won't let you do this," he breathed. His jaw clenched and unclenched in time with his fists.

"Ah, it's already happening, it's almost 9:45 now," she said as she pushed herself up off the couch. "Rami told me that I had to wait for you, but if you aren't going to cooperate, then I'm leaving without you." She started toward the door.

Before she had taken three steps, he was standing in front of her.

"You are not going!" He grabbed her shoulders.

"Let go of me!" she gasped.

"You have no idea what you are getting into!" he growled. She stared at him wide-eyed.

"You think you know about vampires? You've asked a few questions and think you know enough that you'll be safe meeting one alone?" He gave her a little shake. "You know nothing of the danger you are putting yourself into! Even with us so close, you will be *alone*. If he wants to kill you, there is no chance that we could get to you first." His hands were suddenly on her neck. "He could snap your neck in a heartbeat and be gone in the next!"

He felt her breath quicken and her pulse increase beneath his palm. There was finally fear in her eyes. He had wanted her to be afraid, to understand, but now he felt ashamed for scaring her. He let go of her neck and stepped back.

Whitney watched him as he tried to calm down. She reached out and gently laid a hand on Madraeus' chest.

"I just don't want him hurting anyone else. He threatened my grandma," she said quietly. "I'm not going to sit and wait while she's in danger. And I know that I will be as safe as I'm going to get if you guys are there."

He closed his eyes.

"I know that you won't let him hurt me," she continued. "You pretty much promised me that, I'm going to hold you to it."

He wrapped his hand around hers and held it to his chest. Madraeus slowly exhaled. He felt defeated and exultant all at once.

He would go with her.

"Alright, let me finish getting dressed."

# TRAPPED

Whitney sat at the picnic table facing the playground, although she couldn't see much of it in the dark. It looked creepy at night: all bars and sharp edges.

She glanced at the time on her phone again. It was almost ten after eleven already. She had been sitting here for ages, and she was getting cold. The park closed at eleven, and she really didn't relish the idea of getting caught there by the police.

Whitney looked out across Duck Lake. It glowed orange in the light from the streetlamps. She wondered where Philtzer's wolves were hiding. She couldn't hear anything in the still night beyond the normal traffic noises, but even those were muffled by the trees.

Whitney shivered. She never knew that quiet could be so scary.

Madraeus silently dropped from the tree, not more than thirty feet from Whitney. She jumped at the sound and watched him walk toward her out of the shadows.

"What are you doing?" she asked with her heart in her throat.

"He's not coming. It's time to go."

"Damn, I was so sure he'd come."

"It doesn't matter, come on." Madraeus guided Whitney down one of the paths.

"Thank you for trying anyway," she muttered.

"You didn't give me much choice."

Shadows poured out of the trees as they walked. Whitney edged closer to Madraeus unconsciously. Within moments, they were surrounded by wolves. Disappointment hung in the air as the pack escorted them to the edge of the park and then faded away again.

"Where are they going?" Whitney asked, feeling a moment of panic.

"Back to join Rami," Madraeus said quietly. He looked around, still on his guard. "They are going to make a sweep of the park. They might still get lucky tonight."

"Oh." Whitney didn't know about that part of the plan.

Whitney walked silently beside Madraeus. She was too disappointed to attempt a conversation. Before she knew it, they were stepping out of the elevator.

Whitney stopped outside her apartment door. She turned and looked at Madracus. His eyes were dark.

The situation felt so much like the end of a date that she wondered at her own sanity. Although sitting in a park waiting for a homicidal ex-boyfriend while being watched by vampires and werewolves was hardly what she would call a date. Besides, she was sure he only felt contempt for her anyway. He had made that quite clear earlier, but just the same, she felt that awkward, electric feeling.

At a loss for what else to do, Whitney turned and opened the door.

"Well," she started, "goodnight, I guess. Thanks again for trying."

Before he could answer, something grabbed her and pulled her inside the room.

"Whitney!" Madraeus snarled.

The door slammed shut.

Whitney stumbled. Whatever had grabbed her had let go the instant she was in the room.

She jumped as Madraeus pounded on the door.

Whitney blinked, trying to adjust her eyes to the darkness. The faint light glowing from the stove in the kitchen wasn't enough to help her. Her other senses zinged into overdrive, trying to sense her attacker's location.

She heard a faint movement to her right.

She started backing slowly away. She knew her apartment better than any intruder would, especially in the dark. If she could make it to the kitchen, she could get out.

"Uh, uh, uh," came a voice from the darkness.

"Justin?" Whitney breathed.

"If you keep backing away like that, I may get the idea that you didn't want to talk to me after all."

Whitney froze.

She fought the panic that welled up.

"You didn't come to the park," she accused the darkness.

"Nope," he laughed. "I didn't want to run into all your friends."

His voice was coming from a different spot now.

"Friends?" she asked, trying to gauge where he was.

"Yeah, that little trap you set up. You lied to me, Whit." He was off to her left now. He was getting closer. Then she heard a sound to the right. It was from near the door.

*There must be two of them.*

They had her surrounded. She backed up a little more. Hands grabbed at her.

*Three of them?*

She twisted away.

"No more playing," Justin said.

He pounced.

She screeched and squirmed.

Whitney was determined not to go down without a fight, but he was stronger than her.

He got a grip on her throat and squeezed. Terror spurred her on. She kicked and punched. She scratched his face and tried to knee him in the groin.

The kitchen door bursting open barely registered in her mind before they were tackled. Justin let go of her. Whitney sucked in air only to have it knocked back out of her when she landed hard against the coffee table.

Crashes and snarls echoed around her in the darkness.

Whitney tried again and again to suck in enough air. She struggled to her knees only to be knocked over again by a flying body.

She scrambled away, but a hand clamped around her ankle. She kicked with her other foot as hard as she could. She felt the impact and heard the bone crack.

*I hope that wasn't Madraeus!*

Growling and smashing sounds were all around her. She needed light. There was no way she could defend herself in this darkness.

Someone grabbed her by the hair and yanked her to her feet. She tried to scream, but nothing came out of her tortured windpipe.

Whitney launched an elbow backward into their ribs. She could tell by the grunt that it was Justin. She tried to elbow him again. Justin snarled at her, but suddenly he was ripped away, taking a handful of hair with him. Whitney fell again as she heard him crash against the wall. She whipped around toward the sound.

She had to get a light on. She fumbled across the floor until she found a wall. She had become completely disoriented. She moved along, feeling her way, afraid that any minute something would grab her again.

Suddenly, it was silent.

Whitney stopped and listened. She could hear someone breathing hard across the room. She prayed it was Madraeus. She shifted in the opposite direction just in case.

Her foot hit something solid. Cautiously, she reached down and felt a lamp. She flicked it on.

Right in front of her lay Justin's werewolf, or at least its head.

She tried to scream, but it only came out as a hiss. She stared at the head. Its jaws were spread open in a permanent snarl. The tongue lolled out one side. Her eyes slowly slid over and followed the trail of blood spilling from its neck. The thing's body lay a few feet away.

Bile bubbled up into her throat, making it burn. Her throat throbbed. It felt like she had swallowed glass. She wrapped her cold hands around her neck. It helped the pain a little.

Her head was pounding. She looked around again. Her beautiful apartment now looked like a butcher shop. She started to shake.

Across the room, Madraeus crouched over another body. He turned toward her.

What breath she had gotten back was stolen away. His face was a mask of evil. His eyes were black, staring orbs. His fangs were out. Blood covered his face and shirt. His hands were curled into claws.

The full realization of what he was hit her.

Madraeus stepped toward her. Panic took over, and she scrambled backward on all fours away from him.

Madraeus stopped. He held his hands out palm up.

"Whitney?" She stopped at the sound of his voice. Whitney stared at him wide-eyed as his face returned to normal.

# WHAT A MESS

"Whitney," he began softly, "Whitney, it's alright, I won't hurt you." He took a step forward. When she didn't move, he took another step.

"Are you hurt?" he asked as he stepped slowly closer.

She shook her head. She inched her way along the wall, trying to put some distance between her and the carnage, but it was everywhere.

He knelt in front of her and held his hand out. She stared at it like it was a snake.

"Whitney," he spoke softly again. "It's alright, it's just me. You're safe now."

She looked at the carnage around him again, then her eyes flicked to his blood-soaked shirt. Slowly, she looked up; her eyes found his. She swallowed, then reached up and grasped his hand.

He helped her stand and held her hand against his chest. He pulled her into his embrace. All the rage and fear that had engulfed him when she disappeared through the door eased. Madraeus let out a shuddering breath and then turned to survey the devastation. Blood covered the floor and was splattered on what was left of the broken and scattered furniture.

Justin had brought two men with him: one werewolf and one vampire. The werewolf was no longer a concern, but Justin and the other vampire needed to be restrained before they became conscious again.

"I need to secure them," he whispered into her hair. When he started to move away, Whitney clung to him.

"Whitney, I need to take care of them," he tried again.

Madraeus gave Whitney's hand a squeeze and then moved over to Justin. He picked up a smashed lamp and yanked the cord out of the bottom. Quickly, he tied Justin's hands behind his back.

Madraeus moved over to the other vampire. He glanced around for another cord, but there wasn't one, so he pulled the vampire's belt off and used it.

Madraeus turned back to Whitney but hesitated, searching her face.

"We need to get you out of here." His voice made her jump. He held out his hand.

It seemed like forever before she finally moved away from the wall. She stepped forward through the broken debris. When she reached Madraeus, he wrapped an arm around her shoulders and guided her away from the carnage.

He escorted her down the hall and through the study into his apartments. Steering her into his bedroom, he set her down in his favorite chair near the fireplace. Working efficiently, he flipped on the fire, went to the closet, and pulled out a robe. He turned back to his dazed receptionist and tossed the robe over the arm of the chair.

He knelt in front of her. "Your clothes have blood on them," he said, brushing the hair back from her face.

"I'll bring you some water. Do you think you can change into this while I'm gone?" He patted the robe.

Whitney nodded.

He hated the glazed look in her eyes. "Alright, I'll be right back."

Madraeus took his time getting a glass of water from the kitchen. Whitney was just tying the belt of his robe with shaking hands when he returned. She gave him a weak smile and sank down onto the chair. He reached over and pulled the blanket off the bed. He tucked it around her and held out the glass. Wrapping his hand around her shaking one, he helped her drink. She winced when she tried to swallow.

"Thank you," she rasped.

"I have to go take care of Justin." He brushed her hair back from her face again and cupped her cheek. "You just stay here. It's going to be alright, it's almost over."

Quickly, he gathered up her clothes and slipped out. He threw Whitney's clothes in the washing machine in his laundry room, and then Madraeus made his way back to Whitney's apartment. As he walked into the living room, he heard Justin groan.

Madraeus walked over and squatted down in front of Justin. He grabbed a handful of hair and lifted his head off the floor. Blood was trickling out of the side of his mouth, his nose was smashed, and there were scratches down the side of his face.

"So, you're the mighty Justin? Humph." Madraeus let go of his head, letting it hit the floor with a thump.

He then walked over to examine the head of the werewolf. He didn't recognize the wolf. Madraeus frowned. Philtzer would know if he was local or an import.

From out in the hallway, he heard the elevator doors open. Instantly, he was on alert.

"Ray?" Rami called through the door.

Madraeus moved to open the door. Philtzer and Thomas followed Rami in.

"Whoa, boss!" Philtzer whistled. "You had a party?"

"Oh yeah, big party, Philtzer, sorry you missed it." Madraeus rolled his eyes, realizing too late that he sounded like Whitney.

Philtzer grinned at him.

"You recognize that wolf?" Madraeus jerked his head toward the body.

Thomas and Philtzer kicked broken bits of furniture out of their way as they moved over to examine what was left of Justin's wolf.

"I don't know this one."

"Not at all?" Madraeus asked.

Philtzer looked up at Thomas, who shrugged, then shook his head. "Nope."

"Alright," Madraeus gestured toward the two vampires, "if you would be so kind as to show our guests to their rooms."

Philtzer saluted and hopped over the debris. Thomas grabbed Justin, and Philtzer grabbed the other vampire. They carried them out the kitchen door.

"You alright?" Rami rumbled.

Madraeus nodded. "Yes, just a couple of scratches. He only brought two friends."

"And Whitney?"

"She is resting in my room," he said. "Justin tried to choke her before I got through the door. Her neck is going to be bruised, and she can barely speak. I'd like to go back and check on her if you can start on clean-up."

"Go," Rami sighed. "I hate cleaning up these messes. I miss the old days when we just burnt down the building."

***

Madraeus opened the door to his room slowly so he wouldn't startle her. He expected her to be a mess: hysterical or even crying. He did not, however, expect her to be asleep.

Madraeus shook his head. This woman was a marvel.

Careful not to wake her, he lifted her from the chair and carried her to the bed. She whimpered a little and curled into him, clutching his shirt front. He laid her down and gently pried her fingers from his shirt. She shivered, so he pulled a second blanket up over her.

He sat down on the edge of the bed.

*It's over now.* Madraeus sighed.

It was time to keep his promise to send her away. He just wasn't sure if he could.

He watched her sleep, memorizing her face.

He knew he couldn't stay here for much longer. There were things to do. Eventually, he tore himself away from her bedside and went back to help Rami.

It took several hours to sweep up the broken furniture, roll up the ruined carpets, and wash the blood off the walls. Madraeus called in more helpers to get it done. They hauled everything away, including the body of the werewolf, to be burned in an incinerator at an industrial park across town.

Rami repaired the kitchen door while the others set to re-painting and re-carpeting. Furniture was a little more difficult at this time of night, but enough was scavenged from the other apartments to make it appear normal in case of visitors.

Madraeus was well aware that the police were still interested in Whitney. They didn't want to take any chances. Although he had no idea what to tell them if they saw her neck, it was going to show bruises tomorrow.

As the sun rose, they closed the door on Whitney's apartment. Inside, it looked like nothing had happened.

"Are you going to sleep?" Rami asked Madraeus as they walked back to the study.

Madraeus shook his head. "No, I'm going to have a little chat with Justin."

"Very well," Rami sighed. "I will check the security tapes. I want to know how they got in."

# Let's Forget the Questions

Madraeus took the stairs two at a time. When InfiniCorp had first purchased its new home in downtown Denver, the Council of Races had renovated the 27th and 28th floors to fit their needs. As a home base for council business, it included two state-of-the-art conference rooms, multiple offices, filing rooms, cold storage, several apartments, an arsenal, and four well-fortified holding cells. Madraeus had no illusions about what his position as the head of the Council of Races required, and at this moment, he relished his duties.

Justin and his vampire accomplice were each confined to a cell. Although he would question both of them, right now Madraeus only wanted a piece of Justin.

He swung the cell door open. Justin squinted against the sudden glare. Madraeus stepped in and closed the door. He flicked on the overhead light, filling the room with a buzzing fluorescent glow. Justin hung by his wrists from chains mounted on the wall. His feet barely touched the floor.

Madraeus leaned against the door with his arms crossed over his chest. They sized each other up for a moment.

"Do you know who I am?" Madraeus asked quietly.

"Yeah, I know who you are," Justin smirked. His face was already starting to heal.

Madraeus nodded. "Good."

Justin blinked in surprise.

"You don't scare me," Justin protested. "She said you're a wuss. You're weak!"

"Would that be Cecelia's opinion?"

Justin's eyes widened at his own slip of the tongue. Madraeus smiled.

"She lied." Madraeus pushed himself away from the door and wandered closer. "You have made some very stupid mistakes."

"I haven't made any mistakes!" Justin scoffed.

"Ah, so that's why you are chained to a wall?" Madraeus lifted one eyebrow, earning a glare from Justin.

"Did you know that I had this room specially designed?" Madraeus waited for a response, but when he didn't get one, he continued. "Didn't think so. I had a set of vents installed, ingenious actually; they redirect the sunlight into this room." He wandered over to a panel on the wall.

Justin shifted nervously.

"Cecelia told you about the sun, right?"

Madraeus slid the panel open and turned back to see Justin's face filling with panic. He started struggling against his chains.

"I'm not going to tell you anything!" Justin growled.

"I don't remember asking you to."

Justin's eyes widened.

"You can't just torture me." Justin shook his head in denial.

"I thought you said you knew who I am?" Madraeus tilted his head to the side. "You hurt Whitney. You threatened her family. You've made a public nuisance of yourself and nearly exposed us all. I cannot let that pass."

"So just kill me already!" Justin spat.

Madraeus let his eyes go completely black. "Oh no. You're not going to die for a long, long time."

Justin frantically yanked at his chains. Madraeus calmly turned a knob. A beam of light shot across the room and landed on Justin's thigh. He screamed as his flesh hissed and smoked.

*Yesss,* a voice hissed in Madraeus' mind.

Madraeus turned the knob again, and the light disappeared.

"What do you want?" Justin screeched, "I'll tell you anything!"

"Really?" Madraeus sneered. "One tiny little burn and you're willing to spill everything? Without even being asked?"

"Yes! Yes, please," Justin whined. "Oh shit! It hurts!"

"How pathetic." Madraeus turned the knob again. Another beam of light seared Justin's leg.

*Burn him.*

"AH!" he screeched. "What's wrong with you? I said I'd tell you everything!"

"And I said that you weren't going to die for a very long time," Madraeus smiled. "Do you know what is really great about this device?" he asked over the top of Justin's cries. "It only injures you a little, and since you are a vampire, you'll heal, so we can start over again tomorrow, and the next day, and for as long as I want."

"You bastard!" Justin spat. "I'll kill you!"

"Not likely." Madraeus gave a short laugh. Another beam of light landed on Justin.

*Yesss.* The voice hissed in the back of his mind but was drowned out by Justin's screaming.

"Cecelia will come for me!" Justin gasped when he could speak.

"Also not likely, you are an incidental toy to her." He shook his head.

"She promised that I—" A flash of light cut off what he was going to say.

"Oh, I'm sorry, she promised you what? Power? To rule beside her?" Madraeus taunted. "Wake up, she says that to everyone."

Justin screamed as another section of his leg was burned.

Madraeus walked around the room for a moment, allowing Justin to recover. Then he pulled a pair of pliers out of his pocket and snapped them open and shut a couple of times. He leaned in close to Justin.

"Now about those fangs. Let's make sure you never bite anyone again."

"You're a sick son of a bitch!" his captive panted.

"No," Madraeus snarled. His face was only inches from Justin's. "I'm just really pissed off."

***

Madraeus trotted down the spiral staircase that separated the living room from the kitchen. He headed for the refrigerator and grabbed a bottle of blood.

"Well?" Rami asked hopefully.

He was sitting at the kitchen counter. Madraeus chugged half the bottle before answering.

"He is ready to say anything, but I think he can wait until tomorrow."

"Is this really necessary?" Rami grumbled. "Couldn't you just find out where Cecelia is and what she is planning without dragging it out? Without the torture?"

*No. He dessservesss thisss.*

"No," Madraeus snapped, "he deserves this. He hurt Whitney."

Rami shook his head and stood.

"And what will it do to Whitney," Rami put his hand on Madraeus' shoulder, "when she finds out what you have done to him?" Rami turned and left without waiting for an answer.

Madraeus watched him walk away. He shook his head, realizing that he had heard the hissing voice again. He looked down at his blood-soaked shirt. Rami was right, she would hate him.

He suddenly felt drained. He ripped off his shirt in disgust and stalked off toward the shower.

# TRADE?

Whitney groaned. Everything hurt. She was getting really sick of waking up in pain. She opened her eyes and looked around. Blue walls, fireplace? She was in Madraeus' room.

She whimpered.

She was also getting sick of waking up in other people's bedrooms. She didn't remember moving to the bed, but at least she wasn't going to be stiff from sleeping in the chair.

Gently, she felt her neck. It still hurt. A lot. She said an experimental 'hello'. It sounded like a raspy burp.

*No answering phones today,* she sighed.

She looked around for a clock. There wasn't one.

*Great,* she thought, *I'm probably late for work. If I still have a job.*

She couldn't believe that this nightmare was finally over. They had caught Justin.

She was free.

*But what now?*

She wondered if she would keep her job, or if they would send her away because she no longer needed protection.

*Do I want to stay here?*

After everything that happened, she should have wanted to leave, but surprisingly, she didn't.

Although she could live without the constant injuries, she liked it here. She liked the people, and she liked doing something that mattered. It wasn't like so many of the jobs she'd had where she just filled a space. She could affect people's lives here: human and non-human.

She couldn't imagine what it would be like to go back to the normal world. Back to friends and fun. Back to only worrying about what was in fashion or spending money just to alleviate boredom. She didn't think she could fit back into that world knowing what she did now. It was all so frivolous. It was like Philtzer said: there was so much more to life.

Whitney felt restless. She heaved herself out of bed, groaning aloud from all the aches and pains she had collected. She looked down and realized that she wasn't dressed. Running a finger down the blue silk, she remembered it was Madraeus' robe.

Whitney whimpered. The lines weren't just getting blurred in this job; they were getting erased. She needed to decide where she stood with Madraeus at some point, but when she did, she wanted to be dressed.

Wrapping the robe tighter around her, she hobbled to the door. Whitney opened it a crack and peeked out. The main room was empty. Quickly, she left the bedroom and headed for her apartment.

As she approached her kitchen door, she slowed. It was completely whole. Whitney frowned. She vaguely remembered Madraeus bursting through it last night. The memory of all the carnage and violence made her hands shake as she reached out to open it.

She gaped at the sight of her apartment. It was spotless, but it wasn't *her* apartment. The carpet was a different color, and the walls were painted a pale shade of blue now. The furniture had been replaced, and there wasn't as much of it as there had been.

She moved forward slowly, inspecting every inch of the room. Every bit of evidence from last night was gone. It was like it never happened. She reached up and touched her throat to remind herself that it had been real.

Whitney went into the bathroom to examine her neck. It was discolored, and there were finger marks on either side. Her head was tender where her hair had been pulled out. She winced as she pulled the robe back and felt her ribs where she had landed on the coffee table. They were turning purple.

She sighed. She had never been this beaten up in her life.

Shaking her head, she walked to her bedroom. Thankfully, it hadn't been touched last night. She rummaged around and found a comfortable pair of jeans and a lightweight turtle-neck sweater. There was nothing she could do about her voice, but she could at least hide her bruises.

As she was pulling on her sneakers, her personal phone rang. She glanced at the number and went still. It was the number that Justin had called her from. She let it ring, too frightened to answer it. It went silent for a moment, then started to ring again. Finally, she answered it.

"Hello, Whitney," a sultry voice purred.

"Who is this?" she rasped.

"Oh, you don't sound like yourself at all," the voice sympathized. "That's too bad."

"Who is this?" she tried again, trying to place the voice. It sounded familiar.

"Surely you recognize a catty bitch when you hear one," she snarled.

*Catty bitch?* It took her a moment to remember who she had called a catty bitch, but finally, it dawned on her.

"Cecelia?" Whitney whispered tentatively.

"Oh, so I see they told you who you insulted," Cecelia laughed.

"What do you want?" Whitney held her throat, talking hurt.

"Ah, that is the question," Cecelia purred.

Whitney waited. She heard Cecelia sigh when she didn't answer.

"You have someone that I want," Cecelia explained. "I would like you to go find Justin for me and bring him downstairs."

"No way," Whitney rasped.

"Oh yes, you will," Cecelia's voice became hard, "if you want to see your grandmother again."

Whitney's blood turned to ice. She closed her eyes and prayed that this was just a nightmare. It was supposed to be over now. They had caught Justin.

"Whitney, are you still listening?"

Whitney forced herself to pay attention.

"You will bring me Justin, or you will find pieces of your grandmother scattered from one side of this city to the other."

"No!" Whitney's scream came out a hiss. "You leave her alone!"

"Or you'll what? Call me a name? Please!" Cecelia laughed. "You'll do exactly what I say. You have no choice."

"But I don't even know where they took him. How am I supposed to do this?" Whitney cried.

"You'll find detention cells upstairs in Madraeus' apartment. When they sleep, take him out the back elevator. We will be waiting for you at the bottom. You will not tell anyone, or that will be the end of dear granny."

"Wait," Whitney started, but the phone went dead. Frantically, she called her grandmother's house. Precious seconds ticked away while the phone rang, and rang, and rang again.

She paced around her room and then into the living room. She tried again. Still no answer.

"No! No! NO! NO!" she cried.

She couldn't let them hurt her grandmother, but there was no way she was going to be able to sneak Justin out unnoticed.

She had to think. Her brain was frozen. She yanked the curtain open, letting the sun in. She looked toward the street, trying to see any cars with tinted windows, but it was too far down for her to see.

*What am I gonna do?*

# BETRAYAL

MADRAEUS PADDED BACK TO his room with a towel wrapped around his waist. His shower had left his body clean but not his conscience. Rami's parting words had been turning over in his head with a vengeance. Whitney would hate him if she found out what he had done to Justin. He would lose her forever.

He had lost control. He had wanted revenge on Justin, and that damned voice had risen up again, urging him to do it. It was like all the evil inside of him was connected to that voice. It reared its ugly head like a poisonous snake, time and again.

He hated that hissing voice. He had done so many evil things while under the influence of it. He couldn't allow that evil to control him. He had fought it for too many centuries.

Madraeus growled in frustration. He had to find a way. His future with Whitney depended on it. He stopped. He had promised to send her away to keep her safe. He knew he should, but he wasn't sure he could. He took a deep breath and quietly pushed open his bedroom door.

The bed was empty.

"Damn it!" He stalked across the room and yanked open the dresser drawer. He dressed quickly. "Why does she never stay where she's put?"

After a quick search of his living quarters and the office, he strode down the hallway toward Whitney's apartment.

"She had better be in there."

He thrust open the kitchen door and stopped dead. A sunbeam glowed in the air at the edge of the tile. It barred him from further progress into the room. It was coming from one of the living room windows around the corner. He gave another growl of frustration.

"Whitney? Are you in here?"

"Yeah," she croaked. He winced at the sound of her rasping voice.

"Would you mind coming in here, please?" he sighed.

As she rounded the corner, the sun glinted off the phone screen in her hand. Light flashed across the kitchen. Madraeus instinctively ducked, but the light seared his cheek. He hissed at the pain.

She clapped her hands over her mouth.

"Oh my gosh! I'm so sorry," she croaked as she rushed forward. Gently, she reached out to touch his cheek. Her hands were cold and trembling.

Madraeus took in her panic-filled eyes and frowned in confusion.

"It's alright," he gestured to his cheek absently, "this is nothing." *Nothing compared to what I did to Justin*, his conscience asserted. He cleared his throat, trying to banish that thought.

"I didn't mean to—"

He placed a finger on her lips. "You shouldn't use your voice too much if you can help it."

She nodded, but she still looked frightened.

He gestured to her neck. "Is it bad?"

Whitney shrugged and pulled the collar of her sweater down for him to see. He winced at the marks.

"We should have Dr. Kirkland take a look and make sure there is no permanent damage."

Whitney nodded, looking away.

"Are you alright? You seem upset. Is it because of what happened in here last night?"

"I..." her voice scratched. She made a vague nodding-shrugging movement.

"If it bothers you, what are you doing in here?" Madraeus frowned.

She gestured at her sweater.

"Ah. Yes, you needed clothes." He added, "I put your things from last night in the laundry in my apartments."

She nodded, biting her lip.

Madraeus knew something was definitely bothering her. He looked her over, trying to find the answer. She seemed nervous as well as scared. Her passivity, coupled with the wild look in her eyes, bothered him.

"Come on, you shouldn't be in here alone." He slipped a hand around her back and guided her into the darkness of the hallway. "I'll call Dr. Kirkland since you can't talk. Although I must say, it is a unique experience for you to be so quiet."

He periodically stole glances at her. It occurred to him that she might be afraid of him, of what he had been last night. He didn't know what to say to calm her fears, but he had to try something. Her fear was killing him.

When they reached his apartment, he turned toward her. Madraeus searched her face.

"Whitney," he cupped her chin, "about last night."

Her eyes darted around his face. She was like a frightened rabbit searching for an escape route.

"You know that wasn't me," he started, unsure how to explain. "It was me, but that wasn't all of me. That was just one side of me. I am more than that monster. I don't want you to be scared of me."

She bit her lip as tears welled up in her eyes.

"My poor Whitney," he growled, pulling her into his embrace. His heart swelled as she returned it fiercely. "It's going to be okay." She hugged him like she was pulling every ounce of strength she could from him.

"I need to sleep," he said quietly into her hair. "The daylight drains me, but I will call Mrs. Myers to come sit with you." He pulled back and cupped her face again. "Do you want me to wait with you until she gets here?"

Whitney hesitated like she wanted to say something but then shook her head.

"You are safe. Justin is locked away upstairs. You don't need to worry anymore," he said before turning away.

He almost turned back to invite her to stay with him, but he didn't want to frighten her any more than she already was. When he reached his door, he looked back at her. "Just stay here, alright? I want you to be here when I get up... for a change."

***

Whitney watched him disappear into his bedroom.

*He thinks that I'm afraid of him?*

He couldn't be farther from the truth. It was true that seeing him last night in full-monster mode scared the crap out of her, but she wasn't afraid of *him*.

Regardless of how much she wanted to reassure him, right now, she had to remain silent. His misinterpretation was the only thing saving her right now. If he knew the true source of her fear, it would mean her grandmother's death.

A hysterical sob escaped her lips. She clamped her hands over her mouth. Silent tears ran down her cheeks. She hated lies and secrets. She wished she could still be here when he got up, but if she let Justin out, Madraeus would see it as the ultimate betrayal.

With a breaking heart, she turned to scan the room. She didn't have much time. If Madraeus called Mrs. Myers, she would be on her way. Once she was here, there would be no chance of getting to Justin.

Quietly, she made her way up the spiral staircase next to the kitchen. It was the only way up that she could see. She stepped cautiously onto the thick carpet of the upper living room. She had no idea where to go; there were so many doors. Resigned to trial and error, Whitney started opening doors.

After a few tries, she managed to find a conference room, a lobby that led to the back elevator, and two unused bedrooms. She hadn't yet run into anyone. She wondered if her luck would hold.

Whitney started to open another door but heard snoring from the other side. She held her breath as she slowly let the doorknob slide back into place. She backed away down the hallway directly behind her. While she listened for signs of discovery, she noticed the walls next to her. She tapped one with a fingernail experimentally. They were made of metal. Maybe these were the cells that Cecelia had mentioned.

Quickly, Whitney followed the wall around the corner to the doors. There was a small sliding window in the middle of each door. She lifted the bar and slid back the first one to reveal an empty cell. She didn't bother sliding it back; she was running out of time. Any moment could bring discovery.

The second door she tried was the one she was looking for. She could see Justin in the shadows at the back of the cell. Whitney glanced around to make sure no one was coming, then pulled open the heavy metal door. It swung silently on well-oiled hinges. Light spilled in from the corridor, illuminating the bloody mess that was Justin.

# GET ME OUT OF HERE

WHITNEY STOPPED AND STARED. Burns and cuts covered Justin's body. His nose was broken, and dried blood was smeared down his face. The smell of burnt flesh hung in the air. She turned away, holding her mouth. She was going to be sick.

"What's the matter?" Justin grinned, showing the gaps where his fangs should have been. "Don't like what your little boss did to me?"

Whitney turned back slowly. Horror crept over her face. Whitney shook her head in denial. She couldn't believe that Madraeus would be that cruel.

"I thought you'd be here a lot sooner. Unlock me," Justin commanded.

Whitney backed up a moment. She didn't want to go near him.

"Come on, Whit, unlock me. Key's by the door." He rattled his chains, "You can't leave me here like this."

"I know," she shook her head, "I can't."

Justin sagged with relief. "I knew you loved me."

"No, I don't," she rasped, "but I do love Grammy, and I'm going to trade you for her."

She grabbed the key and stepped forward.

"Whatever." Justin grinned at her again as she unlocked his shackles.

He hit the floor with a grunt. Whitney bent to pick him up, but suddenly he was standing.

"You're so predictable." He grabbed her by the arm and propelled her to the door. He scanned the hallway, then pushed her out in front of him.

She tried to dart away, but he grabbed her arm and twisted it behind her back. She cried out, and his other hand clamped down on her mouth.

"You are so easy to manipulate," he continued as they entered the elevator.

He let go of her after the doors closed. She rushed to the opposite wall, trying to stay as far away as she could.

"I told Cecelia that your grandmother was the key to getting you to do anything."

"Bastard!" she spat, launching herself at him. She pummeled him with fists and feet.

He reared back. "Oh, please."

He shoved her over backward. She landed hard, jarring her bruised ribs. Whitney slowly picked herself up off the floor and glared at him. When the elevator doors opened, Whitney made a run for it. She didn't get past the door before Justin had a hold of her hair.

"No, you don't!" He hauled her toward a waiting black sedan with tinted windows. "In you go."

Whitney was pushed into the back seat, closely followed by Justin. The car was on its way out of the parking garage within minutes.

Whitney wedged her back into the corner, trying to keep her distance from Justin.

"Don't worry, Whit, as much as I would like to jump you right now, I can't bite." Justin said, "You should relax, it's a long ride."

Whitney said nothing as she wrapped her arm protectively around her ribs. There was no way that she could match him physically. She was going to have to be smart about this. She bit her lip.

Her cell phones were in her pocket. All she had to do was wait until he was distracted, and then she would call in the cavalry. She would make this right.

The car sped up the winding roads into the mountains. It seemed like ages before Justin relaxed his guard. His head nodded, and his eyes fluttered. Slowly, his head sank down onto the back of the seat.

Whitney waited a few more miles and then cautiously pulled her cell phone out. She slid it under her leg to hide it. She didn't know if this was going to work, but she had to try something. She glanced out the window, trying to see a landmark of some kind. They were on a dirt road. The mountains rose into sheer cliffs on either side.

She glanced at Justin. He was still sleeping. She glanced down long enough to dial InfiniCorp's number. When she looked back at Justin, he was only inches from her face.

"Uh-uh, no cheating," he warned as he slid his hand down her leg and took her cell phone from her hand. He held it up in front of her.

"Toss it out the window." When she hesitated, he wrapped his fingers around her throat. "Wanna repeat of last night?" Terrified, she shook her head and rolled down the window enough to toss the phone out.

"Now just sit there and be good," he said as he slouched back into the corner.

Whitney willed her breathing back to normal. She stared out the window again, trying to see where they were. She still had her personal phone, but she would have to wait to use it. She couldn't risk losing her last chance for help. She diligently watched for landmarks, but they were in the back of beyond. There wasn't even so much as a fence off the side of the road.

Finally, the car started to slow. Whitney craned her neck to get a look at their destination.  A huge building loomed ahead of them. It looked old and rickety, leaning against the side of the mountain. One part of the building was three or four stories high. The other half of the building was only one story and stretched out along the ground to one side. Several pick-ups and a couple of cars with tinted windows were parked off to the side. A large semi-truck and trailer were backed up to the building.

Several huge guard dogs patrolled the yard. Whitney blinked and then squinted. She corrected her assessment. They weren't dogs, they were wolves.

Justin suddenly sat up straight, making Whitney jump. He grinned at her, enjoying her fear.

She hated him.

"Well, here we are, home sweet home," he said as the car pulled into the single-story section.

When the car came to a stop, Justin gestured toward the door. "Out."

# TRICKED AND TREATED

Reluctantly, Whitney opened the door and stepped out. A group of people lounged around the interior of the building. They all stared at her. None of them seemed too friendly. A few even licked their lips.

Whitney shivered.

"You impress me, little Whitney," an increasingly familiar voice purred.

Whitney turned to face Cecelia, who smiled as she came forward. "You managed to achieve my demands in record time. I have to say that your desire to save your grandmother was commendable, stupidly executed, but commendable nonetheless."

"Where is she?" Whitney rasped.

Cecelia raised an eyebrow and then smiled. "Oh, isn't that cute?" She looked around to include everyone in the joke. "The little rabbit is so brave."

Whitney didn't bother looking around as the crowd laughed at her.

"Didn't he tell you?" Cecelia asked with false sympathy, flicking a look at Justin. "We never had your grandmother."

They all laughed again as shame scorched her face. They had played her like an idiot. Anger flooded Whitney.

She balled up her fists and launched herself at Cecelia. She almost managed to land a punch on Cecelia's jaw, but Cecelia reacted too quickly. She merely slapped Whitney, but the force of the blow knocked Whitney to the ground.

"You are a feisty one." She looked from Whitney back to Justin. "Maybe I picked the wrong human to turn."

She took in his beaten and battered state. A look of disgust filled her face.

"Why haven't you fed to heal yourself?" she snapped.

Justin showed her his teeth. "He took my fangs."

Cecelia's face lit up. "So, he hasn't been tamed," she murmured thoughtfully. "Did you tell him anything?"

"No!"

Cecelia watched him for a moment.

"Where are Dillon and Jarvis?" she asked.

"Dillon is dead. I don't know about Jarvis." Justin shrugged.

Cecelia frowned at him for a moment.

"Spark?" Cecelia growled.

The woman with brilliant white spiked hair standing behind Cecelia snapped to attention. Cecelia jerked her head toward Justin.

Whitney staggered to her feet as Spark and another man came forward and grabbed Justin by the arms. Disbelief clouded his face as they turned him toward the door.

"No! Wait!" he shouted as he struggled to break free of them. "What are you doing? Cecelia! You promised me!" His feet skidded in the loose dirt as they dragged him ever closer to the open door at the end of the building. "Cecelia!"

Whitney looked back at Cecelia; she was smiling. She happened to glance down at Whitney.

"He is of no use without his teeth." She winked.

Whitney watched in horror as they dragged Justin out into the sun-filled yard. They returned to the shade of the building without even a backward glance. He jerked and convulsed as he tried to run back to the safety of the shade.

Whitney wanted to cover her eyes, but she was frozen. His screams echoed through the building as, layer by layer, the sun burned him into dust.

"Now that's done, let's talk about you," Cecelia purred. Whitney didn't even turn; she just kept staring at the smoking heap that had been the love of her life for the last year.

"Bring her to my office," Cecelia said as she turned and left.

Someone stepped forward and took her by the arm. Shock made her compliant as she was marched after Cecelia into the dim building.

She expected them to go up, but once inside, she saw that the interior of the building was mostly hollow. There were a few small rooms built around the edges, but she could see all the way up to the roof three stories above them. The middle of the room was filled with a scaffolded framework built around a large hole in the ground. Cables supported a platform above the hole.

Understanding dawned on Whitney as she was pushed onto the platform: this was an old mine. They must have used this shaft to haul up the ore in the old days; however, the elevator seemed brand new.

Whitney's heart started pounding hard as they descended into darkness. It was very disorienting to be suspended in total blackness.

The only hold on reality she had was the hand clamped around her elbow, and she knew that was connected to some very sharp teeth.

Minutes ticked by as they continued downward, then slowly the light increased. The elevator came to rest at the bottom of a large cavern.

Whitney looked around quickly for possible escape routes. Shafts led in several directions off of the cavern. In the center, they had set up what looked like a lounge area. Couches and chairs stood on luxurious rugs under colorful canopies. It reminded her of a bazaar. People were everywhere.

Whitney stared in astonishment.

She wanted to look some more, but she was being pulled away. Her guard dragged her along behind him into a tunnel as they followed Cecelia. The noise faded behind them as they went deeper into the darkness. As they neared a new source of light, Whitney heard music.

Her escort thrust her into a room that was more lavish than Madraeus' study. Plush carpet covered the floor, and a chandelier hung from the rock ceiling, making the room glow. False walls had been constructed to give the cavern a real 'room' feeling. The room was filled with antique furniture, priceless art, and crystal. Music wound its way through the air, echoing oddly off the rock looming above them.

Whitney didn't like the room one bit.

Cecelia crossed the room and sat in an elegant chair.

"Please have a seat," she gestured toward an empty chair.

Whitney slowly crossed the room and sat.

"You should feel privileged. I don't normally entertain mortals, but you, Whitney, interest me."

Whitney glared at her.

"Nothing to say?" Cecelia raised her perfect eyebrows. "Hmm, I was told that you tended to be rather vocal. 'Mouthy' was the word, I believe."

Whitney still glared at her.

"Oh well, it doesn't matter." She waved her hand in the air. "You've given me a lot of entertainment. I thought you would just be a hook to dangle in front of Madraeus, but you've shown a lot of fire." Cecelia smiled. "Perhaps you would like to change sides?"

Whitney frowned.

"No? Then what should I do with you?" Cecelia watched her for a moment as if waiting for her to start pleading for her life.

When Whitney wouldn't take the bait, she frowned.

"Personally, I would string you up for dear Madraeus to find, but I have an army to feed, and I don't like wasting food. You will be put to pasture with the rest of the cows."

Whitney's eyes widened.

Cecelia smiled at her reaction. "But before you go, I want to let you know just how badly you'd been played, and not just about your grandmother." Cecelia explained, "I hand-picked you."

Whitney stared at her in disbelief.

"I took your boyfriend, which was remarkably easy by the way. I bought the recording studio, so I could put you out of work. I did it all."

Whitney shook her head. Cecelia couldn't be the cause of all the recent disasters she'd experienced. There was no way she could have manipulated her life so thoroughly.

"Why?" Whitney rasped.

"Oh! She speaks!" Cecelia exclaimed with a grin. When Whitney didn't share her joke, she shrugged. "Why, little one? Because I needed Madraeus distracted. You were just pathetic enough that his misplaced chivalry would assert itself. He'd never admit it, but he likes being the hero." She smiled. "And then to make him think you were betraying him. Although that part didn't really work out, if you had just come with Justin when he had asked, it would have. But you had to be stubborn. Ah well, the betrayal turned out so much better this way. Poor Whitney, just a pathetic little pawn."

All the terror, anger, and angst that she had been through in the last few weeks rushed through Whitney's mind.

*All that, just so that I could be just a pathetic distraction!*

"You bitch!" Whitney hissed, lunging for Cecelia again, only to be caught and pulled, struggling, back into her chair. She winced as the pain in her ribs flared to life again.

"You are just full of spirit, aren't you?" Cecelia grinned, then leaned forward. "Don't worry, you'll have plenty of time to cool your temper." She laughed and gestured to the guard behind Whitney. "Put her with the others."

The man grabbed Whitney's arm and bodily hauled her out of the chair. She struggled uselessly. A tinkle of laughter followed Whitney as she was pulled into the darkness.

# DINNER TIME

Whitney was dragged through the darkness of yet another tunnel. She couldn't see a thing.  All she could do was listen to the sound of her captors' feet kicking through the loose rocks of the shaft floor, but even that was drowned out by the thumping of her terrified heart.

By the time they finally stopped, Whitney was totally terrified and completely confused. She wasn't sure how far they had come or which direction was out. She heard the sound of a key in a door. Then she was thrust forward onto the floor. She heard the door slam behind her, and the key scraped again.

Whitney sat up and looked around, but it was so dark she couldn't make anything out. She put her hands out, trying to get her bearings in the darkness. Then she noticed the smell. Human feces and the worst body odor she had smelled since having worked in that gym, scrubbing the men's locker room, invaded her nose. She put her hand over her nose and mouth to try and keep out the smell. Suddenly, she heard breathing near her. She froze. Hair stood up on the back of her neck.

"Hello?" a voice said from the darkness.

"Who's there?" Whitney whispered.

"My name's Sandra." She heard movement coming toward her, then a hand touched her arm.

Whitney jumped.

"Oops, there you are. Hard to tell in the dark." The hand patted her arm. "You okay?"

Whitney nodded, then felt silly, realizing the woman couldn't see her.

"Yeah," she rasped.

"What's your name?"

"Whitney."

"Well, Whitney, welcome to your new home," Sandra huffed. "Come on, the wall is over here."

Sandra guided her forward slowly. Whitney put her hands out, trying to feel her way. Once they were against the wall, Whitney slid to the floor. Despair washed over her. She felt used up. She had promised herself that she would be stronger like Rami, but apparently, she hadn't gotten smarter. She hated herself for falling into Cecelia's trap so easily.

"So how did you get caught?" Sandra interrupted her thoughts.

"Huh?"

"The monsters, how did they catch you?" she asked again. "I was hiking with a group. Now we are all in here." Whitney heard her gesture in the dark. "Well, most of us are still here anyway."

"Most of you?"

"Yeah," Sandra sighed. "There are only a couple of us still alive. So how did they get you?"

Whitney groaned, "I was an idiot."

When she didn't say any more, Sandra patted her arm again. They were sitting shoulder to shoulder. The cold from the rocks started to seep into her legs and back. She couldn't bring herself to say anymore.

*Keeping secrets must be a learned skill,* she thought.

"It's alright, it doesn't matter," Sandra said with the air of someone who was resigned to her fate. "There's nothing you can do about it now."

Whitney shifted a little, trying to find a comfortable position against the rock wall, only to be poked by the phone in her pocket. Whitney felt a surge of hope.

She dug into her pocket and pulled out her second cell phone. Light from the screen flared. Whitney blinked against the sudden brightness. The screen happily declared that there was no signal available. Instantly, all her hopes crashed.

"Great." She groaned and turned it off again.

"Hey, it was worth a try." Sandra patted her arm again. Whitney pushed to her feet, turned on the phone again, and aimed it around. They were in a cell built into the rock. Three of the walls were made of rock, and the front was a barred door. Through the bars, she could just make out other cells. People-shaped shadows moved in the darkness.

She aimed the phone at her new friend. She gasped. The woman was gaunt and pale. Her cheeks were sunken, and her eyes were huge. Her greasy hair, which might have been blonde at one time, hung limp around her face.

"What happened to you? How long have you been down here?" Whitney whispered in horror.

"I don't know. What day is it?" Sandra asked.

"Um, it's April 19th," Whitney said as she turned off her phone and sank to the floor once more.

"About three months, I guess," Sandra said after a moment.

"Three months?" Whitney whispered, leaning her head back against the rock. Her throat hurt.

"Some of us have been here a lot longer," Sandra said matter-of-factly. "Of course, after a while, it starts to get to you, and you go a little insane. By the way, avoid the corner over there, it's our bathroom."

Whitney opened her phone to see the direction that Sandra pointed and wrinkled her nose again. She shoved her phone back into her pocket. When the light winked out, everything seemed so much worse.

Tears welled up in her eyes. This was going to be the end of her life, dumped in a stinking hole. Her grandmother would never know what had happened to her. She started to cry silently.

A buzzer went off somewhere in the darkness.

"What was that?" Whitney asked as she wiped the tears from her face with the back of her hand.

"Dinner bell," Sandra sighed as she pushed herself to her feet.

"Dinner bell?" Whitney echoed. A commotion sounded from the tunnel. It sounded like a mob was coming. "You mean dinner for us?"

"No. I mean, we're dinner," she answered too calmly.

"What?" Whitney scrambled to her feet.

"We are dinner," Sandra repeated as the noise got closer. "Just a word of advice, it hurts less when you don't fight. Just let them feed, and they will go."

"What!" Whitney croaked.

She couldn't believe what she was hearing. People in nearby cells started to wail and scream. The noise was deafening.

She couldn't see anything. The door clanged open. Suddenly, she was grabbed. Hands gripped her arms painfully.

She struggled and twisted, but they were far stronger than her. She was hauled off her feet. Her body arched in the air. Suddenly, her back slammed against the wall, knocking the air from her chest. Someone's shoulder was shoved into her chest, holding her against the wall. The hands pulled at her clothes. She heard something rip. Pain lanced through her as teeth pierced her forearm and shoulder.

Whitney tried to scream with her tortured voice, but it was no use. Moments of agony passed and faded into numbness. She was faintly aware that she was being lowered to the floor, and then true blackness claimed her.

***

"Whitney!" a soft voice intruded. "Whitney, come on, you need to wake up."

Something prodded her hip. Slowly, she clawed her way back to consciousness and was sorry she did. She was cold, but she lacked the strength to shiver. She felt drained.

"Whitney, if you don't get up and start eating, they'll think you are unfit."

Memories filled in the numbness. She was a prisoner. Her cellmate, Sandra, was speaking to her. She had been food for a couple of vampires.

Whitney groaned.

"Come on, that's it, wake up." Sandra poked her again.

Whitney opened her eyes and was surprised to find she could actually see. Faint light was spilling into their cell from the tunnel. Not far from where she lay on the ground sat a tray of food. Her stomach growled. Sandra leaned over and helped her sit up. Once again, she was waking up in pain.

"Come on, you need to eat and get your strength back." Sandra handed her a bowl of oatmeal. She could barely lift it. She pulled her knees up and balanced the bowl on top. She finally managed to scoop some into her mouth. It was cold. Whitney wrinkled her nose.

"I know," Sandra laughed, "but beggars can't be choosers."

Whitney slowly started to spoon up the globular mush and eat. She gagged and gagged again. It took a lot for her to finally get the tasteless goop down. By the time she was finished, she was exhausted.

"You know it's surprising how well they take care of us, considering," Sandra said between mouthfuls.

Whitney couldn't believe she was so cheerful.

"I mean, it's not the Ritz, but they only feed on us every few days. As far as I can tell, there are more cells in other tunnels." She reached forward and pulled the food tray closer. Whitney noticed that there were bits of bread and some cheese. "They alternate so that we can replenish the blood they take."

Whitney watched her munch on some cheese for a moment and then looked around the cell. She could see into the cells across from them. Their fellow prisoners were either sitting up and eating or passed out on the floor still.

"What did you mean earlier when you said they'd think that I was unfit?" she whispered.

Sandra tore off a piece of bread and handed it to Whitney before she answered.

"They keep us to feed on," she shrugged, "if you are too weak to get up and replenish, you go to the dogs."

"Dogs?" Whitney asked tentatively. She was a little put off by Sandra's cheerful matter-of-fact attitude.

"Yeah, the werewolves."

"What?" Whitney couldn't believe what she thought she heard.

"Yeah, they send them out for the dogs to hunt. Anyone too weak or too wild. After a while, this kind of situation can snap your mind."

Whitney wondered if Sandra's mind had snapped or if she was the most practical person on the planet.

"So, we just sit here and eat for the next few days until they feed again?" she asked, slightly nauseous at the idea.

"Yeah, and we get to have a bath on the day before we're dinner." Sandra smiled like it was the biggest treat in the world. "What happened to your voice? You sound pretty hoarse."

"My ex-boyfriend tried to strangle me," Whitney sighed. She couldn't see any harm in telling Sandra that, at least.

"Ah, I had a boyfriend like that once. I super-glued his hands to his chest while he slept, never tried to hit me again."

Whitney couldn't think of anything to say to that, so she dutifully finished off her cheese and bread.

Sandra handed her a jug of water that was sitting on her other side. Whitney downed a good amount and then laid her head down on her knees. She was so tired.

She had to rest a little, then she would work on escape. There was no way she was going to stay here meekly awaiting her fate. She wondered absently if this was what Unkhabami meant about not being alone when the darkness came; if so, it wasn't very comforting.

# GONE AGAIN!

Pounding loud enough to wake the undead jolted Madraeus awake.

"What!" he roared. The door sprang open, admitting Rami.

"Justin's gone!" Rami scowled.

"What?" Madraeus scrambled out of bed.

Mrs. Myers stood in the doorway, wringing her hands.

Fear clenched his gut. "Where's Whitney?"

"Gone!" Mrs. Myers was close to tears. "I've looked everywhere!"

"She woke me to help look. That is when I found Justin's cell empty." Rami sighed. "Someone let him out."

The possibilities shot through Madraeus' mind. He remembered Whitney's nervousness earlier.

"She wouldn't dare!" Madraeus stared at Rami.

"You think Whitney let him go? She would never do such a thing!" Mrs. Myers shook her head.

Madraeus looked at Mrs. Myers. His heart wanted to deny it too, but circumstances said something different.

"Why would she let him go?" Rami asked. "After all we went through to catch him."

"Check the security tapes."

Rami nodded and disappeared out the door. Mrs. Myers followed him.

Madraeus stalked across the room and grabbed his phone. He dialed Whitney's number. He walked out to the kitchen while he waited for an answer, pulled a bottle from the fridge, and took a drink. He reached her voicemail. He tried three more times but still only got her voicemail.

Madraeus was still buttoning his shirt as he took the stairs two at a time to join Rami in the Security Room. Rami was already scanning a tape in fast-forward.

It showed Philtzer and Thomas carrying Justin and the other vampire in, and then, after a pause, they left. After a few moments, they watched as Madraeus entered the room.

Madraeus drained the bottle he was holding while they waited for the tape to speed through events.

Finally, they saw Madraeus leaving the cell. They continued to watch the tape speed through time, trained on an empty corridor, until suddenly they saw Whitney.

"There." Madraeus leaned forward.

Rami slowed the tape. They watched as Whitney checked the cell doors and then opened Justin's. Madraeus clenched his jaw. They saw her enter Justin's cell. Betrayal cleaved his heart in two.

"Ray-" Mrs. Myers began, but he cut her off.

"Are you so sure of her?" he asked, not taking his eyes off the tape.

"Yes," Mrs. Myers said with absolute conviction.

They kept watching. It certainly looked like Whitney was helping Justin escape, but then it all changed. Whitney bolted only to be grabbed by Justin. They watched as he twisted her arm and held his hand over her mouth. They moved into the elevator. The last moment the camera caught was Whitney being thrown against the elevator wall before the doors closed.

Madraeus straightened, staring at the frozen image of the elevator doors.

"Why would she help him to begin with?" Rami asked.

A couple of weeks ago, he would have said it was because she was an idiot, but now that he knew her better. He knew Whitney always had a reason, sometimes they were stupid reasons, but she always had them.

Madraeus turned and stalked toward the door.

"Madraeus, what are you going to do?" Mrs. Myers called.

He paused at the door. "I'm going to find her," he said over his shoulder.

On the way down the stairs, Madraeus kicked himself again.

*If I hadn't let that damn voice take control again, if I hadn't been so bent on revenge, I would have gotten Cecelia's location from Justin before he had escaped.*

He strode into his office and leaned against his desk, then called Marcus.

"Hello, Ray," Marcus answered.

"Marcus," Madraeus sighed, "where is she?"

"Cut to the point, why don't ya," he laughed.

Madraeus said nothing.

"Which one do you want? Cecelia or Whitney?"

"Pretty sure they are both in the same place." Madraeus rubbed his forehead. "Whitney had her phone when she left, at least we think she did."

"I can hack into the emergency services network and track her like the authorities would."

"You can do that?"

"Use Emergency Services for nefarious reasons? Absolutely." Madraeus could tell Marcus was grinning from ear to ear.

"Lovely."

"Oh, and Madraeus?" Marcus stopped him. "You might want to get some of the witches to scry for Cecelia. I think that she might be using magic to shield her location."

Madraeus huffed, "Magic?"

"Yeah, you got a problem with magic?"

"Let's just say that I've never been a fan."

"Well, whatever your opinion, you need to give it a shot. I've used every available tool and resource I've got and came up with zilch. There has to be something or someone hiding her. She can't just disappear into thin air. Everybody leaves a trail, no matter how small, and she's left nothing."

"Alright, I'll look into it." Madraeus sighed and snapped his phone shut.

"Magic," he snorted. Madraeus shoved away from the desk. He paced the length of his study. Anger at the mess they had gotten into boiled up.

Madraeus grabbed an empty glass that was sitting on his desk and hurled it across the room, shattering it against the wall.

At that moment, Rami walked into the study with a sullen expression. He glanced at the glass pieces that were scattered across the rug, but he didn't say anything.

"You want to find us some magic?"

"What?" Rami cocked his head.

"Marcus thinks that the only way to find Cecelia is to get the witches looking. He says that she must have magic protecting her," Madraeus scoffed.

Rami's eyes widened. "You do not think so?"

"It's one of the most unreliable entities in the universe. It's herbology and intuition at the best of times and parlor tricks and lies at the worst." Madraeus threw his hands in the air. "People use magic as an excuse to ruin other people's lives and for malicious mischief."

"My friend, I know you do not believe, but if she is using magic, then we must be wary." Rami shook his head. "Bami warned us that she was digging up the old sources, and many of those are powerful in magic."

Madraeus still wanted to shrug off the idea that magic was the answer, but Rami was right: Unkhabami had warned them.

He paced to the end of the room and back, then leaned on his desk. He had the horrible feeling that this was just the beginning of a really bad day.

"Very well," he said over his shoulder. "Do what you need to. I'm going to talk to our guest upstairs."

# PINS AND GRANNIES

Madraeus wiped the blood from his hands as he descended the stairs. It had been a full week since Whitney's disappearance, and he was beyond frustrated.

His captive was still uncooperative. He had learned his name was Jarvis, but that was all. He would only say they were chasing the wrong rabbit and asking the wrong questions. They had no idea what it meant.

Madraeus had been very thorough in his methods of persuasion, but to no avail. Either Cecelia had groomed Jarvis well to be evasive even under torture, or she had taken precautions to prevent him from speaking. Madraeus did not doubt that she had expected either this vampire or the werewolf, or both, to be caught. They were merely pawns that she was playing with. Cecelia had always been an expert in picking her expendable henchmen.

Marcus hadn't had any luck in locating Whitney's phone signal either. The signal kept showing near Leadville, Breckenridge, and I-70. The wolves had been out searching for any clues in those areas but had come up empty-handed so far. There was only so much ground they could cover per day.

Rami had pulled in a coven of witches to find Cecelia. He had set them up in the conference room and supplied them with whatever they had asked for. Madraeus thought it looked like a voodoo carnival. It didn't really surprise him that they had been at it for days, and they couldn't find anything.

He threw the blood-soaked towel into the washing machine a little harder than necessary as he passed.

Madraeus walked into his study to find that most of the room had been packed into crates for the move, but there were still several piles of books and papers on his desk. He sighed and continued on into Rami's office.

The boxes from the Dreaded Filing Project that Whitney and Rami had sorted were still sitting stacked against the wall.

"Whitney was on to something." Rami gestured to the wall.

Madraeus glanced at the world map Rami had tacked up. It was covered in little red pins.

"When she was working on her Dreaded Filing Project, sorting it into regions and divisions, there were spikes in shipments to certain areas and then sudden drops or they stop altogether like a large group on the move."

"Right, she said that."

"I've looked through each file and added a red pin to the map for each invoice. Then made a note for each pin's corresponding date." He held up the pages filled with dates and locations. "These are the oldest down around this way." He traced the trail of red pins across South America and up through Mexico to North America. "And here is the latest." He pointed to Denver.

"We could have been tracking her all along," Madraeus growled.

"Yes, I'm sorry, Ray, I should have noticed." Rami shook his head.

"No, there was no way to know." Madraeus frowned at the map. "What about those?" He pointed to the individual pins scattered across the map.

"I don't know." Rami shook his head.

"Alright, keep looking. I'm going to make a pass through Leadville tonight and see if I can find anything." Madraeus rubbed his forehead as he walked back into his office. "You might cross-reference your missing person's list with those pin locations; maybe they'll correlate."

"Yes, I—" Rami started but stopped when he heard Philtzer shouting in the hallway.

"You can't go in there!" Philtzer yelled again.

"You just try and stop me," challenged an unfamiliar woman's voice.

Madraeus frowned. Philtzer was not much of a front desk guard if he just let some random mortal woman past him.

*Whitney never let anyone through, even when they were supposed to be here*, he thought moodily.

A moment later, a short woman with graying hair and a cane appeared in the doorway. Philtzer was right behind her.

"I'm sorry, Boss, I couldn't stop her."

"Are you Mr. Ravilla?" she asked.

"Yes."

She looked him up and down, then glanced at Rami, her eyes momentarily widening at his size, but then she returned her gaze to Madraeus.

"Good. Where is my granddaughter?" She thumped her cane against the floor.

Madraeus sized up the woman who had bullied her way past Philtzer. She was short and square, but there was nothing about her that spoke of laziness. He suspected that most of her girth came from her reliance on that cane.

There was a resemblance to Whitney in the eyes, both in color and determination. He had seen that look before in Whitney's eyes, and he hadn't been successful against it there either. This is where Whitney got it. No wonder she had gotten past Philtzer so easily.

"Please, Mrs. Martindale, come in." He gestured to the chairs near the chess table.

Carefully, she stepped over and took a seat. Rami cocked an eyebrow at him from across the room as Madraeus slid easily into the chair opposite her.

"I'm glad you know who I am. Now I would like to know where my granddaughter is, and I don't want any of this 'she's working on something important' run around that I have been getting from your man in the front office."

Madraeus regarded her for a moment. "I'm sure that he wasn't intentionally giving you the runaround."

"Don't you start with me! I know when I'm being snowed. There is something going on here that you don't want anyone to know about. I haven't seen or heard from Whitney since the day before that funeral. She gives me the excuse that she is instrumental in your business dealings, but she ends up in the police department. How will that help your business? And another thing, I don't appreciate your people hanging out around my house watching me. It's creepy." Elizabeth Martindale tapped her cane on the floor and glared at Madraeus.

He couldn't help it, he smiled.

His smile made her scowl. "This isn't a game. I haven't gone to the police yet, but I will if I don't get Whitney and the truth right now."

Madraeus thought for a moment. If Whitney could handle the truth, maybe this woman could too. They seemed to be cut from the same cloth. However, if she didn't, they would have a terrified mortal on their hands. He hadn't quite decided yet whether to divulge the truth to her or not when another commotion in the hall caught his attention.

# UNEXPECTED VISITOR

"Wait a minute!" Philtzer yelled a second before Unkhabami strode into the study.

"I told you to keep her by your side! Now look at the disaster you have brought upon us all!" she raged.

Philtzer stood behind her. He threw up his arms in defeat, then turned and left.

Unkhabami continued to rant at Madraeus, lapsing into her native language most of the time.

Rami's jaw dropped as he listened to her. He understood her dialect. Madraeus did not. But from the look on the giant's face, Madraeus was certain that none of it was complimentary.

He stole a glance at Mrs. Martindale. She was watching the woman with a mystified expression. He didn't blame her. Unkhabami was something to behold when she was angry. He sighed. He had better put a stop to this scene before it got worse.

"Unkhabami!" Madraeus raised his voice as he stood. The priestess stopped abruptly and stared at him. "We have company." He gestured toward Mrs. Martindale.

Unkhabami's eyes widened for a moment, then she leaned forward and stared into the older lady's eyes. Her nostrils flared.

"You are related to Whitney Martindale," she pronounced and turned to Madraeus. "You had better tell her, then we can get down to business."

He glanced at Mrs. Martindale.

"Yes, please tell me." Mrs. Martindale turned a triumphant eye on Madraeus.

If she was concerned that Unkhabami could tell who she was with just a look, she didn't show it. Madraeus sat and steepled his fingers, watching Whitney's grandmother for a long time. She didn't flinch or squirm like most people did when he went quiet. She merely sat and waited, returning his regard expectantly. She was indeed a unique lady.

"Mrs. Martindale, what I am about to tell you is in the strictest confidence." She nodded when he paused. "It is also going to be hard for you to believe. I would ask that you let me finish before reacting. I can prove what I say."

"Alright." The older lady nodded again.

Madraeus took a deep breath and then blew it out again slowly.

"Mrs. Martindale, your granddaughter has been kidnapped by a very dangerous vampire." He watched for a reaction to his pronouncement, but she didn't even blink. Madraeus glanced at Rami.

"Did you hear what I said?" he asked, puzzled by her lack of reaction.

"Yes, I'm waiting for you to get past your childish games and tell me the truth."

Madraeus gave a short laugh of disbelief. "Madame, I assure you this is no childish prank. You are sitting in a room with two vampires and one were-cat right now. Your granddaughter was kidnapped by a vampire."

Mrs. Martindale frowned at Madraeus with growing impatience. "This is not a joke, sir. Where is my granddaughter?"

"Oh, for goodness' sake, woman!" Unkhabami exclaimed.

She shook slightly like a dog shedding water and shifted into a jaguar.

Mrs. Martindale surged out of her chair, grasping her cane to her chest. She stared wide-eyed at the giant cat.

Unkhabami hissed at her once and then shifted back into human form. "Now, you believe. Let us get down to business."

Mrs. Martindale slowly sank back down onto the chair. Madraeus watched her closely for signs of a heart attack or fainting, but she only sat very still. Finally, she turned her wide eyes to Madraeus.

"You have some convincing evidence." She glanced warily at Unkhabami. "You say Whitney was kidnapped? What are you doing to get her back?"

"Finally!" Unkhabami gave an impatient gesture.

"We are using all available resources to find her, but so far no luck." Madraeus hated to admit his failure.

"I warned you not to let her out of your sight. It was very important to keep her close." Unkhabami reprimanded him. "You did not listen."

"Why? Did you know that this was going to happen?" Mrs. Martindale demanded.

"I have seen many possible futures. This one could have been avoided." She glared at Madraeus.

"Futures?" Whitney's grandmother looked to Madraeus for an explanation.

"Unkhabami is what you would consider an oracle of sorts."

"Bami, we did our best to keep her close, but she has a mind of her own," Rami rumbled.

"Whitney always does," Mrs. Martindale huffed and tapped her cane again.

Madraeus almost smiled. The lady was taking this all in stride.

"This will bring war," Unkhabami warned.

"Are you saying that my little girl is going to start a war?" Mrs. Martindale objected.

"No, the war has been going on for years without battles," Unkhabami waved her hand. "Whitney is the spark. Her actions will ignite a chain reaction that will destroy all that we know."

"Unkhabami, I think that is an exaggeration," Madraeus sighed. He was used to the doomsayer routine, but he didn't think it necessary to frighten Mrs. Martindale.

"You should have listened to me years ago when I told you to kill her." Unkhabami glared at Madraeus.

"What!" Mrs. Martindale surged out of her chair again.

"Not Whitney, Madame, Cecelia." Rami soothed as he crossed the room.

"Who's Cecelia?"

"We do not have time for any of this!" Unkhabami grumbled. "If you had listened to me-" she started to rant again.

"Unkhabami!" Madraeus surged out of his chair, making Mrs. Martindale jump. "I have the utmost respect for you, but if you insist on blaming me, then nothing will be accomplished. I suggest you turn your talents toward finding Ms. Martindale instead of ranting at me!"

Unkhabami hissed at him, baring her fangs. Madraeus stared her down. He seemed to grow in size without actually moving. Mrs. Martindale stared wide-eyed at the two of them. After a long moment, the priestess backed down.

"Very well," she muttered. "What do you require of me?"

"Cecelia's location eludes us." He glanced at Rami. "Some think she is shielded by magic."

Unkhabami's eyes narrowed at his admission.

"We have a coven in the conference room searching, but there has been no luck. If you have something to add to the mix, please do so."

"Coven?" He heard Mrs. Martindale whisper.

"I cannot use my power to search. Mine is a healing magic." She glanced at Rami. "There is nothing I can add to your mix."

"Oh, but there is," he smiled as inspiration struck. The more he thought about it, the better it sounded.

"You have other power." Madraeus nodded, crossing his arms with a look of devious determination.

"You do not even believe in magic," she accused.

"I don't need to. You believe."

Unkhabami blinked at him apprehensively.

"I know that most of your visions are not based on facts. You see what will happen if someone carries out their intentions. I am asking you to see the result of my intentions."

"That kind of prophesying is like trying to grab a cloud, the slightest shift in your thoughts, and that future wisps away. There are too many possible outcomes to every action," she cautioned.

"I will not change my intentions." Madraeus gave a minuscule shake of his head. "If you see where I am when I find her, then we will work backward from there to find her location."

"The amount of power to focus on one individual intention is enormous. I cannot do it alone." She waved her hand dismissively.

"The coven?"

Unkhabami frowned at him, thinking. "It will take time to get ready."

"Fine."

"Be it on your head if you see what you do not want to know," she hissed before turning to leave.

Madraeus watched her go, then turned to Mrs. Martindale. She was staring up at him curiously. The look was so reminiscent of Whitney that a pang went through his chest. He avoided her eyes as he reseated himself.

"Perhaps you should start at the beginning, Mr. Ravilla," she prodded.

# DEAD ENDS AND MAGIC

*DEAD ENDS. THAT'S ALL there seems to be anymore,* Madraeus thought.

Thomas and Hamilton had tried to find out about the attack that Detective Sanders had mentioned. Unfortunately, one victim had disappeared and the other had died.

They couldn't find Justin.

They couldn't find Whitney.

They couldn't find Cecelia.

No one knew anything about missing people.

Madraeus growled in frustration.

He hoped that Unkhabami was ready for her ritual. He was tired of searching haphazardly for needles in the Rocky Mountain haystack.

He didn't put much stock in regular magic, but prophesying was something that he had come to believe in, sort of. It was just as shifty and unreliable, but it had saved him in the past. It was a long shot, but at this point, long shots were all that was left.

Madraeus headed for the kitchen. It was just past dawn. He needed food, then off to bed for a couple of hours of rest. He needed sleep. It had been days since he had slept more than a couple of hours. He was wearing down, and it could prove fatal.

He opened the fridge door and sighed. Elizabeth Martindale had moved the food from Whitney's apartment into his kitchen. He had to shift things around just to reach the bottles of blood.

He had insisted that Mrs. Martindale move in until Whitney returned. It had been easy enough to convince her that it was wasting manpower to have someone guarding her house when they could be out looking for Whitney. The security was better, and if she stayed in an extra room here, he could keep an eye on her.

*Not that it ever worked on Whitney,* he snorted.

They were a lot alike -these two Martindale women. There was definitely a family resemblance in stubbornness. Unfortunately, having Whitney's grandmother around was a constant reminder of Whitney's absence. He missed her terribly. It was like there was a hole in his world. He ached to have her back, no matter how annoying she was.

Madraeus drained the bottle and left it on the counter. As he walked to his room, he tried to convince himself that he wouldn't have to wait much longer. He told himself that after the ritual, he would have a direction.

He turned on the gas fireplace in his bedroom, then slumped backward onto the pillows and stared at the flames. He would find her. He had to. There didn't seem to be much point in existing without her.

Madraeus let his eyes drift closed. Someone pounded on his door. His eyes popped open again. Madraeus sighed and hauled himself out of bed. He moved to open the door, dragging his feet all the way.

"Good afternoon, Ray," Rami greeted him.

"What time is it?" he blinked.

"3:23," Rami said as he glanced at his watch.

"What?"

"I woke you because Bami is ready for her ritual," Rami explained.

"Oh," optimism flooded through him, "I'll be right there." He turned back to his room.

"Ray, are you sure about this?" Rami asked. "There are some things that you can't unsee."

Madraeus looked back at his friend. "If there is any chance to find Whitney, it doesn't matter what I see."

Rami nodded sadly. "Just remember that things are not set. They can change."

Madraeus laid a hand on the giant's shoulder. "My friend, we have been through much in these centuries, and I know that you are concerned but," Madraeus hesitated to admit his feelings even to Rami, "I have to find her."

Rami clapped his friend on the shoulder and nodded. "I will wait for you in the conference room."

Madraeus got dressed quickly and strode to the conference room. He didn't relish the idea of going through a magic ritual. He had always taken whatever measures necessary to keep the taint of magic from his life.

Madraeus stepped into the conference room and groaned. Rami was right, some things couldn't be unseen.

It had been a voodoo carnival in here before, but it was worse now. Unkhabami had transformed it into one of her primeval huts from the Congo.

What had once been an elegant room of carved wood paneling, plush carpets, and state-of-the-art communication technology was now a murky cave filled with a brown, pungent haze that glowed orange from too many candles.

The double-wide oak conference table had been shoved against the wall. It was now covered with bowls and jars and bottles containing indiscriminate ingredients. There were multicolored candles and smoking bits of herbs scattered around the room. Through the brown cloud, Madraeus could see they had decorated the walls with runes and symbols.

"All we need now are some bugs and snakes," he muttered.

Then he caught sight of the thick mass of dirt in the middle of his conference room's luxurious carpet. It was about four inches thick and spread out in a large circle.

He was going to kill Unkhabami. They were never going to get this room clean again.

Out of the shadows, Rami approached, skirting the pile of dirt. Whitney's grandmother trailed behind him with an uncertain expression on her face. Madraeus gestured toward the dirt menacingly.

"I know, I know," Rami held up his hands, "but it is necessary."

"Necessary?"

"Let me explain." Unkhabami emerged from the haze.

Madraeus crossed his arms and waited.

"This ritual needs to be done grounded on the Earth, but since you cannot leave until sunset, and we are pressed for time, I have brought the Earth to you."

Madraeus refrained from snorting while she continued her explanation. Unkhabami gestured to the center of the dirt where a small round table stood. Its legs were partially buried in the dirt. In front of it stood three bowls. The large bowl in the center held water, but the other two were smaller, and he couldn't see what was in them.

"You will sit on the small table. You are to be grounded but also suspended. The small bowl on the right holds some of Whitney's hair."

Madraeus glanced sharply at the priestess.

"It's from her hairbrush," Rami soothed.

"The bowl on the left will have some of your blood and some of mine," she explained.

Madraeus narrowed his eyes suspiciously.

"It is to bond you to the vision. You will be able to see all that I see then."

Unkhabami leaned closer. "There is danger in this ritual. You will see all possible futures. It may cause you some," she paused to consider her word choice, "disorientation and pain."

"That's fine." Madraeus waved away her warning.

"There is also a possibility that you will be forever linked to Whitney Martindale."

"In what way?" he asked. He could feel her grandmother's eyes boring into his back.

"You will be magically bonded to her futures for a short time. This magic is not easy to dismiss. It is," she searched for the right word again, "sticky. It is often hard to shed once you have donned it. The experience may not end with the ritual. It is possible that you will always be connected to her on a temporal level."

"What does that mean?" Mrs. Martindale asked.

"There may be residual after-effects. It will be like experiencing a momentary hallucination of Whitney's futures. They may come in overwhelming flashes, or you may experience just a vague feeling," Unkhabami explained.

"Will any of this affect Whitney?" Elizabeth Martindale asked fearfully.

"I do not know." Unkhabami shrugged. "I have never tried this with a vampire before."

Madraeus looked at Elizabeth Martindale. He raised his eyebrows, letting her know that he was waiting for her permission. She looked terrified, but after a moment she nodded.

"Let's get started," Madraeus growled.

"Very well." Unkhabami shrugged as if she had done her duty to warn him and no longer felt responsible. She gestured for the members of the coven to come forward and take their places.

Madraeus glanced at Mrs. Martindale. She looked like she would rather be anywhere but here.

"You don't have to be here," he offered. She watched him for a moment as if trying to decide if he was trying to get rid of her, then shook her head.

"No, if this is the only way to find Whitney, then I'll stay," she said as they stepped back to let some of the witches by.

"It's not the only way, but we're running out of options," Madraeus sighed. "The longer she is gone, the more dangerous it becomes for her."

"Do you care for my granddaughter?" she asked suddenly. He thought for a moment. It would be better for him to say no, but he couldn't bring himself to lie to this woman.

He glanced around, then leaned closer and whispered in her ear, "More than is safe, for either of us."

He walked to the middle of the dirt circle and stepped up onto the table. He lowered himself down and sat cross-legged in the middle.

Rami ushered Mrs. Martindale to the edge of the room near the door where the conference room chairs had been shoved aside. As they sat down, Elizabeth grabbed Rami's hand. He squeezed it in reassurance. Then they turned their attention to the rite.

Madraeus watched Unkhabami fold her long limbs into a position that mirrored his own. Then she produced a knife and held out her hand. He hesitated no more than a moment before placing his hand in hers. She sliced down the length of his index finger and turned his hand over above the empty bowl on the left.

Madraeus looked around one last time. There were colored candles placed at the four cardinal points around him, and there were symbols that he hadn't noticed before drawn in the dirt around the table. The coven of thirteen witches was now standing in a ring around the dirt mound. They linked their hands with fingers intertwined and held them at shoulder height.

Unkhabami brought his attention back to her as she sliced her own finger and mixed her blood with his in the little bowl.

"Remember, you must not alter your intentions of finding her. You must stay focused no matter what you see."

He nodded and took a deep breath, letting it out slowly.

"Close your eyes. Shed your skepticism. You must concentrate on Whitney and then just watch with your mind's eye." Her voice was becoming hypnotic.

Madraeus closed his eyes. He could hear the witches droning around him, but he couldn't tell what they were saying.

"Concentrate on Whitney," Unkhabami reminded him.

Madraeus let the rhythm of the voices lull him into a kind of trance. He focused all of his thoughts, his very being, on Whitney.

*My name is Madraeus Nicoteles Peltrasius Ravilla,* he forced his brain to think. *I will find Whitney Martindale.*

Madraeus gave no notice of the rumble that filled the room from the thirteen women as they swayed back and forth.

*No.* The hissing voice distracted him for a moment.

He shook his head. *My name is Madraeus Nicoteles Peltrasius Ravilla. I will find Whitney Martindale. I will hold her in my arms. I will tell her that I love her.*

Suddenly, his mind was swarming with images. Flashes of Whitney battered him. Each flash was only a few seconds long, and they overlapped each other, making a jumble of images.

He saw her laughing.

He saw her crying.

He saw her fighting for her life.

His heart beat faster.

She was different ages.

She was with children.

She was dying.

He saw her death in a hundred different ways. It tore his heart every time he saw her die.

The snapshots of her possible lives and deaths came faster and faster. He cried out.

*NO!*

A flash of a massive snake burst across his vision. He felt a stabbing in his brain.

He screamed.

Suddenly, the lights flared, not just the candlelight, but the electric lights that had been turned off at the request of the witches flashed on too.

Then it stopped. Everything was silent.

Madraeus collapsed into oblivion.

# WHAT A HEADACHE

Whitney was making progress, at least, she told herself she was. She had been scratching tiny bits of dirt away from the hinge holding her cell door with a sharp rock.

She had been at it for days, but in reality, she hadn't even worn a stripe of the dirt away. She kicked the door near the hinge in frustration.

It didn't move.

She kicked it again and again, then rattled the bars with all her strength, but nothing moved. After a few more kicks, she flopped down on the ground, panting.

A heaviness pressed down on her, making her head throb. Living in the constant near-darkness was starting to grate on Whitney's nerves. She constantly saw shadows in the darkness, although no doubt it was just her eyes trying to find something to see. She was surrounded by eerie sounds and rank smells. She hated the smell of her own body, but everywhere she turned, there it was, and that wasn't the worst of it.

The worst part was feeding time. It was painful and terrifying. Whitney hadn't yet been able to submit docilely to the feedings. Sandra stood passively and let them feed, but she couldn't. She fought them every step of the way. Fighting made it hurt more, but she couldn't just lie there and take it.

Her feelings of failure and stupidity overwhelmed her, and she finally let her tears fall. Whitney kicked herself hourly for believing that Cecelia had had her grandmother.

*Grammy. She must be freaking out with worry right now,* Whitney thought.

She wondered if anyone was looking for her. She wondered if her grandmother had gone to the police. *That would be bad.*

Then another thought occurred to her: *What if Grammy went to Madraeus? That would be worse!*

Whitney pulled her knees up and hugged them. *I'm single-handedly ruining everyone's life!*

She felt guilty for scaring her grandmother and for Lisa's death. She also felt responsible for Justin's death. It may not have been her fault, but she still felt guilty.

She sniffled and rubbed at her wet cheeks.

"Don't get discouraged, Whitney," Sandra offered from behind her.

Guilt didn't make her stay in Casa de Vamp any easier, but it kept her going. She was determined to make up for her mistakes.

"You are getting farther than I ever did. At least you have a plan. I just sat here."

"If I had fought more to start with, I wouldn't be in this situation," Whitney grumbled.

She rattled the door once more with her foot and then sat down to resume working on the hinge.

Whitney didn't really know where she planned to go if the hinge finally gave out, but she stayed vigilant. She had watched for tunnels as they were herded to the lake and back for their bath. There were several along the way, but she had no idea where they led. For all she knew, they could be dead ends.

She knew that Madraeus would still be looking for Cecelia even if he wasn't looking for her. It was only a matter of time. If she could get out and lead them back here, maybe she could make up for her most recent stupidity.

Suddenly, the torches up the passageway flared. Whitney screamed and fell backward. She held her head and curled into a ball. Sandra rushed to her side.

"Whitney?"

After a moment, Whitney pushed up off the floor. She braced her hands on her knees and groaned.

"Are you alright?" Sandra asked, helping her stand.

"I... I guess," Whitney staggered to the wall and leaned on it for support. "What the hell was that?"

"What happened? Are you sick?" Sandra followed her and felt her forehead.

"I don't know," Whitney groaned as the remnants of the worst headache she'd ever had faded. "I was just kneeling there, and then it was like a semi ran over my head."

Her vision wobbled. She slid to the floor, resting her head on her knees.

"Oh man," she groaned.

As she fought a wave of nausea, she became aware of the growing noise around her. Excited voices were coming from the cells around them. Whitney looked around in the dim light.

"What's going on?" she asked.

Sandra said as she pressed her face against the bars, trying to see down the tunnel in either direction.

"Someone is coming!" Sandra whispered and hurried to the back wall of the cell.

Whitney looked up from her knees to find Cecelia standing outside her cell door. She was looking up and down the tunnel as if searching for something; then a man stepped up to Cecelia and whispered in her ear. She turned and looked at Whitney with a suspicious look on her face. They watched each other for a moment, then Cecelia stepped up to the door.

"What were you doing?" she demanded.

Whitney let her hands flop to the floor and made an exaggerated show of thinking.

"Well, let's see, I just got back from the spa, and I was thinking about going to a movie later." Whitney turned to Sandra. "Did you wanna come? I hear there is a great new vampire film called *They Suck Rotten Tomatoes*."

"That sounds lovely!" Sandra nodded. "I heard there's a double feature. They're also showing *When Harry Staked Sally*."

"Nice!" Whitney grinned at Sandra.

"Very funny," Cecelia growled. "What were you really doing?"

"Oh, you're right, I shouldn't tell stories like that, I was actually climbing Mount Everest." Whitney smiled despite the fact that her vision was still wobbling.

"I thought we were riding unicorns?" Sandra cocked her head to one side.

"That's how we got to Mount Everest, remember?"

Cecelia sneered at her, "Laugh all you want. I can find worse ways for you to spend your time here." She jerked her head toward one of the guards down the tunnel. He came running at her summons.

"Watch this one, constantly. I want to know if she is up to something," she murmured, then disappeared down the tunnel into the darkness, leaving the guard staring into Whitney and Sandra's cell.

"That was fun." Sandra crossed her ankles and closed her eyes.

Whitney glanced at Sandra. They would no longer be able to chip away at their hinge. All hope of escape was now lost.

# POINT ME IN A DIRECTION

Madraeus groaned. He had forgotten how much pain a body could live through. His head ached and his body felt drained, but most of all, he felt sick inside. It was the same hollow, self-hating nausea that he had felt when he had killed his first human for blood.

A Hell like none he could have dreamed up was lodged in his brain. His overloaded mind scrambled to categorize the images he had seen. Already, he was having a hard time differentiating between real memory and future visions.

He yearned for the peace of death. He had seen so many futures all related to Whitney. Most of them he didn't want to live to see again. Seeing her die over and over had almost killed him. Seeing the futures where she was happy with a husband and children had ripped his heart to shreds. He didn't want to remember what he had seen. He didn't want to know which would be the true future. He groaned again and rolled over, burying his face in the pillow.

From far away, he heard a soft voice whisper, "Do you think he will be okay?"

"I hope so," Rami whispered back.

"He is dealing with what he did not want to see," Unkhabami murmured from the other side of the room.

"Does this happen to you when you are... seeing things?" Elizabeth Martindale asked quietly.

"A little, but I was born to this. My mind naturally sifts through the visions. I do not tag along on someone else's power," Unkhabami said.

"So, if you do this so well, did you see anything to help find my Whitney?" Elizabeth asked.

"I believe so, but without Madraeus," Unkhabami shrugged, "none of it will come to be. It was his intentions that we searched on. If he is not there to fulfill what we saw, then it is all just a mist that floats away. We must wait for him to follow through with his intentions."

Madraeus cringed inwardly and tried to crawl back into the darkness in his head. He didn't want to be alive or aware. He didn't want to be the only one who could make a move. He had no idea which future to choose. He kept second-guessing himself. The hissing voice intermingled with the images telling him he was making the wrong decision.

He groaned again and shied away from opening his eyes. That would only start him on whatever course he was going to take, which would only lead them to any number of disasters.

"I'm going to make some coffee," Elizabeth exhaled irritably.

He heard a door open and shut, and then the room fell silent again. There was expectancy in the silence. He moaned and curled up in a ball, trying to flee the physical pain of existing.

"Say something to him," Rami snapped at Bami. "You know that he needs guidance, some kind of reassurance."

"He was warned." She seemed unconcerned.

"Bami, it does not become you to be spiteful." Silence fell again. After a moment, Madraeus heard movement. Instinct warned him that someone was moving toward him, but he couldn't bring himself to react.

"You must concentrate," Unkhabami said, sitting down beside him on the bed. "The feelings of being overwhelmed will fade. You must understand that the futures that you and I have seen are only possibilities. Some of them may never come true."

Madraeus groaned again.

"You must pull yourself together and step forward," Unkhabami hissed. "Her futures will happen whether you sit here moaning in self-pity or not. It is up to you to act on your intentions." She leaned forward and breathed next to his ear, "You must hold Whitney Martindale in your arms and tell her that you love her."

Unkhabami's words seemed to tangle around his consciousness. They pulled and tugged until he stood in a darkened room. His back was against steel bars set into a rock opening. Whitney sat against the wall in front of him. Her face was drawn and pale, and her body abused. She looked around wildly, then looked up at him.

*She can't be seeing me.*

He glanced away and saw a tunnel outside the bars. There was a man standing in the tunnel watching them.

Madraeus' eyes opened with a gasp.

Rami rushed to his side. "Ray? Are you alright?"

Madraeus stared sightlessly at the ceiling for a moment before speaking.

"I think she is in a cave."

"A cave?" Rami looked to Unkhabami in confusion. She returned his gaze without expression.

"There were tunnels in the rock."

"Perhaps a mine shaft? There are plenty of those in the mountains."

"What time is it?" Madraeus asked as he tried to sit up. Rami put a hand behind his shoulders to help.

"Nearing seven," Rami replied.

"I'm going." Madraeus pushed off the bed and staggered to his feet.

"Going where? It is near seven in the morning." Rami grabbed Madraeus' arm to steady him. "Besides, you can barely stand."

"I need a list of the mines near where Marcus found her phone signal. Tell everyone to search." Madraeus sounded hoarse.

"Are you sure you are capable?" Rami searched his friend's face.

"What choice have I got?" he replied. Madraeus turned to Unkhabami but found he had nothing he could say.

She merely regarded him down the length of her nose. He looked away and walked unsteadily out of the room.

Mrs. Martindale was standing in the kitchen, watching him approach. After seeing what the future held for Whitney, he couldn't bring himself to meet her eyes. He felt ashamed.

He moved past her toward the refrigerator, all the while feeling her gaze. He poured himself a drink. He managed to get a couple of swallows down before becoming too conscious of Mrs. Martindale watching him. He couldn't finish the glass.

"I'm leaving to find her as soon as it is dark." He looked toward her without meeting her eyes. "I won't be coming back until I have her."

"I'll be waiting."

Madraeus nodded. She didn't say another word as he crossed the room and left through his study.

***

Light from the waning moon filtered through the pine trees, casting jagged shadows. The search teams had randomly divided up the list of mines along the length of Interstate 70. Philtzer and Madraeus pulled off the road and checked the map again.

"The mine should be up that way." Madraeus pointed out the driver's side window. "We'll walk. If they're there, we don't want to tip our hand."

"You know chasing ski bunnies is a lot more fun," Philtzer complained as he shed his clothes and tossed them into the car before changing into wolf form.

Madraeus barely noticed. His mind was still jumbled, and nausea still plagued him.

*How did the Weavers live with the curse of prophesying?*

It made being the evil undead a picnic. His limbs felt heavy, but the fresh, chilly air was helping a little. Mentally, he chastised himself for not feeding more before he left. He had never considered himself to be a coward until he had faced Mrs. Martindale's expectant gaze.

The road switched back and continued to climb. Philtzer zigzagged back and forth across the road with his nose to the ground. There wasn't much of a breeze tonight, so they hadn't caught many scents on the wind. They rounded another bend in the road, and Madraeus almost tripped over Philtzer. He had been so lost in thought that he didn't even notice that Philtzer had stopped in front of him.

The wolf glanced back at him, laying his ears flat against his head, then pricked his ears forward again towards the trees off the edge of the road. Madraeus watched the hackles rise on Philtzer's back, but he didn't growl. He shook his head and scanned the trees. If he didn't pull his thoughts together, he was going to get them killed.

Philtzer slowly stepped forward into the ditch with his head low. He reached out with all his senses, trying to detect what Philtzer was after but couldn't catch it. Werewolves had a much better sense of smell than vampires.

Madraeus followed, stepping silently. Philtzer led them through the trees up the slope. Several times, the wolf froze and then slowly continued forward. Finally, Philtzer sank down into a low shrub at the edge of a clearing. He glanced up as Madraeus appeared silently beside him.

About a hundred yards away, several wolves patrolled a wide open space sloping up to an old shaft house. It stood tall and black against the night sky. Faint light glowed from the open door of the lower building. The wolves wove in and out of the parked cars sitting out front. Madraeus could hear quiet words here and there in the stillness.

This was it. This was Cecelia's new lair. He signaled Philtzer to begin retreating. As much as he would like to charge in there right now, they had to get back and bring reinforcements. Cecelia was no fool, she would be well-guarded. Inch by silent inch, they faded back from the tree line.

Awareness prickled the back of his neck. They were no longer alone.

A low growl came from the shadows. Philtzer spun toward the trees on the left as a wolf launched out of the darkness and landed on Madraeus' chest. He scrambled to get a hold on the wolf, but his foe twisted and turned. Philtzer surged in with teeth bared.

From the woods behind them, they heard a warning howl. They would be outnumbered in moments.

They lost precious seconds in a three-way wrestling match. Just as Philtzer ripped the throat out of the sentry, the woods were flooded with more wolves.

"Run!" Madraeus shouted to Philtzer as he knocked aside an attacking wolf. Another one lunged at his leg, pushing him sideways.

Madraeus twisted away from the wolf only to be tackled by another one.

Philtzer snarled and rolled, fighting off his own set of attackers.

"Go!" Madraeus roared. Madraeus threw a wolf against a tree and smashed another in the jaw.

Philtzer howled and broke for the road. He dodged trees and leaped over rocks. The sounds of the fight were receding, but he could hear several of the wolves crashing through the trees behind him.

# GLOATING AND MORE GLOATING

MADRAEUS STAYED CROUCHED AND ready. The wolves stopped attacking and circled him. Blood oozed down his legs and arms from lucky bites. Several wolf bodies lay at his feet.

Suddenly, they came at him all at once. He couldn't stand against the force of bodies. He hit the ground hard. Madraeus looked up to find that some of them had changed into human form.

They grabbed his arms and twisted him around. Someone must have gone for rope because he felt his wrists being tied.

Madraeus stopped fighting. He knew that he had no chance of winning against these odds. His strength was depleted from the ritual, and he was not up to fighting condition from lack of blood. Not feeding may have been the last mistake of his life.

The wolves were taking no chances. They dragged him up the slope to the shaft house, clamped iron cuffs on his ankles, shackled his wrists behind his back, and then chained the two together. A tiny part of him was flattered that they thought him such a threat, but the rest of him was angry.

They took him down into the mine. Once at the bottom, he was confronted by a gathering of Cecelia's army. It surprised him how many there were.

*Where had they all come from?*

Some he knew. Rage at their betrayal boiled in Madraeus' chest. However, amongst the traitors, there were many more that he didn't know.

The guards hauled him past the crowd, down a darkened tunnel, and into a garish, glowing room. Cecelia lounged in a chair at the far end. She smiled when she saw him.

The man holding his arm shoved him from behind. Madraeus had to shuffle forward to keep from falling. His chains rattled in the stillness as he pulled himself up to his full height to face Cecelia.

She stood and sauntered forward, making a slow circle around him.

"You are bleeding on my carpet," she hummed playfully as she reached out and poked a finger into the gash on his shoulder.

Madraeus clenched his teeth.

"I'm surprised that you came yourself. I was beginning to think that you had lost your nerve. But when I saw what you had done to Justin, I knew that you hadn't been tamed yet." She licked his blood off her finger. "Yummy."

Madraeus just waited.

"I can't even tell you how well this has all worked out." She circled him again. "I knew that chasing after Justin would distract you, but this little drama has had no end of entertainment."

"Distract me?" Madraeus baited, but she only smiled at him.

From behind him, he heard scuffling and a familiar voice protesting and complaining, "Let go of me, you big cow!"

He shifted to the side in time to see a man and a woman pulling a squirming Whitney along between them into the room.

The guards stood her across from Madraeus. She ripped her arm out of the woman's grasp and kicked for her shin, but the woman evaded her foot easily, only to jerk her upright.

Whitney looked terrible. The shadows beneath her eyes and the hollowness of her cheeks were amplified by the glow of the chandelier. Her clothes were covered in dirt and stains. There were holes in her jeans. Through rips in her sweater, Madraeus could see multiple bite marks peppering her skin. In that moment, he could have killed every living thing within a hundred miles.

Whitney's eyes lit up when she saw him, but her expression quickly turned to alarm as she took in the amount of blood covering his clothes.

"Well, isn't this cozy!" Cecelia smiled.

Madraeus glared at her.

"Time for more gloating?" Whitney snorted. Cecelia turned an icy glare on her, but Whitney continued, "Can't you do anything without bragging about it?"

"Watch your tongue!" Cecelia snapped.

"Why? What are you going to do? Lock me in a mine shaft? Hello, been there done that," she scoffed, rolling her eyes.

Madraeus smiled. Whitney really could be a pain when she put her mind to it.

"Silence or I will cut out your tongue!" Cecelia snarled, but then quickly she smiled. "Meat doesn't need a tongue anyway."

Whitney opened her mouth, but Madraeus stopped her. "Whitney, don't. She really will cut out your tongue."

"Yes, listen to him, my feisty little rabbit."

Madraeus' eyes snapped to Cecelia when she said 'rabbit'.

Cecelia smiled. "He knows intimately what I am capable of."

Whitney just shrugged and rolled her eyes again, but kept her mouth shut.

"Alright, Cecelia, tell me what you want?" Madraeus growled, pulling her attention away from Whitney.

"Don't presume to order me." Cecelia returned to her chair and watched Madraeus. "You, who think you are the savior of our people, you are nothing! I have led you around by your nose, and you don't even have a clue why! Running around all this time chasing the wrong rabbit!" she giggled.

Madraeus frowned, *What's with the rabbits?*

"What do you want?" Madraeus snarled.

"I want to be free. I want an end to the ridiculous restrictions you have placed on us, denying our very nature! We are predators! We should be free to hunt unrestricted!"

"You know that will only bring about a war with the mortal world. They would wipe us out," Madraeus scoffed.

"No, they won't, not this time. You have been preaching that same old tired drivel for centuries. Soon, I will have the means to stand against their reprisal. The mortal world is populated by nothing but cattle. We will pen them up as they deserve," Cecelia hissed, earning murmurs of approval from the guards holding Whitney and Madraeus.

Madraeus' mind was racing. *Is this why she is after the Old Sources?* She was right, he had been a fool to go chasing around after one vampire when he should have been watching for Cecelia's next treachery.

"In your bungling, you have helped my cause more than you know. You have managed to put us on the front page of the papers. The police are watching you, and the council doesn't trust you. Already our numbers are growing because you have made a fool of yourself."

Cecelia stood and wandered around behind Whitney. "And then we have little Whitney here."

Whitney shifted to keep an eye on her.

"Do you think he is here to rescue you?" Cecelia whispered in her ear. "What do you really know about this man?" Whitney glanced at Madraeus, but he was glaring at Cecelia. "This man is the one who tortured your boyfriend, Justin. He ripped his fangs out! You saw the shape he was in. How can you think that he would care what happens to you?"

Madraeus clenched his jaw and balled his hands into fists.

Cecelia moved around to Whitney's other ear. "He has killed more people than you could count. He has tortured not only his own kind but mortals too. Women just like you. They trusted him, and then he lured them to their doom. Just ask him about little Mary."

At the mention of her name, Madraeus stepped forward, intent on strangling Cecelia. The guards grabbed him. They held him back even as he struggled to go forward.

Cecelia smiled, "You see, he can't stand that I am telling you the truth."

Whitney swallowed hard and blinked.

"You put your faith in this man?" Cecelia scoffed.

Madraeus didn't dare look at Whitney. He focused all his anger on Cecelia.

"You see him, and you think that you are saved?" Cecelia whispered into her ear. "He is going to kill you."

Whitney shook her head in denial. Madraeus stopped struggling and stared at the floor, breathing heavily.

"You see how he is losing blood? He must feed if he is to heal." Cecelia looked Madraeus up and down. "He looks like he might last another day without blood, but after that," she shrugged, "he will use every drop of your blood to survive. You are nothing more than a meal to him. Never doubt that.

Madraeus lifted his eyes to Whitney's and waited. He made no move to deny what Cecelia said. He just held her gaze as he waited for her to condemn him.

For a long time, Whitney stared at him. Finally, she turned and looked at Cecelia. "You are so full of shit."

Madraeus blinked in surprise. He had not expected her to believe in him.

Cecelia smiled and moved over to Madraeus. "You see? You've made another one fall for you." She shook her head, "You make this so easy. I won't even have to lift a finger this time. You will be the one to destroy your own happiness. Eventually, you won't be able to control your hunger or your instinct to survive, and you will kill her." Cecelia moved in close to whisper, "You will watch the light fade from her eyes and know that you are responsible for another innocent woman's death."

Madraeus growled menacingly.

"You see all the extra benefits? I get to destroy the council, I get revenge on this little one for all her insults, and I get to see you brought low all at the same time." She danced away from him as he lunged for her again. Cecelia laughed, "Take them downstairs."

# ROOM FOR TWO

As one, Madraeus and Whitney started to struggle, but their captors still hauled them from the room.

Firelight from the torch Cecelia carried danced along the uneven walls of the tunnel. Madraeus threw his weight against one guard and then the other, trying to knock them off balance, but only earned an elbow in his face. His head snapped back from the blow. His vision swam as they moved deeper and deeper into the mountain.

As they passed a cell full of people, a woman asked in disbelief, "Mr. Ravilla?"

Madraeus looked around to find the owner of the familiar voice. His previous receptionist pressed her face against the bars, staring at him in confusion. The guards propelled him farther down the tunnel. He glanced at Whitney; she was craning her neck to see who knew him.

They stopped outside the cell holding Sandra.

"Spark, take that one out," Cecelia ordered.

The woman holding Whitney stepped forward and opened the cell door. She moved inside and hauled Sandra to the opening.

Whitney took the opportunity and kicked at her remaining captor's knees. He shook Whitney like a rag doll as Spark moved Sandra to another cell.

"I don't want you to have any other food options besides our dear Whitney," Cecelia explained to Madraeus.

Whitney was shoved in first. Then they threw Madraeus to the cell floor.

"Unlock him. I want him free to hunt," Cecelia directed from outside the cell.

Three men held him down while the woman, Spark, unlocked his chains.

Spark left the cell first and made ready to swing the door shut.

The men holding Madraeus down exchanged looks, and then as a group, they bolted to the door. Madraeus was up like a shot. He launched himself at the cell doorway, but Spark had been ready and slammed the door closed as soon as the last man was through. Madraeus bounced off the bars with a snarl.

Spark shifted into a snow-white wolf. Her hackles stood straight up as she snarled at him while the other guards backed away from the front of the cell. They didn't want to be in range if the bars gave way.

"Now, now, children, play nice," Cecelia said as she placed the torch into a bracket on the wall. "I'll leave the light. I don't want you to miss the look in her eyes when you finally kill her."

"Non siamo finiti, Cecelia!" Madraeus growled through the bars.

"Yes, we *are* finished. Farvel min venn." She blew him a kiss as she sauntered back up the tunnel. All but one of the guards turned to follow her. He resumed his place across from Whitney's cell.

Madraeus rattled the cell door again, making the man jump. Madraeus' frustration erupted. For several minutes, he attacked the cell door. Pushing, pulling, yanking, and shaking with all his might, he only succeeded in making the bars rattle in their moorings. With a roar, he turned and slammed his back against the bars.

All the energy seemed to drain out of him. He closed his eyes and breathed in the deep, earthy smells of the tunnel. Other scents intruded: the odor of sweaty, unwashed bodies, and fecal matter. Madraeus wrinkled his nose and opened his eyes.

He looked around and took in his surroundings: a rock-walled cell with bars at the front.

*Well, at least I'm in the right place.*

He glanced behind him; more cells lined the walls of the tunnel, and each one contained people. Firelight from the torch cast eerie shadows on their faces, and they all seemed to be looking in his direction. Perhaps these were Unkhabami's missing people.

"Madraeus?" Whitney whispered.

He looked toward the sound of her voice. It was just like his vision. Once again, he took in her battered body and felt his anger flare. It must have shown on his face because she immediately started apologizing.

"I am so sorry!" she blurted. "I didn't mean for any of this to happen! Please, don't be mad."

Madraeus stepped toward her. She cringed and held her hands up, backing away as she continued.

"They said they had Grammy, and I didn't know what to do. They said they would shred pieces of her all over the city if I talked to you, so I had to go it alone. I am so sorry."

Madraeus stopped in front of her.

"I know I'm a pain in the ass, but I am sorry," she continued to babble. "Believe me, I have kicked myself over and over again for not having the sense to trust that you would help me. You always have.

I was even too stupid to at least scream before he got me out of the office."

"Whitney," Madraeus said quietly, but she still kept talking.

"I didn't even think you would come looking, especially after letting Justin out, not that I'm not grateful, but I just didn't... Oh! I can't believe you're here!" She threw herself into his arms, making him grunt from the impact. "I can't believe you came!" She clung to him for a moment, but before Madraeus could return her embrace, she shoved away again. "What am I doing? Did I hurt you? I'm so sorry."

"Whitney?" Madraeus reached out and grabbed her by the shoulders. She gasped, and he released her immediately. Frowning, he reached out and gently moved aside a piece of her torn sweater to reveal bruises covering her arms.

"I'm sorry!" She hurried to explain, "I couldn't bring myself to just let them feed off of me."

"You shouldn't have had to," Madraeus whispered.

Whitney stared up at him for a moment. "So, you're not mad at me?"

"I didn't say that."

"Oh." She hesitated, biting her lip. "So... is what she said true? Are you going to kill me?"

"What?"

"Madraeus," she let her eyes roam over his body, "you're bleeding all over. You told me that you need blood to heal. I'm your only source. She made sure of that."

"I'm not going to kill you to stay alive." Madraeus clenched his fists.

"I would understand if you have to," she said without meeting his eyes. "After all, you barely know me; and I know I can be really obnoxious and annoying, and you probably already want to kill me," she shrugged. "I'd prefer if you didn't, but I also know that if it comes down to survival, you gotta do what you gotta do."

"Whitney, although I have thought about it many times, I'm not going to kill you. I hope to be out of here long before feeding off of you becomes necessary," he lied. There was no way that they would be out of here before he was desperate to feed. As it was, he was starting to feel the pangs of hunger. Standing next to her was only increasing his need.

"Really?" she looked up hopefully.

"Philtzer was with me in the woods. He made a run for it."

"He left you?" she shouted. Madraeus glanced at the guard who was watching them with interest.

"I told him to," Madraeus answered. "He had a better chance of bringing help than I did."

"Why?" Her question hung in the air.

"Sunrise is only hours away. If I was the one to go, then I would have been caught without shelter." The lie was true enough to protect her.

Madraeus turned and looked back at the guard. He was still staring at them. He could only hope that Philtzer had gotten away.

"So, what happens now?"

"Now, we wait." He turned and sat, settling himself against the wall.

"Well, I'm not very good at that," Whitney complained.

Madraeus looked up at her. "I've noticed."

Whitney paced to the front of the cell and tried to see down the tunnel.

"Who was that woman?" she asked without turning around.

"What woman?"

"The one in the first cell that knew you."

"She was your predecessor," Madraeus sighed.

"My predecessor?" Whitney looked at him over her shoulder. "You mean the receptionist that disappeared?"

"Yes."

"Great. I'm part of a trend," Whitney sighed and turned back to the bars. "Sandra?"

"Over here." Her voice came from the left. "They put me two cells down. Who's your new roommate?"

"Who's Sandra?" Madraeus asked.

"The girl who was in here before you," she answered and then called down the tunnel, "He's my boss."

"Your boss? That's a little weird," Sandra laughed.

"You have no idea," she called back before the guard stepped forward and pushed Whitney back from the bars.

"Quiet!" he snarled.

"Don't touch her!" Madraeus growled. He was suddenly standing in front of Whitney, glaring at the guard.

"Back off!" the guard warned.

"Come in here and make me," Madraeus taunted.

"What? You think I'm stupid?" the guard scoffed. "Like I'm gonna fall for that."

Whitney laid a hand on Madraeus' arm. "Come on, taunting them doesn't do much good. Believe me, I've tried. It's not like the movies where all the henchmen are gullible."

Madraeus let her lead him to the back of the cell. They sat back down on the cold ground. Whitney pulled her knees up to her chest and hugged them.

"This Sandra, tell me about her." Madraeus stretched his legs out.

"Well, she's been down here about three months. Can you believe it? I've been going stir crazy and it's only been a week. It has been a week, right?" She cast a glance at Madraeus.

"Yes."

"Anyway, she's either crazy or the most practical person ever."

"Really?" Madraeus gave a short laugh.

"Yeah. Nothing fazes her," Whitney grinned. "So Philtzer took off, huh?"

"Last time I saw him there were half a dozen or so wolves chasing him down the mountain," Madraeus said, rubbing his shoulder.

"Half a dozen!" Whitney exclaimed. "You're not worried?"

"No, the kid is well acquainted with evading pursuit." Madraeus winced as he probed his shoulder.

"What do you mean?"

"Angry boyfriends."

"Somehow that doesn't surprise me."

# WELCOME TO MY CELL

Whitney shivered.

"Cold?"

"Yeah." She looked at Madraeus and shrugged. "At least we have some light now."

"What do you mean?"

"When I first got here, it was dark all the time. They come in the dark to feed. It's creepy. I know they can probably see us but..." her voice trailed off.

Madraeus felt sick inside for what Cecelia was doing to these people.

"Why do you have light now?" he asked.

"I think... I don't know, something happened earlier." She gestured toward the door. "We had just come back from our bath—"

"Bath?" Madraeus interrupted.

"Yeah, they take us down to this underground lake and let us clean up a little. I think it's because they don't like the smell when they're eating." Whitney wrinkled her nose.

Madraeus nodded. "Go on."

"Anyway, we hadn't been back very long when the torches all flared up and I got a wicked headache. I felt like I was going to be sick. I actually fell down." Whitney pushed her hair back from her face.

Madraeus shifted uneasily.

"Cecelia came down asking me what I was doing. I wasn't doing anything, but she set a guard on us." She glanced at Madraeus. "What?"

"Nothing." He shook his head. *Could she have been affected by the ritual even this far away?* Madraeus wondered.

She leaned closer to Madraeus and whispered. "It really sucks because me and Sandra were working on getting the hinge in our door loose. Too late now." She gestured toward the guard.

He was watching them intently.

"He can hear you, you know," Madraeus warned.

"Really?" she glanced at the guard.

"He's a vampire." Madraeus nodded. "We have very good hearing."

"Oh." Whitney looked back at the guard and stuck her tongue out. The guard only shook his head and frowned.

"So, how did you find me?" she asked after a moment.

"Unkhabami's ritual," Madraeus muttered. He hoped she would leave it at that.

"Really? What kind of ritual? Wait, it wasn't one of those 'sacrifice a chicken' things, was it? Unkhabami kind of gives off that creepy voodoo vibe."

Madraeus had to agree about the creepy voodoo vibe. "Not exactly, but it was magically based."

"Magic? Like real magic?" Whitney grinned like a little kid. Madraeus nodded. "Dude, that's so cool!"

"Hmm," Madraeus couldn't keep the skepticism out of his voice.

"What? You don't think it's cool?"

"I am not that fond of magic."

"Why not? It's awesome!" She elbowed him.

"Ow!" She had managed to hit him directly in one of his wolf bites.

"Oh sorry!" She rolled over onto her knees. "Here let's see what we can do for those. I should have done that right off, but here I am yakking."

She pulled some of his shirt away from the bite on his shoulder. There was a jagged rip in the flesh near the top of his shoulder. She winced.

"I don't know what to do. There's no water or anything."

"Don't worry about it," he said, removing her hand. "I've already started to heal."

Whitney sat back on her heels. "I thought you needed blood to heal."

"It would be better that way, but I will heal very slowly without it."

"Why do I feel like there's a 'but' to that statement?" She eyed him.

Madraeus sighed. He didn't want to tell her that his body would start to consume itself, and he would be in intense pain while it happened. Instead, he said, "But it will make me very weak."

Whitney bit her lip. "You should feed."

"No." He shook his head. "Let's talk about something else."

"Why are you always so stubborn?"

"Why don't you do as you're told?"

"Madraeus," she started to protest, but he cut her off.

"Leave it," he warned.

Whitney crossed her arms and huffed, "Fine! Why don't you like magic?"

"Because it is shifty and manipulative, people use it to fool themselves into believing they have control of the world instead of facing reality."

"But you used it," she challenged.

"That is not the same thing," he growled.

"How so?"

"Because in this case, Unkhabami and I tried to divine your future in order to find you now."

"Huh?"

"The priestess set up a divining ritual based on my intentions of finding you. She prophesied that I had found you. I merely had to go looking and follow through," Madraeus shrugged.

"So, you tried to manipulate your reality by messing with my future?"

"No!" Madraeus snarled, although when he thought about it, that was exactly what he had done. This conversation was slowly moving out of his control. Things seemed to do that around Whitney.

"Wow!" Whitney smiled after a moment. "You were that determined to find me? Why?"

Madraeus stared at her, refusing to answer.

Whitney shrugged. "Well, at least you found me. So, when do we get out?"

"I don't know." Madraeus looked away. "I didn't see that part."

"Are you saying that we may never get out of here?"

"Maybe." Madraeus let his head fall back against the rock behind him. "I don't know. I saw so many of your futures, I can't say what is real."

"My futures?" Whitney asked. "I have more than one? What was I doing?"

He stared up at the ceiling for a long time before answering. Madraeus let his head loll to the side to look at her.

"You don't want to ask me that."

"Why?" Her brow wrinkled. "Were they that bad?"

"No. Not all were bad," he whispered. *Some were wonderful— for you*, he thought sadly.

He let his eyes drift over her face. He didn't want to think about her futures without him. Not when she was so warm and close right now. His desire for her flared to life. It was fueled by his need for blood.

His eyes darkened as he stared at her. His nostrils flared slightly.

"Whitney?" Madraeus rasped.

"Yeah?"

"Will you please move away from me?" His voice was strained.

"Sure." She scooted about a foot away from him. "Why?"

"Because you are too tempting right now." He closed his eyes and turned his face away.

"You are worse off than you said, aren't you?"

Madraeus steadfastly refused to answer.

"Do you need..." she offered, but he shook his head.

"No, I'll be alright if you just keep your distance."

"Okay," Whitney said uncertainly looking around the tiny rock room. "How?"

Madraeus kept his eyes closed. Whitney scooted a little farther away and hugged her knees, watching him.

"So stupid," she mumbled.

"What is?" he asked without opening his eyes.

"Everything. Me. Apparently, I'm the most perfectly pathetic creature on the planet," she grumbled.

He looked at her. "What are you talking about?"

"Cecelia. She told me that she handpicked me because I was just pathetic enough to fit into her plans," Whitney complained.

"What do you mean?" Madraeus sat up.

"She told me that she picked me, took my boyfriend and turned him, bought out the recording studio so she could put me out of work, all so she could make me pathetic enough for you to hire me. I guess that explains the missing receptionist down in cell one too. She needed her out of the way." Whitney sniffled and blinked the tears away. "And here I am Miss Pathetic. I'm so useless, all I'm good for is to distract you from whatever stupid thing she is doing."

"You're not useless. It's not your fault you got tangled up with us. I've been at this a long time, Whitney. I should have known something was going on." Madraeus shook his head.

"I'm sorry for distracting you from your duties."

"Don't be. You didn't really have a choice in all this. She has tried this kind of thing before," Madraeus sighed. "She thinks that if she can make it look like I can't do my job, then the council will replace me, leaving the field open for her to step in, but the council knows that she is a fanatical, power-hungry diva. They'd never let her take over."

"But will they replace you because of all this?" Whitney shifted against the wall.

"I don't care. I am so tired of trying to have all the answers."

"How can you say that?" Whitney protested.

"Whitney, I am tired. I have been chasing conspiracies for over 200 years. I don't want to do it anymore." Madraeus shook his head.

"But I think you've been doing a great job."

For a long time, he looked at her. His eyes were completely black. "You don't know me. Everything she said was true. My past is as dark as hers. I have done horrible things."

*Wonderful thingsss.* His voice trailed off as the voice hissed in his head. He closed his eyes against it.

She watched him. "Who's Mary?"

Madraeus went absolutely still. He stayed silent so long she leaned forward to see if he had passed out.

"Mary was," he struggled to speak, "my wife."

"What happened?" Whitney whispered.

"I fell in love with her and foolishly thought that we could have a life together, even cursed as I was. She wasn't afraid. I thought we had a chance until Cecelia found out. She was jealous that I would give to a mortal what I denied her. She tortured Mary and killed everyone in her village." Visions of Mary's brutalized body hanging from a post outside his door made him choke to a stop. "I was so overwhelmed by grief and guilt. I couldn't function. It was days before I could even let go of her body long enough to bury it."

"I'm so sorry," she whispered. "I shouldn't have asked."

Madraeus shook his head. "I was a fool. I should have killed Cecelia then."

"Why didn't you?"

"It's complicated."

"She's horrid! How complicated could it be?"

"Very," he rasped.

"What kind of answer is that? If she is so nasty, just stop her!"

"Whitney, just leave it," he growled.

"No. Do you know how many lives you could have saved?"

"Whitney! I am well aware of the situation. Now leave it." Madraeus snarled, baring his teeth.

Whitney reared back. She scooted as far from him as she could in their tiny cell and stared at him as he tried to regain control.

# EAT AND RUN

WHITNEY PACED AROUND THE front of the cell. Madraeus had lapsed into silence a while ago. She assumed he was trying to sleep so he could heal. She couldn't believe what he had told her about Mary and Cecelia. It broke her heart.

Whitney looked toward the other cells and frowned. Something was off.

"Sandra?" she called.

"Yeah?"

"Yesterday was bath day, right?"

The guard was staring at her. It would only be a moment before he told them to stop talking again.

"Yeah, why?" Sandra asked, but then she must have understood. The vampires should have come to feed by now, but they hadn't heard the buzzer, and they hadn't heard any commotion from any of the other tunnels. "Oh! You're right."

"Hey, shut up."

"Yeah, boss." She bowed mockingly to the guard. "Sorry, boss."

*Why hadn't the vampires come?* Whitney pushed her face against the bars, trying to see up the tunnel. Maybe they weren't coming because they weren't here anymore.

She turned to look at Madraeus. He'd said that Philtzer had been with him and had run for it. If he had gotten away, he would bring the cavalry. She didn't know Cecelia well enough to predict whether she would evacuate or make a stand.

She heard movement. Someone was coming down the tunnel. Out of the gloom, another guard came into view.

"Ooh shift change!" she taunted as he approached.

He threw her an annoyed glance and walked away. The other guard nodded to him as they passed each other.

"See ya later," she called after him. "We'll do lunch!"

"Shut up!" he called over his shoulder.

Whitney looked at the new guard. "Hey there, come here often?"

He just sighed and crossed his arms. She had seen him before. He was younger than the others. He seemed a little uncertain as if he didn't really want to be here. He kept glancing up the tunnel as if he were waiting for someone. There was definitely something going on. She had the feeling that time was running out. They needed to get out of here sooner rather than later.

Whitney knew that she was no match for a vampire or werewolf, but Madraeus was if he could get his strength back. She turned to look at him. His face seemed thinner. His cheeks were sucked in as if his body was consuming itself. Whitney shuddered at the thought. She had to do something to get him to feed.

She wondered if Madraeus would be strong enough to knock the bars loose. He hadn't had any success before. She couldn't count on that.

There had to be a way to get the guard into the cell. She thought about going to work on the hinge again just to see if she could lure the guard into the cell to stop her. Whitney tapped a finger on her chin. She still had her phone. It wasn't working anymore. The battery had run out a long time ago, but they didn't know that. A few days ago, she had thought about using it to lure the guard into the cell, but there had been nothing she could have done once he was in there with her. She gazed at her boss's prone form.

She couldn't, but *he* could.

Whitney walked over to him cautiously. She was a little afraid to wake him. He might have gone beyond the point where he could control his hunger. Slowly, she knelt down beside him and stretched her hand out.

"What, Whitney?" he said with his eyes still closed.

"Oh, you're awake." She hadn't even touched him.

"Yes."

"I have an idea," she started, but he stopped her.

"Don't say it, remember he can hear you," he reminded her.

Whitney glanced over her shoulder and bit her lip.

"Fine." She reached over and grabbed her little sharp rock.

Crawling a little way away, she started to draw in the dirt. She glanced up at the guard a couple of times to see if he was interested. She wasn't disappointed. He was craning his neck to see what she was writing.

"There." She sat back on her heels.

"What?" Madraeus asked without opening his eyes.

"Read," she said.

Madraeus sighed and opened his eyes. They were black orbs like the night of the attack in her apartment. Whitney's eyes widened, but she didn't say anything.

Madraeus propped himself up on one elbow and read what she had written: *If you were at full strength, could you knock the bars down?*

"No."

She scrubbed out the sentence and wrote again: *Can you take out the guard if I can get him in here?*

"Yes."

Whitney leaned forward and erased what she had written. "Like you are now?"

"Maybe."

She sat back on her heels. He didn't sound confident. "Then you need to feed."

"No."

"Yes."

"No. Whitney, I'm not doing it."

"Why not? You afraid you might hurt me?" She pulled her sleeve open to show the bites she'd already gotten. "It's too late for that."

"Whitney, I could kill you," he whispered.

"You've said that before." She waved her hand dismissively.

"No. I mean really. I might not be able to stop."

She looked at his eyes and nodded. "I know."

"No, you don't know," he shook his head, "I can't be responsible for your death. It would be worse than Mary."

Whitney frowned. "Worse than Mary? How? Because you did it and not her?" She gestured in the general direction of the tunnel and Cecelia.

He growled as he flopped back down onto his back.

"Then what does it matter? You don't even like me!"

"Don't like you?" Madraeus exclaimed, pushing himself up again.

"Yeah, you've said many times that I was obnoxious, or insane, or annoying. I know you don't like me, so why should it matter?" She stood and paced away from him.

"You *are* obnoxious, insane, and annoying." She threw him a dirty look. "That doesn't mean that I dislike you."

"What the hell does that mean?" She threw her hands up.

"It means, you idiot, that you drive me crazy in every way a woman can drive a man crazy."

"What?"

"Never mind." He stood up and turned away from her.

"Oh no, you don't get out of this one." She stomped over to him and put a hand on his shoulder, trying to turn him around. He refused to be turned. "Hey!" She gave up and stepped in front of him. "Tell me what you mean."

Suddenly he grabbed her shoulders, pushing her back against the rock. His eyes were black. He was breathing hard. His fangs were out. Whitney gasped and froze. Then just as suddenly he let go and backed across the cell from her.

"We need to get out of here," he whispered, turning away.

*Either I'm getting braver, or my mind is starting to go*, she thought as she slowly pushed away from the wall and stepped closer to him. "You know that there is only one way to do that."

Madraeus shook his head. "Whitney, I can't." He still had his back to her.

"I don't want to do it either, but I don't see any other way of getting out of here. Do you?"

"We could wait for Philtzer."

"If he got away," she reminded him.

He didn't respond.

"And if he comes, do you think Cecelia will still be here? The other vampires haven't come to feed." She stepped closer to him as she spoke. "I'm betting they've left."

Madraeus finally turned and looked at her. He moved to the cell door and stood listening.

Nothing. He glanced at the guard who shifted nervously.

"I'm right, aren't I?" she whispered.

He turned back toward her but still didn't speak.

"I would rather you did it sooner than later. The longer you wait the less control you'll have to stop. You know I'm right."

"Are you sure about this?" he whispered.

"No, but go ahead."

She stepped up to him. She was shaking, and her breathing was unsteady. Madraeus started to lean forward. She tried to stand still but the past week of fighting this very situation started to weaken her resolve.

"Wait. Wait." She stopped him. Whitney bounced a couple of times, popped her neck from side to side, and then shook her arms.

"Okay." She jammed her eyes closed and looked away. She could feel him getting nearer. She tried to hold still, but she couldn't help it. She started bouncing nervously and danced away from him.

"Whitney!" Madraeus growled.

"Alright! Sorry, sorry." She inhaled sharply and blew it out again. "Okay, this time I'm ready."

With a sigh, he started toward her again, but she backed away from him until her back was against the wall. She screwed her face up like she was expecting a blow.

Madraeus frowned and shook his head. The moment he leaned forward she squeaked and dodged to the side.

"Damn it, Whitney!" He slammed his fist into the wall. "Don't tease me!"

"Sorry, sorry, I'm trying," she whined, "but instinct is working against me here!"

Madraeus turned and watched her with black eyes. "I won't hurt you like they did."

"I know." She bounced around for a minute then stamped her foot in frustration. "Okay let's try again." She walked forward and pulled her sweater neck out.

Madraeus laid a hand over hers and pulled it away from her neck. He held it to his chest. She blinked at him in confusion.

"Let's try it my way," he said softly.

"Umm... K, what's that?" she asked, still shaking.

"This." He leaned forward and kissed her. She froze for a moment then melted. With one hand, he cupped her face while he trailed kisses down the opposite side of her jaw. His other hand slid up her back and held her close to him. She wrapped her arms around his waist and closed her eyes.

"Your way is nice," she breathed.

He pulled her in closer to him as he followed the curve of her jaw with his lips. When she softened against him with a sigh, he moved lower down her neck. She hugged him tighter just before he sank his teeth in. She only felt a little prick of pain.

Whitney moaned softly. It felt like he was drawing her very essence up from the tips of her toes, through her heart, and into him. It was the most amazing sensation she had ever felt. She gave herself up to the experience, clinging to him as if she was the one starving and not him.

# MOUNTAIN SHENANIGANS

PHILTZER PANTED AS HE searched the tree line. He had run all night and into the morning. Originally, there had been three wolves chasing him: one had dropped out of the chase after about an hour. The other two proved a lot harder to lose.

He had run down the mountain then back up again, crisscrossed back and forth over small streams, and squeezed through thickets, but his pursuers wouldn't give up. He was starting to lose hope that he could shake them when he finally caught a break.

About an hour after dawn, Philtzer dodged into a thick glade of pine trees where he caught a scent. He swerved to follow it. The closest wolf nearly got him. He heard its jaws snap shut near his tail. Philtzer put on a desperate burst of speed.

The scent was getting stronger. He skidded around a huge rock and collided with the brown bear he had smelled. The bear was not happy with him. It turned to charge when the other two wolves rounded the boulder. The bear turned on the new threat quickly, and Philtzer ran for it while they were distracted.

He ran back toward the last stream he had been through, hoping to confuse the scent of his trail. He had wasted too much time trying to lose those two. He needed to get to a phone.

Philtzer gave one last scan of the tree line, but there was no sign of his enemy. He turned and loped off through the woods. He had left his cell phone in his pants pocket, and that was in the car. He was going to have to backtrack through the woods to find the right road. He wasn't even sure how far he had run. Hopefully, no one had found the car. He didn't want to run all the way back to Denver, and he sure as hell couldn't just change back to a human and take a taxi. They frowned on naked men doing that sort of thing.

Hours later, Philtzer collapsed on the front seat of the car. He had nearly been back to Cecelia's compound before he picked up the trail leading to the car. He had worried that he had spent all night losing his pursuers just to run into new ones because he couldn't remember where they'd parked.

He dug around in his jeans pocket and found his phone. He dialed Rami and then tucked the phone between his ear and shoulder while he bounced up and down trying to pull his jeans on.

"Philtzer? Where have you been?"

"Oh, just running around in the woods."

"Where is Madraeus?"

Philtzer zipped his pants before answering.

"He is the guest of one psycho blonde," he said with a sigh, reaching for his socks and boots.

"Damn!" Rami groaned. "Alright, where are you?"

"Ah," Philtzer looked around. He couldn't remember the road number that they had come down last night, and there were no signs anywhere near him.

"On the side of a road," he offered with a grin.

"Philtzer!" Rami growled.

"Sorry, couldn't help it," Philtzer laughed. He sat down and held the phone with his shoulder again so he could pull on his socks. "Damn, it's cold up here."

"Just tell me where you are."

"I'll need to backtrack on this road to find the number, but you gotta get up here fast."

"How many are we looking at?" Rami's voice sounded unenthusiastic.

"Don't know. There were at least a dozen wolves that jumped us. Some of them are dead already, but I don't know how many are in the actual mine. There could be a bunch. There is no way to tell without getting closer, but that ain't happening."

"Alright, I'll pull in everyone that I can," Rami sighed.

"They may already be on the move. If the wolves that chased me got back in one piece, they'll report that I got away. They'll know that I'll bring reinforcements." Philtzer scanned the trees.

"You think they'll make a run for it?" Rami asked.

"Wouldn't you?"

"Is that road the only way in or out of there?"

"Hell if I know, it took me forever just to get back to the car. We are in the back of beyond up here." Philtzer held the phone away long enough to pull his t-shirt on. "Look, I've been running all night. I'm exhausted. I'm gonna need some sleep before I get in another fight.

"Well, at least no one will accidentally stumble across our little war." Rami tried to be positive. "Get me the road number."

"Right." Philtzer snapped his phone shut and shoved it in his pocket. Quickly, he finished getting dressed and got in the car. The road was narrow with steep ditches on either side, making it impossible to turn around. He would have to back the car down the road. He threw it in reverse and hung an arm over the seat back to see where he was going. He thought it was only a mile or so back to the turn-off, but he wasn't entirely sure.

Philtzer's stomach growled.

"Ho there, boy, steady!" he replied. "We'll get lunch soon enough."

The idea of steak and eggs, or maybe a breakfast burrito, made him increase his speed. He wished he had his bike, then he could just spin around and get to the food.

Philtzer glanced forward for a moment, only to see the looming grill of a semi. The 18-wheeler was bearing down on him with a cloud of dust billowing behind it. The truck didn't seem inclined to slow down.

"Shit!" he yelled, stomping on the gas, but it was too late. The semi-truck clipped his fender as it passed, sending the car spinning off into the ditch. Philtzer held on tight as the car tilted to the side on the steep incline. He was tossed around like a bouncy ball as the car rolled three times before landing on its wheels again.

"Ouch." He pushed himself up off the passenger-side floor. "Ouch." He looked out the windshield and up towards the road. The truck was gone.

He gingerly pulled himself into the driver's seat and tried to start the car. It only clicked.

"Crap." Philtzer managed to get the door open. His bruised and battered muscles protested as he slowly crawled his way up the slope to the road. He looked in both directions, but only saw dust and trees. With no enthusiasm whatsoever, he started walking toward the turn-off. He dug in his pocket for his phone and called Rami as he neared the road sign.

"Rami, you'll never guess what happened to me?" Philtzer chirped with feigned excitement before continuing to describe the crash and what the semi looked like.

"They moved pretty fast," Rami rumbled. Not at all pleased that they may have missed their chance to get Cecelia.

"No saying that was all of them," Philtzer warned.

"True," Rami agreed. "Alright, cavalry is on the way, just sit tight."

"Hey, Rami?" Philtzer asked before he could hang up.

"What?"

"Could you send out some steak and eggs or maybe a breakfast burrito or two?" Philtzer whined like a puppy. "Or maybe one of those triple bacon cheese mushroom burgers, or a—"

"Yes, Philtzer. Goodbye, Philtzer."

# OPENING DOORS

Madraeus felt Whitney sag against him. He held her tighter. He craved her. He knew that he should stop feeding off of her soon, but she was so sweet.

*Yesss.*

Madraeus snapped back to reality. He forced himself to retract his fangs. Savoring his last taste of heaven, he ran his tongue over the bites, sealing them. Carefully, he lowered her body to the floor and sat down. He laid her head on his thigh and smoothed her matted hair.

"My poor Whitney."

Madraeus lowered his head back against the rock and closed his eyes. Absently, he stroked her hair as he felt her blood coursing through him, healing his wounds. He hadn't fed nearly enough, but it was enough to heal a little. He hoped he hadn't done her any serious damage. Now, he had to wait for her to recover. They couldn't go anywhere until sunset anyway. It was daylight out right now; he could feel it even this far below ground. Hopefully, she would be awake by then and not too weak to move.

Madraeus watched through slitted eyes as their guard shifted nervously. He looked up as a woman came down the tunnel and motioned him to follow. They wasted no time in disappearing up the tunnel.

Whitney was right. Cecelia was running.

Madraeus could hear the other prisoners talking quietly amongst themselves. They were confused. He could hear their murmurs.

"The vampires didn't come today to feed."

"Where are they?"

"Are we being left down here to die?"

"What are we going to do?"

Those questions plagued Madraeus' thoughts as well. What was he going to do with all these people? He couldn't very well let them go. They knew too much about the Races already and it was all bad. There was no way they would quietly return to their homes and keep what had happened to them a secret. He would have to find a way to deal with them.

He didn't like killing innocent people, but it may come to that. He looked down at Whitney's head in his lap. She would never forgive him. He had known that this moment would come. He would have to choose between Whitney and his duty. Madraeus squeezed his eyes shut, wishing the choice had been farther down the road.

***

Madraeus sat up. The sun had set; he could feel it. The people in the other cells were sleeping quietly. He looked down at Whitney. She was still asleep in his lap. Gently, he slid out from under her head and stood.

Madraeus yanked on the bars, testing for weakness with little success. Just as he started to turn back to Whitney, movement caught his eye.

A small wolf crept down the tunnel toward the cells. Madraeus watched her. Her movements were very cautious, almost as if she shouldn't be there.

"Hello?" Madraeus said gently. The wolf flinched at the sound of his voice.

"Who are you?" he asked as she stepped closer.

She was a pretty little thing. Her fur was a soft brown color with a few white streaks across her chest, and she had one white fore paw.

She looked around with her ears up. When she saw all the people in the cells, she laid her ears flat back against her head and whined.

Clearly distraught, she sidled sideways coming up against Madraeus' cell. He reached out a hand and scratched her ears. She jumped and turned to face him in one smooth movement. Madraeus left his hand outside of the bars. She edged forward and sniffed it cautiously then backed up, shifting nervously. Her ears were swiveling backward and forward as if she was confused.

Suddenly, she bolted back up the tunnel. Madraeus watched her disappear then pushed away from the cell door. He walked back over to Whitney and bent over her.

"Hey, Whitney, wake up." He shook her shoulder slightly. When she didn't respond, he slid an arm behind her and sat her up. He tapped her cheek gently, "Hey, come on."

Whitney suddenly became aware that someone was touching her, and she started to fight. She flailed her arms and tried to squirm away.

Madraeus held tight. "Whitney! It's me!"

It took a moment before she stopped fighting, but she finally looked up at him.

"Sorry." She rubbed her arm across her face.

"It's okay." He brushed her hair back. "It's after sunset. Do you feel strong enough?"

She looked like she really didn't, but she nodded.

"Good, what was your idea?"

She pulled her cell phone out of her pocket.

"You've had that the whole time?" Madraeus' eyebrows shot up.

"Yeah," she said defensively.

"Then why—" He started only to be shushed by her as she looked for the guard. "He's gone. We're on our own."

She whimpered and flopped back onto the floor.

Madraeus stood. "Are you alright?"

"No, I don't suppose they brought any food down?" she asked hopefully.

Madraeus shook his head. This is what he had been dreading. His strength had returned, but hers was gone. He should never have taken what she offered. He paced to the front of the cell and back again. Once again, he wished he knew whether or not Philtzer had gotten away. If he had, then they just had to wait.

Madraeus stopped and listened.

"What?" Whitney asked as Madraeus moved to the front of the cell.

"Someone is coming." He held up a hand to quiet her as he strained to hear.

Out of the darkness, the little brown wolf appeared. She took a careful look around then trotted up to the bars. A set of keys dangled from her jaws. She gazed up at him taking the measure of him again, looked past him to Whitney, then laid the keys just outside of the bars and backed away.

"Thank you." Madraeus bowed to her.

She turned and shot up the tunnel.

Quickly, Madraeus grabbed the keys and opened the door. He stepped through and checked the tunnel. Whitney immediately pushed herself up and staggered toward the door.

Madraeus turned back to Whitney as she plopped down just outside the door. He frowned. There was no way that she would make it up the tunnel. Even if she did, she would only become a liability. Madraeus squatted down in front of her.

"Stay here. I'm going to see what I can do to clear the way out of here."

"But," she started, not willing to be left behind.

"No buts!" Madraeus growled, "For once in your life, stay where I put you, or I'll lock you back in the cell."

"Fine," she huffed. He stood and quickly ran up the tunnel. Whitney looked around at the other prisoners.

"Damn it." Whitney smacked the ground beside her and shouted, "You could've left the keys!"

Madraeus moved quietly up the tunnel. There was no one in sight. He passed Cecelia's empty office and continued on to the main room where the elevator was. He glanced around. The cavern had been abandoned. Some of the furniture and trappings were still there, but the occupants had left. It was like they had dropped whatever they were doing and ran.

# TO THE RESCUE

Philtzer groaned again.

"Will you stop that?" Rami rumbled in annoyance.

"But I'm hungry," Philtzer whined. "Thomas only brought me a sandwich. One sandwich. A cold sandwich. And you didn't bring me anything when you came."

"I am not your personal caterer." Rami shook his head as he grabbed another quiver of arrows.

The wolves had come to retrieve Philtzer's wrecked car midway through the morning, but there hadn't been enough of them to move against Cecelia. All they could do was wait and watch, but there had been no sign of Cecelia's henchmen all day.

Now that the sun had set, they could finally act.

Rami had gathered almost twenty vampires and werewolves to storm Cecelia's compound. The witches and the pixies had refused to get involved. He had raided the arsenal at InfiniCorp's offices and brought bows and arrows and swords. Guns were of no use. Vampires and werewolves tended to keep going even if they had been shot. Rami always thought that it was unfortunate that the myth of silver bullets working on werewolves was just that, a myth.

It was best to go the old-fashioned route: lop off a head and they stay dead.

Rami handed the quiver to a young vampire named Vivian and looked around at the faces of his 'army'. He had no way of knowing what they were up against. This might go well if most of Cecelia's people had evacuated, but it might be a massacre if they hadn't.

He sighed and thought, *I am not cut out to be a general.*

"Some of you need to circle around to the back side of the compound and cover us with some well-placed arrows. Try not to shoot any of us." Rami winked at Vivian, eliciting a chuckle from several of them.

"I only did that one time!" she snarled as she settled the quiver over her shoulder.

"The rest of us will fan out through the trees on this side and go straight at the front."

While he was speaking, the werewolves had started to undress and transform.

"I can't believe I have to do this again," Philtzer grumbled, yanking off his shirt. "I didn't even get a nap."

"Stop whining," Rami said over his shoulder as he moved up the side of the ditch.

"I'm not whining," Philtzer muttered. He changed into wolf form and trotted ahead of Rami.

Slowly, they made their way up the side of the mountain. Philtzer pricked his ears. There were no night noises, no other animals, or even birds. Apparently, Mother Nature knew something was up. Philtzer slowed his pace as they neared the clearing.

Rami watched Philtzer's hackles rise. This was it. Rami glanced to his left. Eyes glittered in the darkness. He turned in the other direction to find a few faces and more shining eyes.

They were ready. Now they had to wait. The others would have to circle around behind the shaft house to the top of the ridge without being detected. At least there was no wind to give their position away.

Rami settled the handle of the sword more comfortably into his hand. It had been a long time since he had been in battle and never without Madraeus. He was the real warrior. Rami had never had any formal training, only what his friend had taught him. He had learned well enough, but he preferred to remain on the sidelines.

*Ah well*, he thought, *the best-laid plans of mice and vampires.* He smiled in spite of the situation.

Rami scanned the clearing around the shaft house. There were a couple of wolves patrolling, but they were on the far side, away from where his people lay hidden in the trees. It seemed like they waited forever. Suddenly, they heard a howl from the other side of the compound, raising the alarm.

Rami looked up to see the wolves rushing across the bare lot toward the sound of the howl. Philtzer burst from the trees. He sprinted for the nearest enemy wolf and tackled him.

The others were quick to follow Philtzer's example. A few men and wolves ran out of the low end of the shaft house.

Rami gave a yell and charged forward. Arrows zinged through the air around him. Most missed their targets. No one had needed to use these weapons in centuries. They were out of practice.

Cecelia's vampires backed up against the building, out of sight of the archers, giving no target to hit. Her wolves spread out and kept moving. Rami had a moment of panic as he realized how unprepared they were for this fight. This had been a bad plan.

***

Madraeus could hear the battle raging. Snarls and shouts were echoing down the shaft. The elevator had barely reached the top when Madraeus bounded off the platform and sprinted for the nearest open door. The yard was in total chaos. Arrows were sprinkled across the ground, but only a few had found their marks and were sticking out of prone bodies.

Rami and Malcolm, one of Madraeus' vampire bodyguards, were in a sword fight with several of Cecelia's vampires. They had been backed against the building and were cornered. Madraeus glanced the other way and caught a glimpse of Philtzer scrapping with two other werewolves. Similar fights were scattered all over the yard. His people were clearly outnumbered. He knew that Philtzer had a better chance of winning than Rami did, so he headed for the side of the shed.

Cecelia's vampires were so intent on their quarry that they didn't notice him until it was almost too late. He managed to get inside the first one's sword range quickly, turning it into a hand-to-hand fight.

Madraeus fought fiercely. He wouldn't allow his weakened condition to be an excuse. He would not let his friends pay for his mistakes.

Madraeus hit, dodged, and hit again, driving the vampire out into the main yard. The vampire backhanded him, knocking him to the side. Madraeus rolled with it and came back up onto his feet. Next to him, sticking out of the ground, was one of the arrows that had missed its mark. He grabbed it. In one swift movement, he spun around and launched it spear-style at his opponent. The arrow impaled his enemy's neck. Madraeus rushed forward and grabbed the sword from the man's hand. Quickly, Madraeus swung it around and down, beheading him.

Madraeus spun back toward the building only to find Rami slashing through the chest of his opponent.

"You alright?" Madraeus shouted to Rami.

The giant nodded.

Madraeus turned toward Malcolm. He had driven back the two vampires that he was fighting. Malcolm lunged at one, driving the sword through his neck, only to be slashed in the arm by the other one. Malcolm roared in pain. Instead of finishing him off, the second vampire turned and ran for the woods. Ripping his sword out of the dead man's neck, Malcolm charged after the retreating vampire.

Madraeus looked around. Many of Cecelia's wolves were making a run for it. They disappeared into the trees like rats off a ship. Philtzer was ripping the throat out of one of the wolves he had been fighting, the other one was nowhere to be seen.

Madraeus heard another wolf fight going on just off to the left of the building's entrance. Quickly, he headed that way, but when he rounded the corner, he stopped. One of the wolves was the little brown female with the white paw that he had seen in the tunnel. She was fighting against a much larger, brilliant-white female wolf.

Philtzer appeared suddenly at his elbow.

"Who is she?" Philtzer said in awe.

They watched as the two wolves circled each other.

"The white one is Spark, one of Cecelia's. I don't know the other one. She brought me the keys to my cell."

The white wolf must have noticed that the sound of battles had stopped. She pricked her ears forward and turned to see them watching. With a yip, she spun and sprinted for the trees.

The little wolf turned to see what frightened the other away. Her ears shot up and then lay flat back when she saw a very naked Philtzer and Madraeus with a sword watching her. She darted toward the trees, taking a different route than the white wolf.

"Hey, wait!" Philtzer charged after her, changing to wolf in mid-stride.

"Philtzer!" Madraeus shouted, but it didn't even slow him down. Madraeus shook his head and turned back to find Rami stalking up to him.

"Where is he going?" Rami frowned, watching Philtzer disappear into the trees.

"Chasing skirts," Madraeus snorted in disgust.

"Why did they run? They still had us outnumbered," Rami asked, looking around the clearing.

"I don't know."

"Is it over?" Vivian and a couple of others trotted out from behind the building.

"Yeah," Rami called back to her.

"Not quite." Madraeus turned back toward the building. "We have a problem, a few of them actually."

"What do you mean?" Rami asked as he fell into step with his friend.

"There are cells full of people down in the mines. They were being used as cattle to feed Cecelia and her friends," Madraeus explained as they stepped into the elevator.

"Was Whitney with them?" Rami searched his friend's face.

"Yeah."

They rode the rest of the way in silence.

# FINALLY SAFE

Whitney tried to obey Madraeus. She actually managed to sit there for a few minutes before she just couldn't stand it anymore. There had to be something she could do to help. Whitney dragged herself up off the floor. She staggered and fell against the wall. She was too weak.

"This is stupid!" she raged at the thin air. Slowly, she turned, and leaning heavily against the wall, Whitney looked around.

"Whitney?" Sandra called. Her face was pressed against the bars as she strained to see Whitney.

"I'm here. I'm out." She forced herself to put one foot in front of the other as she made her way toward Sandra.

She had almost made it when she heard someone running up the tunnel. It was coming from the opposite way that Madraeus had gone. Whitney saw the flash of a man's face as he burst out of the darkness beyond the block of cells. She only had a moment to gasp before he tackled her. Whitney hit the ground hard. Her breath whooshed out on impact.

"Whitney!" Sandra screeched.

"At least I can take you out!" The vampire who had tackled her laughed wickedly before sinking his teeth into her neck.

Whitney yelped in pain and tried to struggle, but everything was working against her, even her own body. She felt the life being sucked out of her.

Malcolm charged out of the darkness behind the vampire with a roar. The man rolled off Whitney as soon as he heard him and went into a crouch.

"You're too late!" he cackled.

Malcolm looked at Whitney's limp form.

In that moment of distraction, the vampire lunged for Malcolm. It was a stupid attack. Malcolm's sword was poised in front of him. When the vampire charged, he skewered himself. The man made a gurgling noise as he slid down the blade. Malcolm pulled his sword free and quickly beheaded him.

He moved over to Whitney. She was deathly pale and unconscious. He felt for a pulse. It was weak but there.

"Madraeus is going to kill me," he muttered as he looked around. For the first time, he became aware that there were cells around him filled with people. He took in their pale, eerie faces and shivered.

"Whitney?" Madraeus called from up the tunnel.

"Madraeus! Hurry!" Malcolm shouted back.

Out of the dark, Rami and Madraeus came running.

"No, not again!" Madraeus snarled as he landed on his knees beside Whitney.

He picked Whitney's limp body up: "Get a car!"

Malcolm ran up the tunnel with Madraeus close behind.

From behind him, the tunnel was filled with shouts from the prisoners begging not to be left, but he didn't slow his pace.

They all piled into the nearest car that had keys. Tires spun, spraying the side of the building with gravel as they sped out of the yard.

Malcolm drove like a madman.

"Get Dr. Kirkland! Whitney is going to need a transfusion as soon as we get there!" Rami growled before snapping his phone shut. He looked at Madraeus. "You could change her."

Madraeus looked at Rami, then back at Whitney sprawled across his lap.

"No. We'll make it." Madraeus shook his head. "Malcolm, go faster!"

Time dragged on.

Finally, they skidded to a stop, sending gravel flying across Mrs. Myers' steps. They hauled Whitney's limp form into the house. Dr. Kirkland was waiting for them at the door. He didn't wait for them to take her to a room, he shoved an IV into her arm while Madraeus still held her.

"What's happened?" Mrs. Myers fluttered around them as they settled her on the floor just inside the door. Kirkland worked quickly, manipulating the bags of plasma and tubing.

"Cecelia happened," Rami sighed as he watched the doctor work.

"Oh, my poor Whitney!"

"Will she be alright?" Rami asked Kirkland.

He lifted one of Whitney's eyelids and then the other, then checked her pulse again. "Yes. I think we were in time," he said as he continued to examine his patient.

"We must return to the mine." Rami glanced at Madraeus.

He was still kneeling beside Whitney. He didn't want to leave her. She was finally safe.

"Ray, we have to go."

"Why?" Mrs. Myers asked.

"The night is half over. We cannot afford to waste an entire day. There are," he thought about the people in the cells, "loose ends we need to tie up."

He gazed at Whitney's pale face and knew that this was going to be goodbye. As soon as he fulfilled his duty and handled the situation in the mine, he would lose her forever. She would never forgive him.

Madraeus closed his eyes and took a long, deep breath. He squeezed her hand in farewell, then shoved to his feet and swayed.

Mrs. Myers' hand shot out to steady him. "I think you better grab something to eat before you go."

After Madraeus chugged down a bottle of blood, he stepped out of Mrs. Myers' door, only to find the yard filling with vehicles. Thomas stepped out of the nearest car and looked up to see them coming out of the house.

"Is she alright?" he called.

"So far," Rami growled.

"We gathered all the spent arrows and weaponry from the yard and loaded all the evidence we could find into every car we could," he reported. "Vivian is watching over the remains of the vamps and wolves. We moved them into a pile and set it ablaze."

"Any sign of Philtzer?" Rami asked. Thomas shook his head.

"He'll be back," Madraeus muttered.

"We didn't know what to do with all those people," Thomas shrugged.

"I'll deal with them." Madraeus yanked the car door open and got in.

"What are we supposed to do with all this?" Thomas gestured toward the cars behind him.

"Search for any clues to Cecelia's plans, where she's been, or going. Anything you can find. We'll be back soon."

# CHOICES

Once they reached the mine, Vivian, Malcolm, and Rami went to search the mine, but Madraeus stayed at the door of the shaft house and watched the bodies of the fallen Races crumble into ash. As black smoke curled into the night sky, he turned and strode to the elevator. There was more gruesome work to be done.

Madraeus stopped in the tunnel just outside the ring of light given off by the guttering torch. He stared at the eerie faces pressed against the bars as they called for help. There was no good way for this to end.

Taking a deep breath, he stepped into the light. Immediately, the people in the cells started to wail. He moved along the tunnel past the empty cell he and Whitney had occupied.

He yelled, "Sandra!

"I'm here!" The answer came from his left.

He turned towards her. She was pushing her way to the front of the pack. The scraggly blonde woman stared back at him through the bars.

"How is Whitney?" When he didn't answer, she frowned. "You're her boss, right? You were down here earlier. I saw her get tackled by that other guy. Is she okay?"

Madraeus didn't answer. He walked to the front of her cell and began to unlock the door.  Everyone surged towards him.

"Get back!" he shouted. In fear, they scrambled away from him, except for Sandra, who patiently waited for him to open the door.

"Come with me," he said.

"So, is Whitney okay?" she asked again as she stepped out. He locked the door behind her.

"She was alive when I left her," he growled before turning away. Protests and screams for help followed them up the tunnel. Madraeus led her to the cavern that Cecelia had been using as an office.

"Sit." He motioned to the chairs in front of the desk while he moved to sit behind it.

"Huh," Sandra grunted thoughtfully as she sat down carefully.

"What?" He steepled his fingers and stared at the bedraggled woman in front of him.

"Oh, nothing, it's just weird to sit on a chair again."

Madraeus raised an eyebrow and continued to stare at her. She looked much worse than Whitney. Sandra was gaunt and pale. Her filthy skin and hair were matched only by her stench.

"No offense, but will you get on with it?" Sandra said after a few moments.

"Excuse me?"

"Well, you are trying to decide if you want to kill me or not, right?" She returned his gaze frankly. "I just want you to get on with it. I haven't eaten in a while, and I am very tired."

Madraeus blinked in disbelief. "It doesn't bother you that I am thinking of killing you?"

"Not really. The way I look at it, you can kill me, and I won't be hungry or tired; or you can not kill me, and I won't be hungry or tired, so either way I'm good. I just wanna not be hungry or tired. Or dirty," she added as an afterthought.

"Are you really this practical? Or is your mind a little unhinged?" Madraeus started to smile.

"I honestly think it is a little of both at this point," Sandra shrugged.

Madraeus watched her for a moment longer, then asked, "Alright, if you are that practical, what do you suggest I do with all those people?"

Sandra thought about it and then sighed, "I am assuming that since you are here and the police are not, you are one of them?"

Madraeus nodded.

"Whitney seemed to like you, so I am also assuming that you are not all bad."

Madraeus shrugged.

"I'm also assuming that since I've never heard of real vampires and werewolves, you want to stay a secret?"

Madraeus nodded again.

Sandra chewed on the inside of her cheek for a moment, then sighed again.

"At the risk of getting myself killed, I'll tell you the truth. I think they should be put out of their misery. These people have been in Hell, and to let them try and go home to live normal lives? I don't think they'll be able to. And there's no way that you can keep that many people quiet about something like this."

"You just told me that it was all right to kill a lot of people." Madraeus watched her carefully.

"I didn't say it was all right." Sandra sighed. "There is no good way to come out of this."

"I know," Madraeus said quietly after a moment. "The good news is that you will."

"Will what?"

"Come out of it. I'm going to let you go."

"Why?" Sandra narrowed her eyes.

"Because you were there for Whitney," Madraeus said, thinking that if he couldn't save them all, he could at least save her friend. *Maybe she won't hate me as much.*

"However," he leaned forward and held her gaze, "if you breathe one word about this to anyone, it will be the last thing you ever do."

"Fair enough." Sandra swallowed hard. "What about the rest of them?"

"Don't ask." His voice was ice.

Sandra shuddered.

"Vivian?" He called, and after a moment, a young woman stepped into the room. "Vivian, please see that Miss...?"

"Conners," Sandra supplied.

"Miss Conners is escorted to Mrs. Myers' house."

"Sure," Vivian smiled and gestured for Sandra to go ahead of her out the door. Madraeus followed them out of the cavern and watched them as they walked toward the elevator, then he turned and walked into the darkness that led to the cells.

He heard them long before he saw them. The nearest torch had burnt itself out, leaving the room in darkness. There was still enough light coming from farther up the tunnel for him to see by, but they couldn't see him. It was better that way. If they saw what he was going to do, there would be panic. It would only make things more difficult.

Quietly, he unlocked the first cell and stepped inside. Silently, he stepped up behind the closest person and reached out. A quick twist and it was done. One by one, he snapped their necks and let them slide to the floor. With every bone that cracked, he knew that he stepped farther and farther away from any chance of a future with Whitney.

Suddenly, he hated them all.

*Yesss.* The hissing voice reared up in his head.

He hated them for getting caught by Cecelia.

*Kill them.*

He hated them for being weak.

*Yesss.*

He hated them for making him kill them.

*Kill them all!*

It took no time at all to remove sixty-six threats. Then he returned to the office cavern and retrieved another torch. He moved back down the tunnel and set each section of cells ablaze.

Madraeus walked up the tunnel. He felt numb. He heard Rami's voice and turned toward it. Malcolm and Rami were looking through some boxes that had been left under a table in the corner. Rami was scrutinizing a small object in his hand. He glanced up when he heard Madraeus.

"It's done," Madraeus grimaced.

Rami closed his eyes for a moment and shook his head sadly.

"What have you found?"

"Not much, everything is cleaned out except for these papers and this."

"What is it?" Madraeus growled, stepping forward.

"It is a rabbit," Rami said with satisfaction. "Or more precisely three rabbits." He held out the object in his hand.

Madraeus reached out and picked it up. "Rabbits? As in, we're chasing the wrong rabbit?"

It was a small metal disk with three rabbits running in a circle with their ears forming a triangle at the center of the disk. It looked ancient and worn. Madraeus glanced up at Rami in disbelief.

"Not rabbits. Hares." Madraeus almost laughed. He *had* been chasing the wrong rabbit.

"I have seen this symbol. A lot," Rami nodded. "It is in almost all the books about the Old Sources."

"That doesn't surprise me. This is the symbol of the Hares. That genocidal cult built the traps that contain the Old Sources. We should have been chasing the Hares, not Justin."

Madraeus reached out to take the disk but stopped.

All three heads swiveled at once.

Sirens.

"Police?" Rami hissed.

"Cecelia gets the last laugh," Madraeus snarled.

"What do we do?" Malcolm looked between Rami and Madraeus in panic.

"Burn it!" Madraeus growled grabbing a torch and pushing it into the pile of papers next to Rami. "Burn it all. Then we go into the tunnels and hope they don't find us."

Malcolm and Rami grabbed everything they could find that would burn and threw it in the blaze.

"Come on!" Madraeus snarled. "The elevator's almost to the bottom." They dodged down the tunnels, past the smoldering cells, deeper and deeper into the mountain.

"I don't want this to be the end," Malcolm complained.

"It's not!" Madraeus snapped as they dodged down another tunnel. "I have every intention of coming back to hunt Cecelia down. To the ends of the earth if I have to."

"Oh, good. Something to look forward to then." Malcolm grinned as they descended deeper into the endless darkness.

# About the Author

Adriana Pridemore has loved reading and writing all of her life. She has been a journalist, freelance editor/proofreader, and teacher. She currently lives in Montana with her wonderful husband and family, a fuzzy feline queen, and a moose-sized St. Bernard.